Christine Feehan

"A magnificent storyteller" *(Romantic Times)*

DARK SYMPHONY

"Feehan's followers will be well sated by the latest addition to her dark series . . . laced with romance and erotica . . . unconventional and intriguing."

—*Publishers Weekly*

A VERY GOTHIC CHRISTMAS

"[A] captivating story. . . . Christine Feehan has written a gothic novella that is not only a page-turner but is highly recommended!"

—*Romantic Times* Magazine, on "After the Music"

"A modern day gothic tale that will thrill you and chill you . . . plenty of sexual tension and wild romance to heat the blood as well."

—*The Belles and Beaux of Romance,*
on "After the Music"

DARK GUARDIAN

"A skillful blend of supernatural thrills and romance that is sure to entice readers."

—*Publishers Weekly*

DARK LEGEND

"Vampire romance at its best!" —*Romantic Times*

Dark Fire

"If you are looking for something that is fun and different, pick up a copy of this book."

—All About Romance

Lair of the Lion

"Feehan adds a gothic twist to a classic fairy tale in this eerie and engrossing nineteenth century romance . . . steamy sex scenes heat up the page. Feehan's inspired retelling is likely to garner her the attention she deserves."

—*Publishers Weekly*

Dark Challenge

"The exciting and multifaceted world that impressive author Christine Feehan has created continues to improve with age." —*Romantic Times*

Dark Magic

"With each book Ms. Feehan continues to build a complex society that makes for mesmerizing reading."

—*Romantic Times*

The Scarletti Curse

"The characters and twists in this book held me on the edge of my seat the whole time I read it. If you've enjoyed Ms. Feehan's previous novels, you will surely be captivated by this step into the world of gothic romance."

—Under the Covers Book Reviews

Dark Gold

"Imbued with passion, danger, and supernatural thrills."

—*Romantic Times*

Dark Desire

"A very well-written, entertaining story that I highly recommend."

—Under the Covers Book Reviews

Dark Prince

"For lovers of vampire novels, this one is a keeper . . . I had a hard time putting the book down . . . don't miss this book!"

—*New-Age Bookshelf*

BOOKS BY CHRISTINE FEEHAN

A Very Gothic Christmas
(with Melanie George)

Published by Pocket Books

THE TWILIGHT BEFORE CHRISTMAS

Christine Feehan

POCKET STAR BOOKS
NEW YORK LONDON TORONTO SYDNEY SINGAPORE

An *Original* Publication of POCKET BOOKS

A Pocket Star Book published by
POCKET BOOKS, a division of Simon & Schuster, Inc.
1230 Avenue of the Americas, New York, NY 10020

ISBN: 0-7434-7628-X

First Pocket Books printing November 2003

10 9 8 7 6 5 4 3 2 1

Cover design by Lisa Litwack; front cover illustration by Shasti O'Leary Soudant

Manufactured in the United States of America

For information regarding special discounts for bulk purchases, please contact Simon & Schuster Special Sales at 1-800-456-6798 or business@simonandschuster.com

dedication

This book is dedicated to my sister Lisa, who has a special magic all her own.

acknowledgments

Thank you to Heather King and Rose Brungard for the wonderful chilling Christmas poem they so graciously provided to me to use for this book!

Be sure to write to Christine at Christine@christinefeehan.com *to get a FREE exclusive screen saver and join the PRIVATE email list to receive an announcement when Christine's books are released.*

The Twilight Before Christmas

by

Heather King and Rose Brungard

'Twas the twilight before Christmas and all through the lands,
Not a thing has occurred that was not of my hand.

The snowglobe they hold has a secret inside,
Where the mist rolls in place of the snow that's outside.

A chill, colder still than the air they will feel,
As I rejoice in release as I slip past the seal

A wreath of holly meant to greet,
Looks much better tossed in the street.

A town dreams of sweet thoughts while nestled in bed,
Until nightmares of me begin to dance in their heads.

The time, it was right, for a present or two,
And the fog on the sand holds a secret, a clue

As lovers meet beneath mistletoe bright,
Terror ignites down below them this night

And the blood runs red on the pristine white snow . . .
While around all the houses the Christmas lights glow.

A star burns hot in the dead of the night,
As the bell tolls it's now midnight

Beneath the star, that shines so bright,
An act unfolds, to my delight

In the stocking hung with gentle care,
A mystery, I know, is hidden there.

A candle burns with an eerie glow,
As it melts, the wax does flow,

My last gift now, is a special one,
A candy cane for a special son,

He watches and tends and knows the land,
But not enough to evade my hand.

All deeds are now done, forgiveness is mine,
As two people share a love for all time.

chapter 1

'Twas the twilight before Christmas and all through the lands
Not a thing has occurred that was not of my hand

"DON'T SAY IT. DON'T SAY IT. DON'T SAY IT," Danny Granite muttered the mantra under his breath as he sat in the truck watching his older brother carefully selecting hydro-organic tomatoes from Old Man Mars's fruit stand. Danny glanced at the keys, assuring himself the truck was running and all that his brother had to do was leap in and gun it. He leaned out the window, gave a halfhearted wave to the elderly man, and scowled at his brother. "Get a move on, Matt. I'm starving here."

Matt grimaced at him, then smiled with smooth charm at the old man. "Merry Christmas, Mr. Mars," he said cheerfully as he handed over several bills and lifted the bag of tomatoes. "Less than two weeks before Christmas. I'm looking forward to the pageant this year."

Danny groaned. A black scowl settled over Old Man Mars's face. His craggy brows drew together in a straight, thick line. He grunted in disgust and spat on the ground.

The smile on Matt's face widened into a boyish grin as he hurried around the bed of the pickup truck to yank open the driver-side door. Almost before settling into his seat, he cranked up the radio so that "Jingle Bells" blared loudly from the speakers.

"You'd better move it, Matt," Dan muttered nervously, looking out the window, back toward the fruit stand. "He's arming himself. You just had to wish him a Merry Christmas, didn't you? You know he hates that pageant. And you know very well playing that music is adding insult to injury!"

The first tomato came hurtling toward the back window of the truck as Matt hit the gas and the truck leaped forward, fishtailing, tires throwing dirt into the air. The tomato landed with deadly accuracy, splattering juice, seed, and pulp across the back window. Several more missiles hit the tailgate as the truck tore out of the parking lot and raced down the street.

Danny scowled at his brother. "You just had to wish him Merry Christmas. Everyone knows he hates Christmas. He kicked the shepherd last year during the midnight pageant. Now he'll be more ornery than ever. If you'd just avoided the word, we might have gone unscathed this year, but now he'll have to retaliate."

Matt's massive shoulders shook as he laughed. "As I recall you played the shepherd last year. He didn't hurt you that bad, Danny boy. A little kick on the shin is good for you. It builds character."

"You only think it's funny because it wasn't your

shin." Danny rubbed his leg as if it still hurt nearly a year later.

"You need to toughen up," Matt pointed out. He took the highway, a thin ribbon of a road, twisting and turning along the cliffs above the ocean. It was impossible to go fast on the switchbacks although Matt knew the road well. He maneuvered around a sharp curve, setting up for the next sharp turn. It ran uphill and nearly doubled back. The mountain swelled on his right, a high bank grown over with emerald green grasses and breathtaking colors from the explosion of wildflowers. On his left, a narrow ribbon of a trail meandered along the cliffs to drop away to the wide expanse of blue ocean with its whitecaps and booming waves.

"Oh, my God! That's Kate Drake," Danny said gleefully, pointing to a woman on a horse, riding along the narrow trail on the side of the road.

"That can't be her." Matt hastily rolled down his window and craned his neck, gawking unashamedly. He could only see the back of the rider, who was dressed all in white and had thick chestnut hair that flamed red in the sunshine. His heart pounded. His mouth went dry. Only Kate Drake could get away with wearing white and riding a horse so close to the side of the road. It had to be her. He slowed the truck to get a better look as he went by, turning down the radio at the same time.

"Matt! Watch where you're going," Danny yelled,

bracing himself as the truck flew off the road and rolled straight into the grass-covered bank. It halted abruptly. Both men were slammed back in their seats and held prisoner by their seat belts.

"Damn!" Matt roared. He turned to his brother. "Are you all right?"

"No, I'm not all right, you big lug, you ran us off the road gawking at Kate Drake again. I hurt everywhere. I need a neck brace, and I think I might have broken my little finger." Danny held up his hand, gripping his wrist and emitting groans loudly.

"Oh shut up," Matt said rudely.

"Matthew Granite. Good heavens, are you hurt? I have a cell phone and can go out to the bluff and call for help."

Kate's voice was everything he remembered. Soft. Melodic. Meant for long nights and satin sheets. Matt turned his head to look at her. To drink her in. It had been four long years since he'd last spoken with her. She stood beside his truck, reins looped in her hand, her large green eyes anxious. He couldn't help but notice she had the most beautiful skin. Flawless. Perfect. It looked so soft, he wanted to stroke his finger down her cheek just to see if she was real.

"I'm fine, Kate." It was a miracle he found his voice. His tongue seemed to stick to the roof of his mouth. "I must have tried to take the turn a little too fast."

A snort of derision came from Danny's side of the

truck. "You were driving like a turtle. You just weren't looking where you were going."

The toe of Matt's boot landed solidly against his brother's shin, and Danny let out a hair-raising yowl.

"No wonder Old Man Mars wanted to kick you last year," Matt muttered under his breath.

"Daniel? Are you hurt?" Kate sounded anxious, but her fascinating lower lip quivered as if close to laughter.

Determined to get her away from his brother, Matt hastily shoved the door open with more force than necessary. The door thumped soundly against Kate's legs. She jumped back, the horse half reared, and Danny, damn him, laughed like the hyena he was.

Matt groaned. It never failed. He was a decorated U.S. Army Ranger, had been in the service for years, running covert missions where his life depended on his physical skills and his cool demeanor, yet he always managed to feel clumsy and rough in front of Kate. He unfolded his large frame, towering over her, feeling like a giant. Kate was always perfect. Poised. Articulate. Graceful. There she was, looking beautiful dressed all in white with her hair attractively windblown. She was the only person in the world who could make him lose his cool and raise his temperature at the same time just by smiling.

"Is Danny really hurt?" Kate asked, turning her head slightly while she tried to calm the nervous horse.

It gave Matt a great view of her figure. He drank her

in, his hungry gaze drifting over her soft curves. He'd always loved watching her walk away from him. Nobody moved in the same sexy way she did. She looked so proper, yet she had that come-on walk and the bedroom eyes and glorious hair a man would want to feel sliding over his skin all night long. He just managed to stifle a groan. How had he not known, *sensed* that Kate was back in town. His radar must be failing him.

"Danny's fine, Kate," Matt assured her.

She sent him a quick smile over her shoulder, her eyes sparkling at him. "Just how many accidents have you been in, Matt? It seems that on the rare occasions I've seen you, over the last few years, your poor vehicle has been crunched."

It was true, but it was her fault. Kate Drake acted as some sort of catalyst for strange behavior. He was good at everything. *Everything.* Unless Kate was around—then he could barely manage to speak properly.

The horse moved restlessly, demanding Kate's immediate attention, giving Matt time to realize his jeans and blue chambray work shirt were streaked with dirt, sawdust, and a powdery cement mixture in complete contrast to her immaculate white attire. He took the opportunity to slap the dust from his clothing, sending up a gray cloud that enveloped Kate as she turned back toward him. She coughed delicately, fluttering her long feathery lashes to keep the dust from stinging her eyes. Another derisive hoot came from Danny's direction.

Matt sent his brother a look that promised instant death before turning back to Kate. "I had no idea you were in town. The town gossips let me down." Inez at the grocery store had mentioned Sarah was in town, as well as Hannah and Abigail, three of her six sisters, but Inez hadn't said a word about Kate.

"Sarah came back for a visit, and you know how my family is, we get together as often as possible." She shrugged, a simple enough gesture, but on her it was damned sexy. "I've been in London doing research for my latest thriller." She laughed softly. The sound played right down his spine and did interesting things to his body. "London fog is always so perfect for a scary setting. Before that it was Borneo." Kate traveled the world, researching and writing her bestselling novels and murder mysteries. She was so beautiful it hurt to look at her, so sophisticated he felt primitive in her presence. She was so sexy he always had the desire to turn caveman and toss her over his shoulder and carry her off to his private lair. "Sarah's engaged to Damon Wilder." She tilted her head slightly and patted the horse's neck again. "Have you met him?"

"No, but everyone is talking about it. No one expected Sarah to get married."

Matt watched the way the sunlight kissed her hair, turning the silky strands into a blazing mass of temptation. His gaze followed her hand stroking the horse's neck, and he noted the absence of a ring with relief.

Danny cleared his throat. He leaned out the driver's

side. “You’re drooling, bro.” He whispered it in an over-loud voice.

Without missing a beat, Matt kicked the door closed. “Are you going to be staying very long this visit?” He held his breath waiting for her answer. To make matters worse, Danny snickered. Matt sent up a silent vow that their parents would have one less child to fuss over before the day was out.

“I’ve actually decided to stay and make Sea Haven my home base. I bought the old mill up on the cliffs above Sea Lion Cove. I’m planning on renovating the mill into a bookstore and coffee shop, and to modernize the house so I can live in it. I’m tired of wandering. I’m ready to come home again.”

Kate smiled. She had perfect teeth to go with her perfect skin. Matt found himself staring at her while the earth shook beneath his feet. He stood there, grinning at the thought of Kate living in their hometown permanently.

A shadow swept across the sky, black threads swirling and boiling, a dark cauldron of clouds blotting out the sun. A seagull shrieked once. Then the entire flock of birds overhead took up the warning cry. Matt was so caught up in Kate’s smile, he didn’t realize the ground was really rolling, and it wasn’t just her amazing effect on him. The horse backed dangerously close to the road, tossing its head in fright, nearly dragging Kate from her feet. Matt swiftly reached past her and gathered the reins in one hand to steady the animal. He swept his other arm around Kate's waist, anchoring her smaller body to his, to keep her from falling as a jagged crack opened several feet from them and spread rapidly along the ground, heading right for Kate's feet. Matt lifted her up and away from the gaping hole, dragging her back several feet, horse in tow, away from the spreading crack. It was only a few inches wide, but it was several inches deep, very long, and ran up the side of the embankment.

"You all right, Danny?" he called to his brother.

"Yeah, I'm fine. That was a big one."

Kate clung to Matt, her small hands clutching at his shoulders. He heard the sharp intake of her breath that belied her calm demeanor, but she didn't cry out. The ground settled, and Matt allowed her feet to touch the path but retained his hold on her. She was incredibly warm and soft and smelled of fresh flowers. He leaned over her, inhaling her fragrance, his chin brushing the top of her head. "You okay, Kate?"

Appearing as serene as ever, Kate murmured soothingly to the horse. Nothing ruffled her. Not earthquakes and certainly not Matthew Granite. "Yes, of course, it was just a little earthquake." She glanced up at the boiling clouds with a small frown of puzzlement.

"It was a fairly good one. And the ground opened damn near at your feet."

Kate continued to pat the horse's neck, seemingly unaware that Matt was still holding her, caging her body between his and the animal. He could see her hands tremble as she struggled to maintain composure, and it made him admire her all the more. She lifted her face to the wind. "I love the sea breeze. The minute I feel it on my face, I feel as if I'm home."

Matt cleared his throat. Kate had a beautiful profile. Her hair was swept up in some fancy knot, showing off her long, graceful neck. When she turned, her breasts thrust against the thin shirt, full and round and so enticing it was all he could do to keep from leaning down and putting his mouth over the clinging white fabric. He tried to move, to step away from her, but he was drawn to her. Mesmerized by her. She'd always reminded him of a ballerina, with her elegant lines and soft, feminine curves. His lungs burned for air, and there was a strange roaring in his head. It took three tries opening his mouth before a coherent word came out. "If you're really serious about renovation, Kate, it just so happens my family's in the construction business."

She turned the full power of her huge eyes on him. "I do recall all of you are builders. That's always struck me as a wonderful occupation." She reached out and took his hands. He had big hands, rough and callused, whereas her hands were soft and small. "I always loved your hands, Matthew. When I was a young girl I remember wishing I had your capable hands." Her words, as much as her touch, sent little flames licking along his skin.

Matt was certain he heard a snort and probably a snicker coming from the direction of his younger brother.

"I think you've held on to her long enough, bro," Danny called. "The ground stopped pitching a few minutes ago."

Matt was too much of a gentleman to point out to his brother that Kate was holding *his* hands. Looking down at her, he saw faint color steal under her skin. Reluctantly, he stepped away from her. The wind tugged at tendrils of her hair, but it only made her look more alluring. "Sorry, Kate. This is the first time in a while we've had an earthquake shake us up so hard." He raked his fingers through his dark hair in agitation, searching for something brilliant to say to keep her there. His mind was blank. Totally blank. Kate turned back to her horse. He began to feel desperate. He was a grown man, hardworking, some said brilliant when it came to designing, and most women quite frankly threw themselves at him, but Kate calmly gathered the reins of her horse, no weak knees, completely unaffected by his presence. He wiped the sweat suddenly beading on his forehead, leaving a smear of dirt behind.

"Kate." It came out softly.

Danny stuck his head out the window on the driver's side. "Do you want a little help with the old mill, Kate? Matt actually is fairly decent at that sort of thing. He obviously can't drive, and he can't talk, but he's hell on wheels with renovations."

Kate's eyes lit up. "I would love that, Matthew, but I really wouldn't want to presume on our friendship. It would have to be a business arrangement."

Matt hadn't realized she thought of them as friends. Kate rarely spoke to him, other than their strange, brief conversations when they'd run into one another by chance during her high school years. He liked the idea of being friends with her. Every cell in his body went on alert when she was near him, it always happened that way, even when she'd been a teenager and he'd been in his first years of college. Kate had always brought out his protective instincts, but mostly he'd felt he had to protect her from his own attraction to her. That had been distasteful to a man like Matt. He had taken his secret fantasies of her to every foreign country he'd been sent to. She had shared his days and nights in the jungles and deserts, in the worst of situations, and the memory of her had gotten him home. Now, a full-grown man who had fought wars and had more than enough life experience to give him confidence, he found he could speak easily and naturally to any other woman. Only Kate made him tongue-tied. He'd take friendship with her. At least it was a start. "Tell me when you want me to take a look, Kate, and I'll arrange my schedule accordingly. Being my own boss has its advantages."

"Then I'm going to take advantage of your generous offer and ask if you could go out there with me tomorrow afternoon. Do you think you can manage it that soon? I wouldn't ask, but I'm trying to get this project off the ground as soon as possible."

"It sounds great. I'll pick you up at the cliff house around four. You are staying there with your sisters, aren't you?"

Kate nodded and turned to watch the sheriff cruise up behind the pickup truck. Matt watched her face, mainly because he couldn't tear his gaze away from her. Her smile was gracious, friendly even, but he was aware even before he turned his head that the man getting out of the sheriff's cruiser was Jonas Harrington. It occurred to him that he knew Kate far too well, her every expression. And that meant he had spent too much time watching her. Kate was smiling, but she had stiffened just that little bit. She always did that around Jonas. All of her sisters did. For the first time he wondered why Kate reacted that way.

"Well, Kate, I see you caused another accident," Jonas said in greeting. He shook Matt's hand and clapped him on the back. "The Drake sisters have a tendency to wreak havoc everywhere they go." He winked at Matt.

Kate simply lifted an eyebrow. "You've been saying that since we were children."

Jonas leaned over to brush a casual kiss along Kate's cheek. Something black and lethal, whose existence Matt didn't want to recognize, moved inside of him like a dark shadow. He put a blatantly possessive hand on Kate's back.

Jonas ignored Matt's body language. "I'll still be making the same accusation when you're all in your eighties, Kate. Where is everyone?" He looked around as if expecting her sisters to appear galloping over the mountaintop.

"You look a little nervous, Jonas," Danny observed from the safety of the truck. "What'd you do this time? Arrest Hannah and throw her beautiful butt in jail on some trumped-up charge?"

He subsided when Kate turned the full power of her gaze on him. The wind rushed up from the sea, bringing the scent and feel of the ocean. "I had no idea you were so interested in my sister's anatomy, Danny."

"Come on, Kate, she's gorgeous; every man's interested in Hannah's anatomy," Danny pointed out, unrepentant.

"And if she doesn't want them to look, what is she doing allowing every photographer from here to hell and back to take pictures of her?" Jonas demanded. "And just for your information, I wouldn't have to trump up charges if I wanted to arrest Hannah," he added with a black scowl. "I ought to run her in for indecent exposure. That glitzy magazine in Inez's store has her on the cover . . . naked!"

"She is not naked. She's wearing a swimsuit, Jonas, with a sarong over it." Kate sounded as calm as ever, but Matt noted that her hand tightened on the reins of her horse until her knuckles turned white. He moved even closer to her, inserting himself between her and the sheriff.

"She might try a decent one-piece and maybe a robe that went down to her ankles or something. And does she have to strike that stupid pose just to make everyone stare . . ." Jonas broke off as the wind gusted again, howling this time, bringing whispers in the swirling chaos of leaves and droplets of seawater. His hat was swept from his head and carried away from the group. The wind shifted direction, rushing back to the ocean, retreating in much the same manner as a wave from the shore. The sudden breeze took the hat with it, sailing it over the cliffs and into the choppy water below.

Jonas spun around and looked toward the large house set up on the cliffs in the distance. "Damn it, Hannah. That's the third hat I've lost since you've been home." He shouted the words into the vortex of the wind.

There was a small silence. Matt cleared his throat. "Jonas. I don't think she can hear you from here."

Jonas glared at him. "She can hear me. Can't she, Kate? She knows exactly what I'm saying. You tell her this isn't funny anymore. She can stop with her little wind games."

"You believe all the things people say about the Drake sisters, don't you, Jonas?" Danny said. He imitated the opening theme of *The Twilight Zone.*

Matt stared down at Kate's hand. The reins were trembling. He covered her hand with his own, steadying the leather reins she was clenching. "I'll be happy to come look at the mill tomorrow, Kate. Would you like a leg up?"

"Thanks, Matthew. I'd appreciate it."

He didn't bother with cupping his hands together to assist her into the saddle. He simply lifted her. He was tall and strong, and it was easy to swing her onto the horse. She settled into the saddle as if born there. Elegant. Refined. As close to perfection as any dream he could conjure up and just as far out of reach. "I'll see you then. Say hello to your sisters for me."

"I'll do that, Matthew, and you give my best to your parents. It was nice to see you, Danny." Her cool gaze swept over Jonas. "I'm sure you'll be by the house, Jonas."

Jonas shrugged. "I take my job seriously, Kate."

Matt watched her ride away, waiting until a curve in the road took her out of sight before turning on the sheriff. "What the hell was that all about?"

"You know all seven of the Drake women drive me crazy half the time," Jonas said. "I've told you all the trouble they get up to. You're always grilling me about them. Well—" he grinned evilly as he indicated the truck—"Isn't this the third accident you've had with Kate in the vicinity? You should know what I mean."

Jonas had grown up with Matt Granite, had gone through school, joined the Army, the Rangers, and fought side by side with him. He knew how Matt felt about Kate. It was no secret. Matt wasn't very good at hiding his feelings from his family and friends, especially since Jonas had gotten out of the service two years before Matt and Matt had continually interrogated him about Kate's whereabouts and marital status. Matt had been home three years and he'd been waiting for Kate to come home for good, too.

Danny snickered. "You were there back in his college days, Jonas, when he drove Dad's truck into the creek bed and hung it up on a rock. Wasn't Kate about three at the time?"

Matt took a deep breath. He couldn't kill his brother in front of the sheriff, even if it was Jonas. The time he had wrecked his father's truck, driving it without permission, Kate had been about fifteen, far too young for a college man to be looking at her, and he was still embarrassed that his brothers and Jonas had known why he'd wrecked the vehicle. Of course he'd known the Drake sisters, everyone in town knew them, but he'd never *looked* at them. Not in a fascinated, physical, male way. Until he'd seen Kate standing in a creek bed picking blackberries with the sun kissing her hair and her large sea-green eyes looking back at him. The second time he'd wrecked a vehicle had been four years ago. Matt had been home on leave, and he'd been so busy looking at Kate walking on the sidewalk with her sisters, he'd failed to realize he was parked in front of a cement hump and had hung up his mother's car on it when he'd gone to pull out. Now, ignoring his brother's jibe, he moved around the truck to inspect the damage. "I think I can get the truck out without a tow."

"I see you upset old man Mars." Jonas pointed to the tomato smears on the rear window.

"You know Matt, he just had to wish the old man a Merry Christmas." Danny shoved open the door. "He likes to stir the old geezer up right before the pageant. He does it every year. The time Mom made me play the little drummer boy, Mars broke my drumsticks into ten pieces and threw them on the ground and then jumped up and down on them. All my brothers got a kick out of that, but I've been traumatized ever since. I have nightmares about being stomped by him."

Jonas laughed. "Mars is a strange old man, but he's harmless enough. And he gives away most of his produce to the people who need it. He takes it to some of the single moms in town and some of the elderly couples. And I know he feeds the Ruttermyer boy, the one with Down's syndrome who works at odd jobs for everyone. He persuaded Donna to give the boy a room right next to her gift shop. I know he helps that boy with his bills."

"Yeah, deep down he's a good man," Matt agreed. A slow grin spread over his face. "He just hates Christmas." He nodded toward the other side of the truck, and the other two men went to the front to scrape away the mud and dirt and push until they separated the bumper from the embankment. "I didn't appreciate you saying anything to Kate about her and her sisters being different, Jonas." Matt said it in a low voice, but Jonas and he had been friends since they were boys, and Jonas recognized the warning tone.

"I'm not going to pretend they're like everyone else, Matt, not even for you," Jonas snapped. "The Drakes are special. They have gifts, and they use themselves up for everyone else without a thought for themselves or their own safety. I'm going to watch out for them whether they like or it not. Sarah Drake nearly got herself killed a few weeks ago. Hannah and Kate and Abbey were with her and also might have been killed."

Matt felt the words as a blow somewhere in the vicinity of his gut. His heart did a curious somersaulting dive in his chest. "I heard about Sarah, but I hadn't heard the others were there. What happened?"

"To make a long story short, Wilder had people trail him here. They wanted information only he could give them. He helped design our national defense system, and the government wanted him protected at all costs. With Sarah being from Sea Haven, it was natural enough for the Feds to send her in to guard him. These people had gotten their hands on him once before, killed his assistant right in front of him, and tortured him. That's why he uses a cane when he walks. They broke into the Drakes' house, armed to the teeth when he was there, and were ready to kill Wilder and the Drakes to get what they wanted." The anger in Jonas's voice deepened.

"No one said a word about Kate being in the house

at the same time. I knew Sarah was guarding Damon Wilder and that he was a defense expert in some kind of trouble, but . . ." Matt trailed off as he looked back toward the house on the cliff. It was covered with Christmas lights. Beside it was a tall full Douglas fir tree, completely decorated and flashing lights even before the sun went down. When he looked toward the house he felt a sense of peace. Of rightness. The Drake sisters were the town's treasures. He looked away from the cliff toward the old mill. It was farther up the road, built over Sea Lion Cove. A strange cloud formation hung over the small inlet and spread slowly toward land. The shape captured his imagination, a yawning black mouth, jaws opening wide, heading straight for them.

"All of them were nearly murdered," Jonas said. His eyes went flat and cold. "The Drakes take on far too much, and everyone just expects them to do it without thinking of the cost to them."

"I never thought of it like that, Jonas. Now that you mention it, I've seen them all drained of energy after helping out the way they do." Matt didn't take his eyes from the sky. He watched a seagull veer frantically from the path of the slow-moving cloud, braking sharply in midair, wings flapping strongly in agitation. Wisps of fog began to rise from the sea and drift toward shore. "Maybe we all should pay more attention to what's happening with them," he murmured softly, more to himself than to the others.

chapter 2

The snowglobe they hold has a secret inside
Where the mists roll in place of the snow that's outside

INHALING THE MINGLED SCENTS OF CINNAMON and pine, Kate wandered into the kitchen of the cliff house. The sound of Christmas music filled the air and blended with the aroma of fresh-baked cookies and the fragrance of richly scented candles. "Is that Joley's voice?" Kate asked, leaning her hip comfortably against the heavily carved wood cabinet. "When did she make a Christmas collection?"

Hannah Drake spun around, teakettle in her hands. Her abundance of blond hair shimmered for a moment in the last rays of sunshine pouring through the bay window. "Kate, I didn't hear you get out of the shower. I think I was in my own little world. Joley sent the CD as a surprise, although she made a point of saying it was not to go out of the family."

They both laughed affectionately. "Joley and that band of hers. She can sing just about anything from gospel to blues, from rock to rap, but she's so careful not to let anyone know. I think she likes her bad girl image. Did she mention whether she's coming home for Christmas? I know she was touring."

Hannah's face lit up, her smile brilliant. "She's going to try. I can't wait to see her. We keep missing each other in our travels."

"I hope she gets here soon. Talking on the phone just isn't the same as all of us being together." Kate swept a stray tendril of hair behind her ear. "What about Mom and Dad? Has anyone heard from them? Are they coming here for Christmas?"

Hannah shook her head. "Last I heard they sent kisses and hugs and were snuggling together in their little chalet in the Swiss Alps. Libby got in a quick visit with them before she headed out to the Congo. She said she was coming home for Christmas. Mom and Dad promised next year they'd be here with us."

Kate laughed softly as she leaned over to sniff the canister of loose tea. "Mom and Dad are still such lovebirds. What are you making?"

"I was in the mood for a little lavender, but anything is fine." Hannah scrutinized Kate closely. "But let's go with chamomile. Something soothing."

Kate smiled. "You think I need a little soothing?"

Hannah nodded as she measured the tea into a small pot. "Tell me."

"I ran into Matthew Granite and his brother Danny." Kate tried to sound casual, when her entire body was trembling. Only Matt could do that to her. Only Matt moved her. She'd never understood why.

"Matthew Granite? I thought that might be him." Hannah's huge blue eyes settled on her sister with compassion and interest. "How did he seem?"

Kate shrugged her slender shoulders. "Wonderful. Helpful. He offered to look at the old mill for me and help with the renovations." She always enjoyed looking at her younger sister. Hannah wasn't just beautiful, she was strikingly so, exotically so, with her bone structure, abundance of pale, almost platinum hair, her enormous, heavily lashed eyes, and sultry lips. Beauty radiated from her. Kate had always thought Hannah's extraordinary beauty came from the inside out. She watched the graceful movements of Hannah's hands as she went about making tea. "Matt's always so helpful." She sighed.

Hannah reached out to her, clasping Kate's hands in a gesture of solidarity. "Was it the same?"

"You mean with his brothers laughing all the time? Well, only one was with him, Danny." Color crept up under Kate's skin. "Yes, of course. Every time I get anywhere near the Granites they all laugh. I have no idea why. It isn't the same way Jonas is with you. Matthew never needles me. He's always perfectly polite, but I seem to have some humorous effect on his family. I try as hard as I can just to be polite and calm, but the brothers laugh until I want to go check a mirror to see if I have spinach in my teeth. Matthew just glares at them, but it really draws attention to all the silly things I do in front of him." She squeezed Hannah's fingers before letting her hand go. "I've showered and changed, but I came home with my clothes covered with dirt. Poor Matthew just came from work, was dusting himself off, and I had to be two steps behind him. When he tried to open his truck door, of course I managed to get too close."

"Oh, Katie, honey, I'm so sorry. What happened?" Hannah's face mirrored her sister's distress.

Kate shrugged. "The door nearly knocked me over, and he had to apologize yet again. The poor man spends every minute apologizing to me. I'll bet he wishes he never had to see me again."

"No he doesn't," Hannah said firmly. "I think he's always been sweet on you."

Kate sighed. "You and I both know Matthew Granite would never look at me twice. He's wild and rough and an adrenaline junkie. He played every sport in high school and college. He joined the Rangers. I researched what they do. Even their creed is a bit frightening. They arrive at the 'cutting edge of battle' and they never fail their comrades and give more than one hundred percent. The creed says things like fight on even if you're the lone survivor, and *surrender* is not a Ranger word." She shuddered delicately. "He's a wild man, and he does very scary wild things. He's going to look at women who climb mountains and scoff in the face of danger. Can you see me doing that?"

"Kate," Hannah said softly, "maybe he's more settled

now. He went out and did his save the world thing and now he's come home and he's working the family business. He could have changed."

Kate forced a fleeting smile. "Men like Matthew don't change, Hannah. I was telling you my tale of woe. We were just at the point where Jonas drove up. You know how he has to make his little 'Drake sisters' comments. He implied every time I was around something awful happened. It just made the situation worse." She sighed again. "I tried to look as though it didn't bother me, but I think Matthew knew."

"Jonas Harrington needs to fall into the ocean and have a nice hungry shark come swimming by." Hannah dragged the whistling teakettle from the stove and splashed water into the teapot, a fine fury radiating from her at the thought of Jonas Harrington saying anything to upset Kate. The water boiled in the little china teapot, bubbles roiling and bursting with a steady fury. Steam rose.

Kate covered the top of the teapot with her palm, settling the water back down. "You were out on the captain's walk."

Hannah nodded, unrepentant. "The earthquake bothered me. I felt something rising beneath the earth. I can't explain it, Kate, but it frightened me. I was sitting here listening to Joley's Christmas music, you know how much I love Christmas, then I felt the quake. Almost on the heels of it, something else disturbed the earth. I felt it as a darkness rising upward. I knew you were out riding, so I went out to the walk to make certain you weren't in trouble."

"And you felt the wind come in off the sea," Kate said. She leaned her hip against the counter. "I felt it too." She frowned and drummed her fingers on the tiled counter. "I smelled something, Hannah, something old and bitter in the wind."

"Evil?" Hannah ventured.

Kate shook her head slowly. "It wasn't that exactly. Well," she hedged, "maybe. I don't know. What did you think?"

Hannah leaned against the brightly tiled sink, her body so graceful the casual movement seemed balletic. "I honestly don't know, Kate, but it isn't good. I've felt disturbed ever since the earthquake and when I looked at the mosaic, there was a black shadow beneath the ground. I could barely make it out because it seemed to move and not stay in one place."

Kate glanced at the floor in the house's entryway. Her grandmother, along with her grandmother's six sisters, had made the mosaic, women of power and magic, seven sisters creating a timeless floor of infinite beauty. To most people it was simply a unique floor, but the Drake sisters could read many things in the ever-changing shadows that ran within it. "How very strange that neither of us knows precisely whether the disturbance is evil." She shrugged her shoulders and drew in a deep breath filled with cinnamon and pine. "I love the fragrances of Christmas." She tapped her foot, a small smile hovering on her face.

"You're holding back on me," Hannah guessed, her voice suddenly teasing. "Something else happened, didn't it?"

"When the earthquake started, Matthew put his arm around me to steady me, and we just stood there, even after it was over." She grinned at Hannah. "He is so strong. You have no idea. That man is all muscle. It's a wonder I didn't end up in a puddle at his feet! But I managed to look cool and serene."

Hannah pretended to swoon. "I wish I could have seen it. Matthew is definitely hot, even if he is a Neanderthal. I must have come up on the captain's walk just after that, just in time to see the slimy toad of the world arrive in his little sheriff's car." She smirked. "Too bad the wind came up, and his precious little hat went sailing out to sea."

"Shame on you, Hannah," Kate scolded halfheartedly. "Jonas means well. He's just so used to everyone doing everything he says, and we always seem to be in the middle of any kind of trouble in Sea Haven. You're beginning to enjoy tormenting him."

"Why shouldn't I? He's tormented me for years."

There was so much pain in Hannah's voice that Kate slipped her arm around her sister's waist to comfort her. Jonas had known them all since they were children, and he'd never understood Hannah.

She'd been an extraordinarily beautiful, very intelligent child, but she'd been so painfully shy outside of her own home, the sisters had had to work their magic just to get her to school every day. Jonas had been certain she was haughty, when in fact, she'd rarely been able to speak in public. "Well, all in all, it was a good day. You managed to lose another hat for Jonas, and I got to be up close and personal with the hottest man in Sea Haven." Kate hugged Hannah before pouring herself a cup of tea and walking into the living room with it.

Hannah followed her. "Did you get your manuscript mailed off?"

Kate nodded. "Murder and mayhem will prevail in a small coastal town. I forgot to put the tea cozy back on the pot, will you do it?"

Hannah glanced into the kitchen and lifted her arms.

When Kate looked back, the cozy was safely on the teapot. "Thanks, Hannah. I do have to say, Jonas was invaluable to me with the research."

"I know he was, but don't credit him with doing it to be nice or anything." Hannah's large blue eyes reflected her laughter. "He was trying to get on your good side so you'd persuade me to stop messing around with his precious hats."

They both swung around as the front door burst open. Abigail Drake rushed in, a small woman with dark eyes and a wealth of red-gold hair spilling down her back in a thick ponytail. Her face was flushed and her eyes over-bright. The moment she glimpsed her sisters, she burst into tears.

"Abbey!" Hannah set her teacup down on the highly polished coffee table. "What is it? You never cry."

"I humiliated myself in front of the entire Christmas pageant committee," Abigail said miserably. She threw herself into the overstuffed armchair, curled her feet under her, and covered her face with her hands. "I can never face any of them again."

Hannah and Kate rushed to her side, both putting their arms around her. "Don't cry, Abbey. What happened? Maybe we can fix it. It can't be that bad."

"It was bad," Abigail muttered from between her fingers. "I accidentally used *the voice.* I wasn't paying attention. There was the earthquake, and I was so distracted because I felt something under us, something moving just below the surface seeking a way out. I *felt* it." Of all the talents gifted to the sisters, Abigail felt hers was the worst. Her voice could be used to extract the truth from people around her. As a child, before she'd learn to control the tone and the wording of her sentences, she'd been very unpopular with her classmates. They would often blurt out the truth of some escapade to their parents or a teacher whenever they were in her presence. Abigail pulled her hands down and stared at them with her sad eyes. "It isn't an excuse. I'm not a teenager. I know I have to be alert all the time."

Hannah and Kate exchanged a long, fearful look. "We felt the shadow too, Abbey. It was very disconcerting to both of us. What happened at the meeting?"

Abbey drew her legs up tighter into her body. "We were all discussing the Christmas pageant." She rubbed her chin on the top of her knees. "I felt the rift in the earth, a blackness welling up, and the next thing I knew I was asking for the truth." She clapped her hands over her ears. "I got the truth too. Everyone did. Bruce Harper is having an affair with Mason Fredrickson's wife. They were all in the room. Bruce and Mason got in a terrible fistfight, and Letty Harper burst into tears and ran out. She's six months pregnant. Sylvia Fredrickson slapped me across the face and walked out, leaving me standing there with everyone looking at me." She burst into tears all over again.

Kate frowned as she rubbed her sister's shoulders. She could feel the waves of distress pouring off of Abigail. "It's all right now, honey. You're home, and you're safe." At once a soothing tranquillity swept into the room, a sense of peace. The wicks on the unlit candles on the mantel leapt to life with bright orange-red flames. Joley's voice poured into the room, uplifting and melodic, bringing with it a sense of home and Christmas cheer. Kate leaned into her sister. "Abigail, your talent is a tremendous gift, and you have always used it for good. This was a distortion of your talent, not something any of us could have foreseen. Let it go. Just breathe and let it go."

Abbey managed a small smile, the sobs fading at the sound of her sister's voice. Kate the peacemaker. Most thought she prevented fights and solved problems, but in truth, she had a magic about her, a tranquillity and inner peace she shared with others just by the way she spoke. "I wish I had your gift, Kate," Abbey said. She pressed her hand to her cheek. "I didn't mind everyone's finding out about Sylvia—she likes to think she can get any man—but poor little Letty, pregnant and loving her stupid unfaithful husband so much. That was heartbreaking. And at Christmas too. What possessed me to be so careless? I'm so ashamed of myself."

"What exactly did you say, Abbey?" Kate asked.

Abbey looked confused. "Everyone had put in a variety of ideas for acting out the play we do every year and someone asked if they really liked the old script and should we keep it as a tradition or should we modernize it. I think I said, now would be a good time to tell the truth if you want to make any major changes. I meant with the script, not in people's lives." She rubbed her temples. "I haven't made a mistake like that since I was a teenager. I'm so careful to avoid the word *truth*." She scrubbed her hand over her face a second time, trying to erase the sting of Sylvia's hand. "You know if I use that word everyone in the immediate vicinity tells the truth about everything."

"It worries me that we all felt the same disturbance," Kate said. "Hannah saw a dark shadow in the mosaic. You said something you would never have normally said, and a crack opened up nearly at my feet and ran all the way up the embankment."

Hannah gasped. "You didn't tell me that. Kate, it could have been an attack on you. You're the most . . ." She broke off, looking at Abbey.

Kate lifted her chin. "I'm the most what?"

Hannah shrugged. "You're the best of us. You don't have a mean bone in your body. You just don't, Katie. I'm sorry, I know you hate our saying that, but you don't even know how to dislike someone. You're just so . . ."

"*Don't* say perfect," Kate warned. "I'm not perfect. And I think that's why Matthew's brothers always laugh at me. They think I want to be perfect and fall short."

Hannah and Abbey exchanged a long, worried look. "I think we should call the others," Hannah said. "Sarah will want to know about this. She must have felt the earthquake too. We can ask her if anything strange happened to her. And we should call Joley, Libby, and Elle. Something's wrong, Kate, I just feel it. It's as if the earthquake unleashed a malicious force. I'm afraid it could be directed at you."

Kate took a long sip of tea. The taste was as soothing as the aroma. "Go ahead, it can't hurt to see what the others have to say. I'm not going to worry about it. I didn't feel a direct threat. I'm not calling Sarah though. She and Damon are probably twined around one another. You can feel the heat right through the telephone line."

"I can go to the captain's walk and signal her,"

Hannah said wickedly. "Their bedroom window faces us, and for some utterly mysterious reason the curtain keeps opening in that particular room."

"Hannah!" Kate tried not to laugh. "You're impossible."

Hannah did laugh. "And you are perfect whether you want to acknowledge it or not. At least to me."

"And me," Abigail said.

Kate smiled at them. "I'm not all that perfect. I'd like to give Sylvia Fredrickson a piece of mind. She had no right hitting you, Abbey. Even in high school she was nasty."

"I'll take care of Sylvia," Hannah said. "Don't worry, Abbey. She'll spend a long time thinking about how stupid it was to hit you."

"Hannah!" Kate and Abbey chorused her name in protest.

Hannah burst out laughing. "I get the message, Kate. You'll talk to Sylvia, but you don't want me casting in her direction."

Kate grinned. "I should have known you were baiting me."

"Who said I didn't mean it? Sylvia gives women a bad name."

Kate shook her head. "Hannah Drake, you're becoming a bloodthirsty little witch. I think Jonas is having a bad influence on you." She touched Abbey's cheek gently. "Even for this we can't use our gifts for anything other than good."

Hannah made a face. "It's good for Jonas to have to chase his hat. It keeps him from becoming too arrogant and bossy. And who knows what great lesson Sylvia Fredrickson would learn if I tweaked her just a little bit." Before either sister could say anything, she laughed softly. "I'm not going to do anything horrible to her, I just love to see you both get that 'there-goes-Hannah-look' on your faces."

Kate nudged Abbey, ignoring Hannah's mischievous grin. "Guess what I'll be doing tomorrow? Matthew Granite agreed to look over the mill with me tomorrow. I'm hoping none of his brothers will be around to laugh at me, and maybe he'll notice I'm a grown woman, not a gawky teenager. You'd think the fact that I've traveled all over the world and that I'm a successful author would impress him, but he just looks at me exactly the same way he did when I was in high school."

Hannah and Abbey exchanged a quick, apprehensive look. "Kate, you're going to spend the afternoon with him? Do you really want to do that?" Abigail asked.

Kate nodded. "I like to be with him. Don't ask me why, I just do."

"Kate, you haven't been home in ages. Matthew has a certain reputation," Abigail said hesitantly. "He's always been easygoing with you, and he's very charming, but he's . . ." She trailed off and looked to Hannah for direction.

"What? A ladies' man? I would presume a man his age has dated." Kate walked across the room to touch the first of the seven stockings hung in a row along the mantelpiece. It allowed her to keep her expression hidden from her sisters. "I know he's been in relationships."

"That's just it, Kate. He doesn't have relationships. At best he has one-night stands. Women find him charming and mysterious, and he finds them annoying. Seriously, Kate, don't *really* fall for him. He looks great on the outside, but he has a caveman attitude. He was in the military so long, doing all the secret Special Forces kind of stuff, and he just expects everyone to fall in line with his orders. It's probably why he isn't impressed with your world travels. Please don't fall for him," Hannah pleaded. "I couldn't bear it if he hurt you, Kate."

"You're so certain he wouldn't fall for me? A few minutes ago you were saying you thought he might be sweet on me." Kate tried to guard her voice, to keep her tone strictly neutral when there was a peculiar ache inside. "I really don't need the warning. Men like Matthew don't look at women like me." She shrugged. "It doesn't bother me. I need solitude, I always have. And I don't have a tremendous amount of time to give to a relationship."

"What do you mean, Matthew wouldn't look at a woman like you?" Abbey was outraged. "What are you talking about, Kate?"

Kate took another sip of tea and smiled at her sisters over the rim of her teacup. "Don't worry, I'm not feeling sorry for myself. I know I'm different. I was born the way I am. All of you stand out. Your looks, your personalities, even you, Hannah, with being so painfully shy, you embrace life. You all live it. You don't let your weaknesses or failings stand in your way. I'm an observer. I read about life. I research life. I find a corner in a room and melt into it. I can become invisible. It's an art, and I am a wonderful practitioner."

"You travel all over the world, Kate," Hannah pointed out.

"Yes, and my agent and my publisher smooth the way for me. I don't have to ask for a thing, it's all done for me. Matthew is like all of you. He throws himself into life and lives every moment. He's a born hero, riding to the rescue, carrying out the wounded on his back. He needs someone willing to do the same. I'm a born observer. Maybe that's why I was given the ability to see into the shadows at times. A part of me is already there."

Hannah's blue eyes filled with tears. "Don't say that, Kate. Don't ever say that." She wrapped her arms around Kate and hugged her close, uncaring that a small amount of tea splashed on her. "I didn't know you felt that way. How could I not have known?"

Kate hugged her hard. "Honey, don't be upset for me. You don't understand. I'm not distressed about it. My world is books. It always has been. I love words. I love living in my imagination. I don't want to go climb a mountain. I love to study how it's done. I love to talk to people who do it, but I don't want the experience of it, the reality of it. My imagination provides a wonderful adventure without the risk or the discomfort."

"Katie," Abbey protested.

"It's the truth. I've always been attracted to Matthew Granite, but I'm far too practical to make the mistake of believing anything could ever work between us. He runs wild. I remember him being right in the middle of every rough play in football both in high school and in college. He's done so many crazy things, from serving as a Ranger to skydiving for the fun of it." She shuddered. "I don't even scuba dive. He goes whitewater rafting and rock climbing for relaxation. I read a good book. We aren't in the least compatible, but I can still think he's hot."

"Are you certain you want to spend time with him?" Abbey asked.

Kate shrugged. "What I want to do is to take a look at the mosaic and see if I can make out the shadows in the earth the way Hannah did."

"Maybe all three of us can figure out what is going on," Hannah agreed. She followed Kate to the entryway, glancing over her shoulder at Abigail. "Doesn't Joley sound beautiful? She sent us her Christmas CD. She said she might be able to make it home for Christmas."

"I hope so," Abbey said. "Did Elle or Libby call?"

"Libby is in South America," Hannah said.

"I thought you said she was in the Congo," Kate interrupted.

Hannah laughed. "She *was* in the Congo, but they called her to South America. She phoned right after the quake. Some small tribe in the rain forest has some puzzling disease and they asked Libby to fly there immediately to help and of course she did. She said it will be difficult, but no matter what, she's coming home for Christmas. I think she needs to be with us. She sounded tired. Really tired. I told her we would get together and see if we could send her some energy, but she said no. She told me to conserve our strength and be very careful," Hannah reported.

Abbey and Kate stopped walking abruptly. "Are you certain Libby doesn't need us, Hannah?" Kate asked. "You know what can happen to her. She heals people in the worst of circumstances, and it thoroughly depletes her energy. Traveling those distances on top of it with little sleep won't help."

"She said no," Hannah reiterated. "I heard the weariness in her voice. She obviously needs to come home and regroup and rest, but I didn't feel as if she was in a dangerous state." She knelt on the floor at the foot of the mosaic her grandmother and her grandmother's sisters had worked so hard to make.

Relief swept through Kate. Libby always drove herself too hard, and her health suffered dramatically for it. Libby was too small, too slender, a fragile woman who pushed herself for others. Libby worked for the Center for Disease Control and traveled all over the globe. "We'll have to watch her," Kate said softly, musing aloud.

It was one of the best-loved talents of the sisters, to be able to stay in communication with one another no matter how far apart they were physically. They could 'see' one another and send energy back and forth when it was needed. Kate knelt beside Hannah in the entryway.

Kate always felt a sense of awe when she looked at the artwork on the floor. The mosaic always seemed to her to be alive with energy. Anyone looking into the mosaic felt as if they were falling into another world. The deep blue of the sea was really the ocean in the sky. Stars burst and flared into life. The moon was a shining ball of silver. Kate bent close to the mosaic to examine the greens, browns, and grays that made up mother earth.

Only Joley's voice poured into the room, then melted away on the last notes to leave the room entirely silent. The three sisters linked hands. Small bursts of electricity arced from one to the other. In the dimly lit room the energy appeared as a jagged whip of lightning dancing between the three women. Power filled the room, energy enough to move the drapes at the windows so that the material swayed and bowed.

Kate kept her eyes fixed on the darker earth tones. Something moved, down close to the edge of the mosaic, in the deeper rocks. It moved slowly, a blackened shadow, slipping from one dark area to the next. It had a serpentine, cunning way about it, shifting from the edges up toward the surface as if trying to break through. Kate let her breath out slowly, inhaled deeply to fill her lungs, and let her body go. It was the only way to walk in the shadow world that was invisible to most human eyes.

She felt the malevolence immediately, a twisted sneakiness, shrewd and determined, a being honed by rage and fueled by the need for revenge. The turmoil was overwhelming, spinning and boiling with heat and anger. It crept closer to her, awareness of her presence giving it a kind of malicious glee. She held herself still, trying to discern the dark force in the deeper shadows, but it blended too well.

"Kate!" Hannah shook her hard, catching her by the shoulders and rocking her until her head lolled back on her neck.

Abbey yanked Kate away from the mosaic and into her own body. There was a long silence while they clung to one another, breathing heavily, close to tears. The shrill ringing of the phone startled them.

"Sarah," they said simultaneously, and broke into relieved laughter.

Abbey jumped up to answer the phone. "I'm telling Sarah on you," she warned Kate, "and you're going to be in so much trouble!"

Kate gripped Hannah's hand, trying to smile at

Abbey's dire prediction. "Did you feel it, Hannah?" she whispered. "Did you feel it coming after me?"

"You can't go into that world again, Kate. Not with that thing there. I couldn't read what it was, but you have to stay away from it." Hannah held Kate even tighter. "I know what it's like to be afraid all the time, Katie. I can't function in a crowd because the energy of so many people drains me. Their emotions bombard me until I can't think or breathe. You all protect me, you always have. I wish we'd done the same for you."

Kate smiled and leaned over to kiss Hannah's cheek. "I accepted my limitations a long time ago, Hannah, and I've never regretted my choice of lifestyles. I control my environment, and it works for me. I didn't have the need to do all the things you wanted to do with your life. My world is carefully built and has large walls to protect me. You're far more open to the assault. I'll be careful, Hannah. I'm not a risk taker. You don't have to worry that I'll try to find the answers without the rest of you."

"Katie!" Abbey called out. "Sarah has a few things she wants to talk to you about." She held out the phone.

Kate hugged Hannah again. "It will be all right, I promise you, honey. It's Christmas. Most everyone is coming home, and we'll have the best time ever, just like we always do when we're together."

chapter 3

A chill, colder still than the air they will feel
As I rejoice in release, as I slip past the seal

MATT STOOD BESIDE THE ENORMOUS DOUGLAS fir tree decorated with hundreds of ornaments and colorful lights. The tall tree grew in the yard up near the cliffs in front of the house. It was one of the most beautiful sights he'd ever seen, but it paled in comparison to Kate. She stood on her porch, a snowglobe in her hands, smiling at him. Her eyes were as green as the sea, and her long, thick hair was twisted into some kind of intricate knot that made him want to pull out every pin so he could watch it tumble free.

He walked up the porch steps and held out his hand. "Where in the world did you get that snowglobe? The scene inside looks exactly like your house and this Christmas tree."

She put the globe in his hands. Two of her sisters were standing on the porch with her, watching him with serious expressions on their faces. He had been so busy staring at Kate he hadn't even noticed them. His hands closed over the heavy globe, his fingers brushing

Kate's. A tingle of electricity sparked its way up his arm. Almost at once the snowglobe grew warm in his hands. "Afternoon, ladies."

"Hi, Matt," Hannah greeted. Abbey nodded to him.

Although he'd made every effort to clean up after work, scrubbing his hands for a good half hour to get the dirt out from under his fingernails, he noticed with dismay that he hadn't been successful. His nails seemed to be spotlighted from the strange glow coming from inside the glass of the globe. The lights of the tree blazed unexpectedly inside the glass, while an eerie white fog began to swirl. Fascinated, he held the globe at every angle, trying to see how he had turned it on, but he couldn't find a battery or a switch anywhere. Peering closer he noticed a strange dark shadow taking shape at the base of the tree and creeping up the path toward the steps of the house. His body reacted, going on alert as he watched the shadow move stealthily.

"This thing is spooky." He handed the snowglobe to Hannah and took Kate's elbow in a deliberate, proprietary action. Staking his claim. Declaring his intentions. His fingers settled around her slender arm, and his heart actually jumped in his chest. She was wearing some lacy white shirt that clung to the shape of her rounded breasts and left her lower arms bare. The pad of his thumb slid over her petal-soft skin just to feel the texture. She shivered, and he moved his body closer to block the breeze coming in off the ocean. They said good-bye to her sisters and headed for his car.

Kate cleared her throat. "I appreciate your coming to pick me up, Matthew. I could have met you there."

"That's silly, Kate, since we're both going to the same place, and you're on my way. I thought we might discuss the plans for the renovation over dinner when we're finished inspecting the mill." He pulled open the door to his Mustang convertible. The top was securely up. "What were you doing with the globe?"

She smiled up at him and just that easily took his breath away. "We're still putting out our decorations. Hannah just brought the globe down from the attic and was cleaning the glass. It's a Christmas tradition in our family to wish on it."

"What was that strange dark shadow moving in the globe?"

Kate abruptly turned back toward the house. Matt was standing close to her, holding the door open to the Mustang, and she bumped his chest with her nose. For a second she stood there with her eyes closed, then she inhaled deeply. He felt that breath right through his skin, all the way down to his bones. The tips of her breasts brushed his rib cage sending fire racing through his bloodstream and pooling into a thick heat low in his belly. She smelled of cinnamon and spice. He wanted to pull her into his arms and kiss her right there. Right in front of her sisters.

"Matthew." For the first time that he could remember, Kate sounded breathless. "What are you doing?"

He realized his arms were around her. He was holding her captive against him, and his body was growing hard and making urgent demands. He cursed silently and let her go, turning away from her. "I thought you were getting into the car." His voice was rough, even to his own ears. He had never wanted a woman the way he wanted Kate. He didn't feel gentle when he wanted to be gentle. He didn't feel nice and charming when it was usually so easy for him to be charming. He felt edgy and restless and achy as hell. He had a mad desire to scoop her up and lock her in his vehicle, a primitive, out-of-character urge when she looked on the verge of flight.

"You really saw a shadow in the globe?" she asked. "What was it doing?"

It was the last thing he expected her to say, and it sent a chill skittering down his spine. "I couldn't tell what it was. The dark shadow went from the base of the tree up the path toward the porch of the house. It is your house in the globe, isn't it? There's fog or mist instead of snowflakes swirling around. It gives the globe a very eerie effect."

Kate glanced back at her sisters. Hannah set the snowglobe very carefully on the wide banister and stepped away from it. Inside the glass, heavy fog swirled. The lights from the tiny Christmas tree glowed a strange orange and red through the mist, almost as if on fire. Matt watched Kate's sister closely. He had lived in Sea Haven all of his life. He had heard strange things about the Drake sisters. Up close to them, he *felt* power and energy crackling in the air, and it emanated from them. The power filled the space around them until he breathed it. Hannah lifted her arms, and the wind swept in from the sea. With it came soft voices, whose words were impossible to distinguish, but the chant was melodious and in harmony with the things of the earth. The strange light in the snowglobe faded and diminished until it was a soft, faint glow. The voices on the wind continued until the lights behind the glass flickered and vanished, leaving the globe a perfectly ordinary Christmas ornament.

The wind swirled cool air around them. Matt tasted the salt from the sea. He looked down at his fingers curled around Kate's arm. He had pulled her protectively to him without thought or reason. He knew he should release her, but he couldn't let go. Her slender body trembled, with power or with fear, Matt wasn't certain which, but it didn't matter to him.

Kate looked up at him. "I can't explain what just happened with the snowglobe."

"I'm not asking for an explanation. I just want you to get in my car."

She smiled up at him. "Thank you, Matthew. I really appreciate it." She relaxed visibly and allowed him to help her into the warm leather seats.

Kate felt very small beside Matt. Inside the car, he

appeared enormous and powerful. His shoulders were wide enough to brush against her in the confines of the Mustang. When she inhaled, she took the masculine scent of him deep into her lungs. For a moment she felt dizzy. It made her want to laugh aloud at the thought. Kate Drake dizzy from the scent of a man. None of her sisters would believe it. The car handled the tight turns along the coastal highway with precision and ease, flowing around the corners so that she relaxed a little. Being around Matt always made her feel safe. She didn't know why, but she no longer questioned it.

He glanced over at her. "Does it bother you, the way people are always talking about your family?"

"They talk in a nice way," Kate pointed out.

"I know they do. You're the town's treasures, but does it bother you?"

Kate smiled at him. "Only you would ask me that question." She sighed. "It shouldn't bother me. We are different. We can't exactly hide it, and of course people are going to talk about our strange ways. We grew up here, so everyone knows us and to some extent they protect us from outsiders, but yes, it does bother me that people are always so aware of us when we're around." She'd never voiced that aloud to anyone, not even her sisters.

"I miss you when you're gallivanting around the world, Kate. I'm glad you've decided to come home."

Her smile widened. "You're such a flirt, Matthew,

even with me, and I've known you all of my life. You haven't calmed down much since your wild college days. When I was in high school, all the girls said you were legendary at Stanford."

"Well, I wasn't. I should have gone to a college far away from here instead of only a couple of hours. It might have cut down on the talk. And I don't flirt," he said firmly. He wanted to park the car and just look at her. Touch her soft skin and kiss her for hours. The moment the thoughts crept into his head his body hardened into a dull, painful ache. He couldn't get near her without it happening. He was a grown man, and his body responded to her as if he were an adolescent.

"Matthew, you flirt with everyone. And your reputation is terrible. If I wasn't already so talked about, I'd be worried."

"No one talks about me."

She laughed softly. "I can relate the story of you and Janice Carlton by heart, I've heard it so many times."

He groaned. "Is that still going around? That happened long ago. I was on leave, it must have been what? Six years ago? I did pick her up in the bar, she was drunk, Kate. I couldn't just leave her there."

"And how did her blouse get on the bushes outside the grocery store?"

Matt glanced sideways at her. "All right, I'll admit it was her blouse, but come on, Kate, I wasn't in high school. Give me a little credit for growing up. She was as drunk as a skunk and began peeling off her clothes the minute we were driving down the street. She threw her blouse out the window and would have thrown her bra but I told her I'd put her out on the sidewalk if she did. I took her straight home. And in case you want to know why my version was never told, I don't like talking about women who throw themselves at me when they're drunk. In spite of what you've heard, my mother raised me to be a gentleman. We may be a little rough around the edges, but the Granites have a code of honor."

The Mustang swung fluidly into the driveway leading to the old mill on the cliff above Sea Lion Cove. Matt drove straight up the dirt driveway to the long, wooden building and parked. He turned off the engine and slid his arm along the back of her seat. The ocean boomed below the cliffs, a timeless rhythm that seemed to echo the beat of his heart. "Most of the stories about me aren't true, Kate."

Kate stared straight ahead at the old building. Much of the wood was pitted from sea salt. The paint had long since worn away from the steady assault of the wind. She loved the look of the mill, the way it fit there on the cliff, a part of the past she wanted to bring with her into the future. She took a deep breath, composed herself, and turned to take Matt in.

Up close, Matthew Granite was a giant of a man with rippling, defined muscles and a strong, stubborn jaw. His mouth was something she spent far too much time staring at and dreaming about, and the shape of it had managed to slip into her bestselling novels on several heroes. His eyes were amazing. They should have been gray but they were more silver, a startling color that made her heart do triple time. He had the kind of thick, dark hair that made her want to run her fingers in it, and he wore it longer than most men. Kate felt a bit faint looking at his heavily muscled chest, then up into his glinting silver eyes. "Well, darn it, Matthew, all this time I thought I was in the presence of greatness." She managed to conjure up a lighthearted laugh. "It's not nice to destroy a woman's illusions."

He frowned. "I didn't say I *wasn't* the bad boy of Sea Haven."

"I thought Jonas Harrington was the bad boy of Sea Haven."

Matt looked affronted. "I never come in second place." His hand came up, unexpectedly spanning her throat.

Kate was certain her heart skipped a beat. His palm was large, and his fingers wrapped easily around her neck, his thumb tipping her head up so she was forced to meet the sudden hunger blazing in his eyes. It was the last thing Kate expected to see, and his intensity shocked her. "Matthew." She breathed his name in a small protest. It wasn't a good idea. They weren't a good idea.

He simply lowered his head and took possession of her mouth. His kiss was anything but gentle. He dragged her close, a starving man devouring her with hot, urgent kisses. The breath slammed out of her lungs, and every nerve ending in her body screamed at her. Electricity crackled between them, arcing from Matt to Kate and back again. Fire raced over her skin, melting her insides. He took the lead, kissing her hungrily, hotly, his tongue dueling with hers, demanding a response she found herself giving.

Her arms crept around his neck, her body pressing close to the heat of his. She felt so much heat, so much magic she couldn't think straight.

The blare of a horn made Kate jump away from him. Matt cursed and glanced at the highway in time to see his brothers waving, hooting, and honking as they drove by. "Damned idiots," he said, but there was a wealth of affection in his voice impossible to miss.

Kate pressed a trembling hand to her swollen mouth. Her skin felt raw and burned from the dark shadow on his jaw. She didn't dare look in the mirror, but she knew she looked thoroughly kissed. "They saved us."

"They may have saved you, but I'm in dire straits here, woman." And dammit all, he was. What was it about this woman that made him lose control whenever he was around her? Was she really a witch? He was going to have a few things to say to his brothers when he got his hands on them. He wasn't looking forward to the ribbing he was going to get after being caught necking like a teenager with Kate Drake. It didn't help matters that he saw Jonas Harrington cruising by very slowly, obviously looking for them. Damn Danny and his radio. It would be all over Sea Haven if they weren't more careful, and the last thing he wanted was for Kate to run from him because of gossip.

He touched Kate's red face. Her soft skin was raw from his whiskers. "I should have shaved, Katie, I'm sorry. I wasn't planning on kissing you." So, okay, he wanted to kiss her. He'd hoped to kiss her. He'd actually gotten down on his knees briefly last night when no one was around and asked for a Christmas miracle, but she didn't need to know how badly he wanted her.

The way he said Katie, turned her heart over, sending a million butterfly wings brushing at her stomach. "I don't mind."

He caught her face in his hands. "I mind. I need to be more careful with you." Abruptly he let her go and opened the door. It was the only safe thing to do when she looked so tempting. The chill from the sea rushed in to displace the heat of their bodies inside the car.

Kate didn't wait for him to come around and open her door. She was too shaken, too shocked by her reactions to him. It was so un-Kate-like of her. Kate the practical had just made a terrible mistake, and she couldn't take it back. She could still taste him, still had his scent clinging to her body, still felt a tremendous, edgy pressure, a need as elemental as hunger and thirst. She stood in the wind and lifted her face, hoping her skin would cool and that the raging need that was always inside of her would once again find rest.

Matt took her hand and led her up the broken and uneven path to the building. She didn't resist or pull away.

"The structure's sound," she assured him as she unlocked the door. "I want to be able to incorporate as much of the original building as possible when I expand. I was thinking decks outside with some protection against the wind for the sunnier days, and indoors, a large area with chairs and small tables for reading and drinking coffee or chocolate or whatever. There's a large stone fireplace in what must have been an office, and I'd like to keep that too if possible."

Kate covered her anxiety with talk, pointing out the rustic features she wanted to save and as many of the problem areas as she knew about. She was very aware of Matt's hand holding hers securely. Twice she tried to casually disengage, but he tugged her across the room to examine a rotted section of wood near the foundation.

"Where do the stairs lead?" He opened the sagging door and peered down into the dark interior. The stairs appeared to be very steep and halfway down he was certain the walls were dirt. "Is there a light?"

"Of sorts," Kate said. "It's over the second stair down. I can't reach the chain."

"Why wouldn't it be up here?" He pulled the chain gingerly, half-expecting the light to explode. It came on, but it was a dim yellow and made a strange humming sound. "What is that?"

"I don't know, but the fire marshal assured me it was safe in here." She smiled at him. "Isn't one of your brothers an electrician?"

"It will be a while before we need him," Matt said, starting down the stairs. The staircase was solid enough, but he didn't like the look of the wall. Several cracks spread out from the center of the wall in all directions like spiderwebs. He glanced at Kate, his eyebrow raised.

She shook her head. "The earthquake must have damaged it. It wasn't like that when I came down here with the Realtor. I actually came down twice just to make certain the entire place wasn't going to sink into the ocean. I know it's in bad shape, but it's such a perfect location. If I have to, I can pull down the mill and start from scratch. If you think that's the best thing to do, I'll take your advice, but I really want to save as much of the original building as possible."

"It's going to cost more money than it might be worth, Kate," he warned.

Kate shivered as they went down the stairs to the dimly lit basement. It was far colder than she remembered. Always sensitive to energy, she felt an icy malevolence that hadn't been there before. She looked around cautiously, moving closer to Matt for protection. The atmosphere vibrated with unrestrained malicious amusement. "Matthew, let's leave." She tugged at his arm.

He looked down at her quickly. "What is it, Katie?"

There was a caress to his voice, one that warmed her in spite of the icy chill in the basement. "You can wait upstairs while I look around." He felt her shiver and took the jacket she was holding from her to help her into it. "It won't take me very long." He pulled the edges of the jacket together and buttoned it up, his fingers lingering on the lapels, just holding her there, close to him.

Kate shook her head. "It feels unhealthy down here. I don't want to leave you alone. Matthew," she hesitated, searching for the right words. "This doesn't feel right to me, not the way it did before."

His silver eyes moved over her face. He suddenly winked, a quick sexy gesture that sent her heart thudding. "I'll make it quick, I promise."

Kate trailed after him, reluctant to be too far from him in the gloomy basement. It was long and wide and had a dirt floor. "I think this was used as the smugglers' storehouse. There's a stairway leading to the cove through a narrow tunnel. Part of the tunnel collapsed some years ago, but I read in my grandmother's diary that the mill was used to store supplies and weapons and spices coming in off the boats." She pressed her lips together, determined not to distract him as he studied the walls and the floor of the basement.

"What's this?" Matt halted next to a strange covering in the dirt. It was at least two inches thick and looked almost like the lid of a coffin, except it was oval in shape. The surface was rough and covered with symbols, which were impossible to read with the dirt and grime over them. Running straight through the middle of the lid was a large crack.

Kate frowned. "I didn't notice it before. It must have been covered by the dirt. Could the earthquake have shifted that much dirt?" She moved closer to it reluctantly. The icy cold air was coming from the deep crack. "I don't like this, Matthew."

"It isn't a grave, Kate," he pointed out, crouching beside it and brushing at the dirt along the edges. "It's more like a seal of some kind."

She hunkered down beside him. A blast of cold air touched her palm as she passed it above the crumbling rock. She brushed the dirt away from the symbols, trying to decipher the old hieroglyphics. The language was an ancient one, but it was all too familiar to her. Her ancestors, generations of powerful witches, had used such symbols to communicate privately. Her mother had urged them to learn the language, and Kate knew a few of the symbols, but not all. "It says something about rage. The symbols are chipped and worn away. I can make out the words, 'sealed until the day one is born'—" She broke off in frustration, leaning closer to try to figure out the meaning of the words.

"Where did you learn those symbols? Are they Egyptian?" Matt asked.

Kate shook her head. "No, it's a family thing. We

were all supposed to have learned. Do you think this is a well of some kind?"

Matt continued to dig around the edges of the thick lid. "It can't be a well, Kate. Maybe some kind of memorial?" He pushed at the heavy slab. It crumbled around the edges but slid slightly.

"No!" Kate caught Matt's arm, tugging hard. "We don't know what's inside. Something about this doesn't feel right to me. Can't you feel the malevolence pouring out of the crack?" She stumbled back, taking him with her, nearly sprawling on the ground so that he had to catch her as a noxious gas poured from the slit that had opened.

"It's just gas created from decomposed matter that's been trapped for a long time," Matt said, dragging her as far from the crevice as he could get them. He pushed her toward the stairs. "Sometimes the gases can make you sick or worse, Kate. Don't breathe it in." She looked pale, her eyes wide with horror. She stared at the lid without moving, one hand pressed to her mouth. Matt could see that her entire body was trembling.

At once he wrapped his arms around her and drew her close to him. He practically enveloped her entire body, yet she never looked away from the oddity in the basement, mesmerized by the yellow-black vapor streaming from the crack. "It's nothing Kate, just a hole in the ground. It's probably a couple of hundred years old." He remained calm in order to reassure her, but all of his senses had gone on alert.

Matthew obviously couldn't feel the malicious triumph pouring out of the ground, a welling-up of victory, a coup of sorts. She couldn't identify it, had no idea what it was, but she was terrified they might have unleashed something dangerous. Horrified, she watched the dark, ugly vapor swirl around the room, then stream up the stairs toward freedom, leaving behind an icy cold that chilled her to her bones.

"Stop shaking, Kate. It's gas. It happens all the time in these old vents." Matt couldn't bear that she was so frightened. "We find pockets all over the place. You haven't gone into the tunnel, have you? That could have all sorts of gas pockets as well as cave-ins."

"Have you ever seen gas do that? Travel around the room?"

"We're getting some kind of wind off the ocean, Kate. Can't you feel the draft in here? It's very strong."

"I have to take a look at those symbols, Matthew. I think something was sealed beneath that lid, and the earthquake disturbed it." She knew she sounded utterly ridiculous. She probably appeared a crackpot to him, but she was certain she was right. Something had slid out of that vent, something not meant to inhabit the world.

Matt studied her serious face, the fear in her eyes. "Let me make certain it's safe, Kate." He gently set her aside and made his way across the uneven dirt floor to the crumbling rock lid.

"Be careful, Matthew." When he looked at her, she wished she'd kept her mouth shut. She was sounding more and more paranoid.

He sniffed the air cautiously. The odor was foul, but he could breathe easily without coughing. "I think it's safe enough, Kate. I'm not keeling over, and I don't feel faint. I don't know what the hell you think just happened, but if it has you so afraid, I'm going to believe it. Jonas says never to doubt any of you Drakes."

She was grateful that he was trying to understand, but she knew he couldn't. Kate ducked her head, avoiding his gaze, afraid to see the way he was looking at her. She sank down beside the lid and dusted lightly with her fingers, afraid of crumbling the old rock even more.

Matt waited silently as long as he could. There was the sound of the sea booming in the background. The echo of it pounded off the walls eerily. "Does it mean anything to you?" He tried to keep impatience from his voice when all he wanted to do was snatch Kate up and carry her out of the place.

Kate peered closer to decipher the words. Seven sisters. Seven Drake sisters. Her ancestors. They had bound something to earth, committed its spirit to the vent hole to protect something. She couldn't read it exactly as parts of the letters were smashed and worn away, but she was afraid it was the townspeople who needed to be protected. She could also make out something to do with Christmas and fire and one who would be born who could bring peace. Kate looked up at Matt. There was no way to hide the terror in her eyes, and she didn't bother to try. "I need to go home right now."

chapter 4

A wreath of holly meant to greet
Looks much better tossed in the street

MATT SAT IN HIS CAR WITH THE HEATER RUNning and his favorite CD playing low. Joley Drake's unique, sultry voice had taken her up the charts fast. He loved this particular collection, usually finding it soothing, but it wasn't doing him any good now. He gripped the steering wheel and stared up at the blazing lights of the Christmas tree in front of the cliff house. The fog was beginning to roll in off the sea, stretching white fingers toward land and the house he was watching. There were no electric lights in the windows, yet he could see the flicker of candlelight and an occasional shadow as one of the Drake sisters moved past the glass.

The passenger door jerked open, and Jonas Harrington slid into the seat beside Matt, shutting the door against the cold.

"Dammit, Jonas, you scared the hell out of me!" Matt snapped. He hadn't realized just how jumpy he was until Jonas had pulled the door open.

"Sorry about that." Jonas sounded as pleasant as ever. Too pleasant. Matt turned his head to look at his childhood friend. "What are you doing out here? It's cold, and the fog's coming in. You aren't stalking our Kate, are you?"

Matt studied his friend's face. He was smiling, looking amicable, but his eyes were ice-cold. "Of course I'm stalking Kate. Do you think I've lost my mind? That woman belongs with me." He grinned to relieve the tension gathering between them. "I just have to figure out how to convince her of that. What are you doing here? And why didn't I see the headlights of your car?" He glanced in the rearview mirror and noted Jonas had cruised silently up behind him.

"I ran without headlights, didn't want to scare you away. What happened tonight? Why are they all upset?" There was no obvious accusation in the voice, but Matt had been around Jonas his entire life, and he recognized the underlying note of suspicion.

"What the hell are you trying to say, Jonas? Spit it out and quit beating around the bush." Temper was beginning to flare. "I've had a hell of an evening, and you aren't helping."

Jonas shrugged. "I did just spit it out. They're upset. I can feel it. All of them, every single sister. Does it have something to do with you and Kate?"

"What kind of question is that? Hell, yes, I want Kate. And yes, I'd do just about anything to get her, but I sure wouldn't lay a finger on her if she didn't want me to, and I wouldn't *ever* hurt her. Is that what you want to know?"

Jonas nodded. "That's about what I was looking for. I'd hate to have to kick your ass, but if you hurt that girl, I'd have to do it."

"As if you could." Matt tapped his finger against the steering wheel, frowning while his temper settled. "What do you mean, you can feel they're all upset?"

"I've always been able to feel when something's wrong with the Drakes. And right now, something's very wrong." Jonas continued to look at him with cool, assessing eyes.

Matt shook his head. "It wasn't me, Jonas. Something weird happened at the old mill, and Kate was very distressed. She asked me to take her home, and I did." He raked his fingers through his hair, not once, but twice. "I didn't even have a chance to ask her out again. I was just sitting here, trying to figure out whether I should go up to the house and ask her what happened, or go back to the mill and try to figure it out."

"There they are!" Jonas muttered an ugly word beneath his breath. "What the hell do they think they're doing going out in the middle of the night with the fog rolling in?"

Matt could just make out the three Drake sisters swirling dark, hooded cloaks around them as they hurried down the steps. The fog was heavy and thick, an invasion of white mist that hid the women effectively as they rushed down the worn pathway that wound down the hill toward the road. Matt leaped out of his car, losing sight of them in the curtain of fog. He was aware of Jonas swearing under his breath, keeping pace as they angled to cut off the Drakes before they could reach the highway.

Jonas beat him to the women, catching Hannah's arm and yanking her around to face him. "Are you out of your mind?"

Kate's expression went from startled to troubled when she caught sight of them. "Matthew, I thought you went home." She looked uneasily around her at the fog. "You shouldn't be out here. I don't think it's safe. And neither should you, Jonas."

Hannah glared at the sheriff. "Has anyone ever told you you have bad manners?"

"Has anyone ever turned you over their knee?" Jonas countered. "If you don't think it's safe out here, what are you doing running around in the dark?"

Kate indicated the heavy wall of fog. "It isn't like we're going to get very far in this stuff. We have an errand, Jonas, an important one."

"Then you should have called me," Jonas snapped impatiently. Hannah stirred as if to say something but Jonas's fingers tightened around her arm. "I'm really, really angry right now, Hannah. Don't make it worse."

"Jonas," Kate's voice was placating. "You don't understand."

"Then make me understand, Kate," he snarled.

Matt immediately stepped between Jonas and Kate. "I don't think you need to talk to her like that, Jonas. Let her explain."

Kate's fingers curled around Matt's arm. "Jonas worries about us, Matthew. We probably should have called him."

Matt didn't want her calling Jonas; he wanted her to call him when something was wrong. And something was obviously wrong. Before she could pull her hand away from his arm, he covered her fingers with his. "We're already here, Kate. Tell us what you need to do."

Her sea-green eyes moved over his face. He had the feeling she could see more deeply into him than most people, but it was always like that with Kate. He tightened his hold on her hand. "Kate. You trust Jonas. He can vouch for me."

Kate closed her eyes briefly. Matthew Granite was her dream man, and after he witnessed what really went on around the Drake sisters she wouldn't even be able to sustain the fantasy of a relationship with him. She sighed but she squared her shoulders. Some things were just more important than romantic dreams. She took a deep breath. "Something was unleashed today, something malevolent. We think." She looked at her sisters for courage before continuing. "We think the earthquake may have awakened it or at least provided it with the opportunity to rise. It was the shadow you saw in the globe, Matt, and my sisters and I saw in the mosaic. It's very real, and it feels dangerous to us." She stared up at him, clearly expecting him to laugh.

Matt kept his face completely expressionless. He knew the Drakes were different; some said they performed miracles, some said they were genuine witches. Sea Haven was a hotbed of gossip, and the Drake sisters were always at the forefront. But not Kate. Never Kate.

"So it felt dangerous to you, and the first thing you do is rush out into the night in the middle of one of the worst fogs we've ever had," Jonas snapped. "Dammit, Kate, Abbey and Hannah might rush headlong into danger, but you usually show some trace of sense." He hauled Hannah back against him when she tried to squirm away. "I'm not playing around with you, Hannah. Keep it up, and I'll lock you away for the night."

Hannah's beautiful face radiated fury, but instead of taking Jonas to task as Matt expected, she was gasping for breath.

Abbey leaped to her side. "Breathe, Hannah, very slow."

Hannah shook her head, fear filling her eyes. Abbey extracted a paper bag from her purse and handed it to her sister. "Breathe into this."

Looking alarmed, Jonas wrapped his arm around Hannah's waist to support her as she doubled over, clearly unable to breathe adequately. "What the hell is wrong with her? Should we get an ambulance?"

"Would you please stop swearing at her?" Abbey snapped. "Be very careful, Jonas, or I'll ask you questions you don't want to answer."

"Shut up, Abbey, don't you dare threaten me," Jonas growled back.

"Stop it, all of you, stop it," Kate pleaded.

Seeing the anxiety on Kate's face, Matt stepped closer to her and put his arm around her. Hannah breathed into the paper bag for a couple of minutes and lifted her head. She looked ready to cry. "Abbey, if you want to take Hannah back to the house, I'll go with Kate to do whatever it is you all think is so important." He made the offer before he could stop himself. Kate was shivering in the cold fog. She didn't need to be out on such a night. He wanted just to pick her up and take her home and lie down with her by the fireplace.

Jonas pushed back Hannah's wealth of blond hair. "Are you all right, baby doll?" His choice of words should have been insulting, but the gentle concern in his voice made them an endearment.

Hannah nodded but didn't look at any of them, still clearly fighting for air.

"Maybe that's a good idea, Hannah. I'll go with Matt and just look around a little, and you and Abbey pull out the diaries and see if you can find anything that might help us figure this out," Kate said. "Matthew, are you certain you don't mind? I want to walk around town and just get a feel for what's going on."

"I don't mind. Are you going to be warm enough?"

"Just how dangerous is this, Kate?" Jonas asked.

"I honestly don't know," she replied. "I wish I knew. We thought if we went out together, all of us might be able to pick something up, but I already feel it. I think I can track it."

Matt cleared his throat. "Track a shadow?" If they weren't all so serious, he would be thinking it was a Halloween prank. He glanced up at the house. The fog was a heavy shroud, almost obliterating the house. He could see the lights of the Christmas tree, but only as pale, orange-glowing haloes distorted by the blanket of grayish white. He went still. The fog was changing color, darkening from white to a charcoal gray. Just as the fog had done in the snowglobe when he'd picked it up to examine it.

"The fog is bad, Kate. I've never seen it like this," Jonas said. "Stay close to Matt. I'll take Hannah and Abbey back to the house."

Hannah stiffened and looked at Abbey. Abbey smiled. "We'll make it home fine, Jonas. It's just up the hill. We know the path."

"I'm coming with you, Abbey, so don't argue." Jonas turned resolutely toward the house. "Matt, if it feels wrong to you, or you think Kate's in any danger at all, get her back here and don't let her give you any nonsense."

Kate smiled at Jonas. "I never talk nonsense. You take care of my sisters because if anything happens to them . . ."

"I know, I've heard it all before." Jonas waved at her, and the fog swallowed them up, even muffling the sound of their footsteps on the path, leaving Kate alone with Matt.

She looked up at him. "You don't have to do this, you know. I'm capable of walking up and down the streets of Sea Haven."

Matthew stared down into her beautiful sea-green eyes. "But I'm not capable of leaving your side when there's even a hint of danger near you." He lowered his head slowly to hers, drawn as if by a magnet, expecting her to pull away, giving her plenty of time to think about it.

Kate watched his eyes change, go dark with desire, right before his mouth took possession of hers. It didn't matter that the air was cold, and the wind chilled them, their bodies produced a remarkable heat, their mouths fused with fire. He dragged her against his body, his muscular arms enveloping her, holding her as if she were the most precious person in the world to him. He was exquisitely rough, yet impossibly gentle, voraciously hungry, nearly devouring her mouth, yet so tender he brought tears to her eyes. She had no idea how he did it, but she wanted more.

"You're not good for me," she whispered against his mouth.

His tongue slid along the seam of her lips, teased her tongue into another brief, but heated tango. "I'm absolutely perfect for you." He tugged at her cape until her body was pressed tightly against his. "I was born to be with you, Kate. You're supposed to be some kind of a magical woman, filled with the second sight, yet you don't see what's right in front of you. Why is that?" He didn't give her the opportunity to debate, he just kissed her long and thoroughly.

Kate felt her insides melting, turning to a warm puddle and settling somewhere in her lower region as a frustrating and unrelenting ache. Her knees actually went weak. "I can't think straight when we're kissing, Matthew."

"That's a good thing, Kate, because neither can I," he answered, his lips drifting into the hollow of her neck and back up to find her ear.

Heat pulsed through her, but she forced herself to pull away from him. He wasn't for her. She knew that, and once he found out what she was really was like, he'd know it too. She might seem courageous and strong, but when it came to losing him, she knew she'd be very fragile. Starting up with Matthew Granite was a decidedly ridiculous thing for her to do. "Matthew, really, I have to find this malevolent shadow and hopefully help it find some peace or get my sisters to help me seal it back up."

Matt silently cursed dark shadows and evil entities and every other thing that went bump in the night. She obviously believed they had let something harmful loose on the small town of Sea Haven. He was certain it was a pocket of gas; but if it meant walking around town with her at night, holding hands and kissing her every chance he got, well, hell, he was her man. He could do that. And he would even try to keep an open mind.

"Then let's go." He wrapped his arm around her. "I've got a flashlight in my car. This fog is really thick."

"We won't need a flashlight, Matthew. I have a couple of glow sticks. My sister Elle makes them. They work very well in the fog." She pulled several thin tubes from the inside pocket of her cape and handed him one. "Just shake it."

"I forgot about little Elle and her chemistry set. She blew up more missiles on the beach than any other kid at Sea Haven. Didn't she get a full scholarship to Columbia or MIT or some other very prestigious school? One very brave to take her on?"

Kate laughed, warmth spreading through her. "They were very brave, but fortunately they turned out a remarkable physicist able to do just about anything she wants to do. Elle is a genius and utterly fearless. She's not afraid to crawl around in caves looking at strange rock formations, and she's not afraid of taking apart a bomb when she's needed. Unlike me."

"What do you mean?" Matt tightened his fingers around hers.

"My sisters do incredible things and people expect it of us, but I wouldn't want you to think I'm capable of climbing mountains or jumping out of planes because you've heard of all of their exploits." She was feeling her way in the fog rather than following the glow stick. She lifted her face to the droplets of sea moisture, inhaling to try to catch the scent of something foul. "We have to cross the highway."

With the fog so thick there was virtually no traffic. Matt moved with her across the coastal highway and took the shortcut that led to the center of town. She was so serious all of a sudden, so distant from him, that he was actually beginning to believe she was on the trail of something evil. He could sense the stillness in her, the gathering of energy.

The survival instincts he'd honed during his years as a Ranger kicked in. His skin prickled as he went onto alert status. Adrenaline surged, and his senses grew keener. He felt the need for complete silence and wondered if he was beginning to believe in supernatural nonsense. Matt eased the glow stick inside his jacket without activating it. The fog muffled the sound of Kate's footsteps. He was aware of her breathing, of the eerie feel of the fog itself, of everything.

By mutual consent they were silent as they walked along the street. He became aware of a slight noise. A puffing. It was distant and hushed, barely audible in the murky blanket of mist. Matt found himself straining to listen. There was a rhythm to the sound, reminding him of a bull drawing air in and out of its lungs hard before a charge. Breathing. Someone was breathing, and the sound was moving, changing directions each time they changed directions.

Matt pressed his lips to her ear. "There's someone in the fog with us." He was certain someone was watching them, someone quite close.

Kate tipped her head back. "Some*thing,* not someone."

Kate turned toward the residential area. The town looked strange shrouded in the gray-white fog. Heavily decorated for Christmas, the multicolored lights on the stores and office buildings, the houses and trees gave off the peculiar glow of a fire in the strange vapor, giving the town a disturbing infernal appearance rather than a festive one. Matt wished he had brought a weapon with him. He was a good hand-to-hand fighter because he was a big man, strong, with quick reflexes and extensive training, but he had no idea what kind of adversary they faced.

Something hit him in the back, skittered down his jeans, and fell to the street. Matt whirled around to face the enemy and found nothing but fog.

"What is it?" Kate asked. Her voice was steady, but her hand, on the small of his back, was shaking.

Matt hunkered down to look at the object at his feet. "It's a Christmas wreath, Kate. A damned Christmas wreath." He looked around carefully, trying to penetrate the fog and see what was moving in it. He could feel the presence now, real, not imagined. He could hear the strange, labored breathing, but he couldn't find the source.

As he stood, a second object came hurtling out of

the fog to hit him in the chest. He heard the smash of glass and knew immediately that the wreath had been decorated with glass ornaments. "Let's get out of here, off the street at least," he said.

Kate was stubborn, shaking her head. "No, I have to face it here."

Matt pulled Kate to him, shielding her smaller body with his own as more wreaths came flying through the air, hurled with deadly accuracy at them from every direction. He wrapped his arms around her head, pressing her face against his chest. "It's kids," he muttered, brushing a kiss on top of her head to reassure her. "Always playing pranks; it's dangerous in this fog, not to mention destructive."

He hoped it was kids. It had to be an army of kids, tearing wreaths off the doors of the houses and throwing them at passersby as a prank. He heard no laughter, not even running footsteps. He heard nothing but the rough breathing. It seemed to come out of the fog itself. The nape of his neck prickled with unease.

"It isn't children playing a prank, Matt." Kate sounded close to tears. "It's much, much worse."

"Kate." He stroked a caress down the back of her head. Her hair was inside the hood of the cape, but his palm lingered anyway. "It isn't the first time a group of kids decided to play around, and it won't be the last."

The Christmas wreaths lay around them in a circle, some smashed or crushed and others in reasonably good shape. Kate lifted her face away from his chest and took a breath. "I can smell it, can't you?"

Matt inhaled deeply. He recognized the foul, noxious odor of the gases in the old mill. His heart jumped. "Dammit, Kate. I'm beginning to believe you. Let's get the hell out of here before I decide I'm crazy."

She pulled free of his arms. "Is that what you think about me? That I'm crazy?"

"Of course not. This is all just so damned odd."

Her sea-green eyes moved over his face, a little moody, a little fey. "Well, brace yourself, it's going to get damned odder. Stay still."

The fog swirled around them, their faces, their feet, and bodies, spinning webs of charcoal gray matter. As at the cliff house, Matt got the impression of bony fingers, and this time they were trying to grab at Kate. Without thinking, he caught her up and started to run, the urge strong to get her away from the long gray tentacles, but the blanket of fog was thick around them.

Kate pressed her lips to his ear. "Stop! I have to try to stop it, Matthew; it's what I do. We can't outrun the fog, it's everywhere."

"Dammit, Kate, I don't like this." When she didn't respond, he reluctantly put her down and stayed very close to her, ready for action.

She turned in the direction of her home, her face serene, thoughtful, yet determined. She radiated beauty, an inner fire and strength. She whispered, a soft, melodic chant that became part of the night, of the air surrounding them. She wasn't speaking English but a language he didn't recognize. Her voice was soothing, tranquil, a soft invitation to a place of peace and harmony with the earth.

The fog itself breathed harder, in and out, a burst of air sounding like a predatory animal with teeth and claws. The mist seemed to vibrate with anger, roiling and spinning and growing darker. Gray fog whirled around the Christmas wreaths at Matt's feet, spinning fast enough to lift them into the air. Bright green wreaths withered and blackened as if all the life was being sucked out of them. The objects reminded Matt of the garlands at funerals rather than the cheery decorations for a holiday, and each of them seemed to be aimed straight toward Kate.

His breath caught in his throat, and his heart pounded. Kate looked small and fragile under the onslaught of the vicious gray-black vapor. He moved, a fluid glide that took him into the path of the blackened garlands so that they smashed into his larger frame. Kate ignored the fog and the wreaths, concentrating on something inside of herself. She stared toward the house on the cliffs and abruptly lifted her arms straight up into the air. The wind rushed in from the ocean with wild force. It carried the crisp scent of the sea, the taste and feel of the waves, and a spray of salt. It also carried voices, soft and melodious and very feminine. The wind swept through the fogbank, the voices swelling in strength, Kate's voice joining theirs until they were in perfect harmony, in total command.

The spinning Christmas wreaths dropped to the road. The fog receded, heading inland, blanketing the residential homes; but the wind was persistent, shifting directions and herding the fog back toward the ocean. Kate looked translucent, her skin pale and beaded with moisture, wisps of hair clinging to her face, but she didn't falter. Her voice brought a sense of peace, of tranquillity, of something beautiful and satisfying. It filled Matt with longing for a home and a family of his own. It filled him with a deep sense of pride and respect for Kate Drake.

He watched the fog reluctantly retreat until it was far out over the ocean, dissipated by the force of the wind. There was a silence left behind in the vacuum of the tempest. Kate dropped her arms as if they were leaden. She staggered. He leaped forward to catch her before she collapsed, swinging her into his arms and cradling her against his chest.

"It's growing in strength. I couldn't have sent it away if my sisters hadn't helped." Kate looked up at him with frightened eyes.

Matt kissed her. It was the only thing he could think to do. She seemed weightless in his arms. He kissed her eyes and the tip of her nose and settled his mouth, feather-light over hers. "It's all right now, Kate. Rest. You sent it away. Tell me what you need." He could see that every drop of her strength had been used up in fighting the unseen enemy in the fog. She'd made a believer out of him. He was a man of action, having spent several years in the service training to protect his countrymen, yet there had been nothing he could do to stop the evil shadow in the mist. "What is it?"

She rubbed her face tiredly against his jacket. "I don't know, Matthew, I honestly don't know."

"How did you know what to say to it? What language it would understand?"

"I didn't know. I was using a healing chant my family has passed down from generation to generation. I was attempting to heal its spirit."

He stared at her, trying not to look shocked. The dark shadow seemed beyond any sort of redemption to him, something dark and dangerous, looking for a chance to strike out at anything or anyone around it.

Kate looked at the wreaths strewn all over the road. "Strange that he would choose to attack us with the wreaths."

"Strange that it could use them at all. Do you think it's a he?"

She shrugged. "It felt male to me."

The adrenaline was beginning to subside, but he continued to eye the cliffs warily. "I'm never going to look at fog again in the same way."

"A wreath is a continuous circle, Matthew, and it symbolizes real love, unconditional, true affection that never ceases." Her voice was thoughtful.

"I didn't feel love flowing out of the fog," he

answered. He began walking back in the direction of her house, Kate in his arms.

"But he tore the Christmas wreaths off every door on the street and threw them."

"At *us*," he said grimly. "I'm used to looking my enemy in the eye, Katie, fighting him with weapons or my bare hands. I couldn't exactly grab the fog and throttle it, although I wanted to."

"Put me down, Matthew, I'm too heavy for you to carry all that way."

"I was a Ranger for ten years, Katie, I think I can pack your weight with no problem."

She wasn't going to argue, she was just too drained. "Ten years. That's right, you joined right out of college. I've been wandering around so much, and I knew you didn't live here, but your family always made it seem as if you were here."

"I spent my leave here, every chance I could. I picked up my life here again immediately after I got out of the service because the family business was waiting for me. My father and brothers kept me a part of it, even though they did all the work."

"Why did you join the Rangers, Matthew? As soon as I heard, I researched what they were all about. It was very—" she hesitated, searching for the right word—"intense. And frightening. Why would you want to do something like that?"

"I've always needed to push myself to find out my limits. And I believe in my country, so it seemed a perfect fit for me. The Rangers embody everything I believe in. Move farther and faster and fight harder than any other soldier. Never surrender, never leave a fallen comrade, survive and carry out the mission under any conditions."

Kate sighed heavily and turned her face into his shoulder, hiding her expression from him. Something about that sigh gave Matt a sick feeling in the pit of his stomach. He wanted to ask her about it, but by the time he reached the path leading to the house, Kate was asleep.

chapter 5

A town dreams of sweet thoughts while nestled in bed,
Until nightmares of me begin to dance in their heads.

"KATE. KATIE. WAKE UP, HON." THE SOFT VOICE beckoned Kate from layers of sleep. "You need to eat now, wake up."

Kate opened her eyes and stretched, blinking drowsily up at her sister. "Sarah. What are you doing here?" She pushed at the heavy fall of hair tumbling around her face. She always braided her hair before she went to bed, yet it was everywhere. She turned her head and went still. Matthew Granite was sprawled in a chair beside her bed, his silver gaze trained intently on her face. Her stomach did a funny little flip.

A slow smile softened his tough features, lit his gray eyes, and stole her heart. "You're finally awake. I was getting worried."

"You slept in the chair?" Kate couldn't imagine his large body finding a relaxing position in her bedroom chair.

"Well, I did want to share your bed, but I was worried about your sisters giving me the evil eye." His smile widened into a teasing grin. "Jonas slunk out of here a couple of hours ago afraid even to drink a cup of coffee. He warned me one of you might slip an eye of newt into my coffee, so I thought it best to stay in everyone's good graces."

"You like coffee that much, do you? Enough to stay in our good graces?" She couldn't stop looking at him. There was a blue-black shadow along his jaw, and his clothes were rumpled, but it didn't make him any less attractive to her. "Just so I'm not the one slipping the eye of newt to you, why are you sleeping in my room?" She glared at Sarah rather than at Matt.

Sarah held her hands up, palm out. "We all tried to get him to leave last night, Kate, but he wouldn't go. Granite might be his last name, but it's also what he's made of. No one could budge him. Jonas tried scaring him off, but that didn't work either."

Kate tried not to be pleased. She tried to frown at Matt, to pretend displeasure, but there was no way she could carry it off, so she gave up. He just winked at her anyway, looking sexier than ever with the dark stubble shadowing his jaw.

Sarah sat on the edge of the bed. "I hate interrupting, but you have to eat. You expended far too much energy last night. Even Joley called and was feeling drained." She waved a hand toward the drapes, and, to Matt's astonishment, the curtain slid open to allow the morning light to pour in. "I know you don't feel hungry, you never do afterward, but you have to eat for all of us."

Neither Kate nor Sarah seemed to think anything was unusual. Matt blinked several times to test his eyesight.

"How's Hannah?" Kate sat up, thankful she was still wearing her clothes. Matt and her sisters must have removed her cape and her shoes and socks before putting her in her bed, but at least she was safely clad in her slacks and blouse. "I couldn't believe with all of us working on her, she still had an attack. That's the first time I can remember that our joining together failed her."

Sarah glanced at Matt and hesitated. He raised his hands. "If you need to be alone with Kate, I'll go on down to the kitchen and see what kind of trouble I can get into." He stretched out his hand to Kate, resting it palm down on the bed.

"It's just that Hannah is such a private person, Matthew." Kate placed her hand over his. "She was embarrassed that it happened in front of you and Jonas. Especially Jonas."

"It? You mean her asthma attack?" He turned his hand to circle hers with his fingers, knowing she was trusting him with something private. "It was an asthma attack, wasn't it?"

"Not exactly." Kate sighed. "I wish Jonas would let up on her a little bit."

"She seems to be able to dish it right back to him."

Matt leaned over to brush strands of hair from her face. "I don't quite get your relationship with Jonas, but I served with him in the Rangers. Jonas, me, and Jackson Deveau. Jonas is a good man."

"Jackson Deveau is the deputy who scares the hell out of everyone," Sarah informed Kate when she frowned. "You must have seen him a few times. He doesn't ever say much, but he looks lethal. He came to Sea Haven with Jonas when he returned from the Army."

"Jackson's a good man too," Matt said.

Kate hadn't met the deputy because she hadn't been back long, and she tended to wrap herself up in the cocoon of her own world. "I take it Jackson isn't from here originally."

"No, but he often came to Sea Haven on leave with us. He had no family and nowhere else to go when he left the service, so we asked him to come back with us. This town is friendly and tolerant, and Jackson needs tolerance. He's family to us. As for Jonas, you have to understand him. I saw him go in under heavy fire to drag a wounded man out of a battle zone. He carried that man for miles on his back. And Jackson . . ." He broke off, shaking his head. "I know Jonas watches over you all."

"Like a hawk," Sarah interjected dryly.

Matt shrugged. "Maybe it's because he really cares about all of you."

"Don't worry about our relationship with Jonas,"

Kate said. "We all love him dearly, even when we want to conjure up a spell to turn him into a toad."

Matt cleared his throat, rubbed the bridge of his nose, and sat back in his chair. "Can you really do that?"

Kate exchanged a mischievous grin with Sarah. "You never know about the Drake sisters. Really, Matthew, Jonas is intertwined deeply with our family. He always seems to know when something is wrong. He's sensitive to things not seen with the human eye."

Sarah leaned toward Matt. "You felt it last night, didn't you, when you were in the fog with Kate, and we joined with her? You knew something was wrong."

Matt sighed. "I don't know what happened last night, but I sure as hell don't want Kate facing anything like that again." His gray eyes smoldered with something dangerous as he looked at Kate. "I didn't like the way the fog seemed to be attacking you."

Sarah gasped. "What do you mean attacking her?"

"Nothing came at me," Kate denied hastily. "Really, Sarah, it was just throwing Christmas decorations around and Matthew was actually hit a few times. I was never touched."

Sarah looked at Matt steadily. "Why did you think it was after Kate?"

"I stepped in front of her to protect her. The wreaths were thrown, but not very hard in the beginning, yet when Katie began to talk to it, whatever it is, the Christmas wreaths were thrown much more forcefully and with greater accuracy."

"Were you hurt?" Kate looked suddenly anxious, coming up on her knees on the bed to look at him. "Libby's the best at healing, but Sarah. . . ."

"I'm fine," Matt said, but wished he didn't have to admit it. She looked incredibly beautiful leaning toward him with her hair tousled and her eyes enormous with concern for him.

"Kate—" Abbey stuck her head in the room—"Gina over at the preschool says something's wrong, and she needs you. I could hear the children crying in the background. I told her you weren't well, but she said it was an emergency. She said she needed your help. I'll go if I absolutely have to go."

Abbey was clearly apprehensive about going in Kate's place. Matt looked at Sarah. "What does Kate have to do with the preschool?"

"Haven't you noticed Kate has a gift for calming people with her voice? She's able to bring peace to even the most distressed person or situation," Sarah answered.

"Is that what your lives are like? People need you, and it doesn't matter if you're tired or not, you just go to them."

"We were born with certain gifts, Matt," Kate said. "We've always known we were meant to serve others. Yes, it isn't always easy, and all of us have to have ways of protecting ourselves but when we can help, we have to go."

"How do they know to call you?"

Sarah smiled. "You were older than us, Matthew,

ahead of us in school, so you really weren't around when our talents began to develop. I'm sure you've heard the rumors, but you didn't witness what we could do the way other people in town did. Jonas has always connected with us in some way, so it was easy enough for him to believe."

"Kate?" Abbey prompted.

"I'll go. Give me a few minutes to shower and have a cup of tea."

Matt followed her to the bathroom door. "I don't like this, Kate. You look fragile to me. I think Sarah's right. You need to stay home."

Sarah's eyebrow shot up. "Did I say that?"

Kate rubbed a caress along Matt's stubbly jaw right in front of her sisters, then closed the bathroom door on his startled expression. When he turned around, Sarah and Abbey were grinning at him. "She doesn't listen, does she?" he asked.

"Not very well," Sarah agreed. "Kate may be quiet about it, but she goes her own way and does what she thinks is right."

"Do you have another bathroom so I can clean up really fast?"

Sarah grinned at him. "I even have an extra toothbrush. You've got that look in your eye when you look at her."

He followed her down the hall. "What look?"

"You look at her like you can't wait to kiss her," Sarah said. "A toothbrush is definitely in order."

"Does she have something against the Rangers?" Matt asked, remembering the small sigh from the night before. It had haunted him most of the night.

Sarah pushed open a door to a powder blue bathroom. "Of course not. Why would you think that?"

"No reason. Thanks, Sarah." Matt didn't want to think about that strange little sigh of Kate's. She wasn't the type of woman to react that way unless she had a reason. He'd ask her about it later. He hurried through his shower wanting to get back to her.

Kate was still in the bathroom when he returned to her room. He rested his palm on the door, the exact level as her head. "Come out of there, Katie, you're beautiful enough without working at it."

From behind the door she laughed. "How do you know? You took a terrible chance staying. You could have woken up and my mask could have slipped off in the middle of the night."

"I didn't go to sleep. I watched over you."

There was a small shocked silence. Kate jerked the door open and stared up at him. "You must be exhausted. Go home and go to bed."

"I'd rather go with you." He reached out and pulled her to him. Her body fit perfectly against his, as if made to be there.

"Matthew." There was hesitation in Kate's voice.

He kissed her. He didn't want her to voice her reservations. Kissing her was a much better and far more enjoyable idea. It was magic, if there was such a thing, and he was beginning to believe there was. He meant for it to be a brief, good morning kiss, a gentle shut-up-and-just-kiss-me kiss, but she caught fire, or he did, and they both just went up in flames. He wanted more than to kiss her, he wanted to touch her, to claim her soft body, to feel her moving beneath him, her hands clinging . . .

"Stop!"

Matt and Kate drew apart, their hearts racing, and blinked at each other, then looked around in surprise to see Sarah, Hannah, and Abbey in the doorway glaring at them.

"Kate," Sarah said, taking a deep breath. "You know we're all connected in some way. You can't be in such close proximity to us and carry on like that. We're all in overdrive, thank you very much."

Unrepentant, Matt grinned at them as he pulled Kate tight against him. "Sorry about that. We're off to see some preschoolers." Kate hid her face in his shoulder, trying not to laugh. He did the gentlemanly thing and got her out of there quickly, waving at Damon, Sarah's fiancé, as they hurried past him.

"The man should thank us," he whispered, and pretended to wince when Kate smacked his arm.

Kate stared out the window of the Mustang at the white-capped ocean as they drove along the highway toward the exit to the street where the preschool was located. "The fogbank is very thick out over the ocean," she said, a note of apprehension in her voice.

"See how dark it is, more gray than white, and it seems to be churning." She turned her gaze on Matt. "I should have been more careful. Somewhere in the diaries there has to be something about this strange phenomenon."

"What diaries? You've mentioned the diaries before. How can they help?"

"My family keeps a history, books handed down generation to generation. Somewhere this event had to be recorded. The problem is, all of us were supposed to learn the earlier languages used, but we gave it a half-hearted attempt. All of us know a little, but Elle really can read it. We have to decipher the books."

Matt turned the car onto the exit. "You think this thing is coming back."

"I know it is. Can't you feel it on the wind?"

He could only feel how close he was to her. How just out of his reach she always seemed to be. Matt parked the car in the lot at the preschool, and they sat for a moment, absorbing the unnatural silence. There were no children playing in the small yard.

Kate squared her shoulders. "Do you want to wait out here?"

For an answer, he got out of the car and went around to open her door. He wasn't about to miss his opportunity to see more clearly what Kate's life was all about.

Gina Farley greeted them with obvious relief as they entered. Many of the children were sobbing and sniffling as if they'd been crying a long time. Some of the children stared silently at Kate and Matt with large, frightened eyes. Others hid their faces. In the room were several adults, many of whom Matt recognized and nodded to.

There was tension and fear in the room, but Kate smiled at everyone and went directly to the children. "Hello, everyone. I'm Kate Drake." She sat down in the circle and looked at the little ones in invitation.

Matt stood back and watched her. She looked utterly serene, a center of calm in the midst of a violent storm. Immediately the children were drawn to her, pushing and shoving to sit as close to her as they could get. She began talking to them, and a hush fell over the room so that only Kate's magical voice could be heard, bringing a sense of peace and contentment.

"So most of you had a bad dream last night?" Kate's smile was a starburst, radiating light and warmth. "Dreams can be very frightening. All of us have had them. Haley, would you tell us about your dream?" She asked the little girl who had been sobbing the hardest. "Dreams are like stories we make up in our imaginations. I make up stories and write them down for people to read. My stories can be very frightening sometimes. Was your dream scary, Haley?"

It wasn't so much her actual words that were magic as it was her voice. It became apparent to Matt that somehow Kate drew the intensity of the children's emotions out of them. As the room grew calm, and the children quieter, the tension dropped dramatically. It was only Matt who could see the effect on Kate. How draining it was to accept the backlash of emotion not only from the children but their parents as well.

Haley revealed her dream in halting sentences. A skeleton-like man in a long coat and old hat with glowing eyes and bony fingers came out of the fog. He burned the Christmas tree and stole the gifts, and he did something awful to the shepherd in the Christmas pageant. Matt stood up straight when the shepherd was mentioned. His brother, Danny, always played the shepherd in the Christmas pageant. His alarm grew as child after child revealed they'd had a similar dream.

Kate didn't seem the least bit alarmed. Her smile never wavered, and her voice continued to dispel the trauma the nightmares had caused. She told several Christmas stories and soon had the children laughing. As she stood up to leave, Matt saw her sway with weariness. Without a word, Matt waded through the children and slipped his arm around her. She leaned heavily into him as they spent the next ten minutes trying to leave gracefully.

"You look a bit on the fierce and forbidding side," she said once they were back in the car. "I've never quite seen that expression before."

"I was contemplating picking you up and carting you out of there."

Kate laughed softly. "That would have given everyone something to talk about, wouldn't it?" She pressed her fingers to her temples. "Where are you taking me?"

"To the Salt Bar and Grill. You need to eat. Danny's been dating the waitress there, Trudy Garret, so we've spent quite a bit of time sampling the food. It's not bad." He glanced at her and noted that her hands were shaking. "You were using some sort of magic, weren't you? With your voice, and it drained your strength."

"There's always a cost to everything, Matthew." She shrugged without looking at him, closing her eyes and leaning back against the leather seat. "I'm not certain I'll be able to eat, but I'll try."

"You're already too thin, Katie."

She laughed. "A woman can never be too thin, Matthew, don't you know that?"

"That's what women like to think, but men think differently." He parked the car. "I don't mind carrying you."

She opened her eyes then. "Don't you have work to do?"

"I am working. I'm courting you the old-fashioned way. Showing you what a great guy I am and impressing you." He opened the car door for Kate and helped her out, happy to see her laughing. Some of the shadows had disappeared from her eyes.

"You think you're impressing me?"

"I know I'm impressing you."

"Only when you kiss me. I'm really impressed when you kiss me," she admitted, deliberately tempting him. She needed the comfort of his arms more than she needed anything else.

Matt didn't need a second invitation. He pulled Kate's slender body into the shelter of his and lowered his mouth to hers. He brushed her lips gently, back and forth, giving her teasing little kisses meant to prolong the moment. Then his mouth settled over hers, and he kissed her hungrily, like a man starving for more.

Kate's slender arms circled his neck, and her body pressed tightly against his. He knew she couldn't help but feel his body's stark reaction to her, but she didn't seem to mind, burrowing even closer to him so that he felt the warmth of her breasts and the cradle of her hips beckoning with heat.

Tendrils of fog floated in from the sea, ghostly gray strands drifting past them as they stood together on the steps of the restaurant. Kate stiffened, her fingers gripping Matt's shoulders. "Did you hear the weather report? Did they say there would be fog?"

Matt scowled at the mist floating lazily into the parking lot. "We get fog all the time here in Sea Haven, Kate." But it didn't make the hair on his arms rise or his reflexes leap into survivor mode as it had the night before. "I don't smell that noxious odor, do you?"

She shook her head. "But the sun should have burned this fog off. The sky isn't that overcast, Matthew."

"Let's go inside." He held the door open for her to precede him. At once they could hear the wailing of a child in terror. The tension in the restaurant was tangible.

"Oh, Kate! I'm so glad you're here." Trudy Garret beckoned to them from behind the counter, her expression anxious. She was tall and pretty even with the apron she was wearing. Her youthful face was lined with worry.

Danny Granite stood behind her, his arm wrapped around her. He looked relieved to see them. There were a few people in the Salt Bar and Grill, but they were obviously tense and upset over the continual unrestrained sobs coming from somewhere in the back.

"Danny, why aren't you at work?" Matt asked. "Is everything all right at home?"

"Trudy's son had a bad nightmare last night. She can't seem to calm him down, so I offered to come over and see what I could do for him. He's only four years old, a cute little tyke, and I could hear him crying when I called her. I couldn't stand it."

"We haven't been able to calm him down," Trudy said. She was wringing her hands and looking imploringly at Kate. "I'm so glad you came in. Would you talk to him, Kate? Please?"

The cook stuck his head out of the kitchen. "Kate, thank heaven you're here!"

A few of the local patrons broke into applause.

Matt looked at Kate. Her face was pale, her eyes too big for her face, and there were shadows under her eyes. He stirred protectively but didn't speak when Kate put a light, restraining hand on his forearm. She smiled at Trudy. "Of course, I'll be happy to talk to him, Trudy. He isn't alone, many of the children at the preschool had nightmares last night."

Matt slid his hand down her arm, circling her wrist with his fingers. Her pulse was very fast, her skin cool. "While Kate talks to your son, Trudy, maybe you can heat a bowl of soup for her."

"Of course, be happy to," Trudy said. "Right this way, Kate, he's in the back."

Matt followed Kate behind the counter to the back room. The wails grew louder as they approached the small room. Kate opened the door. Matt winced at the high-pitched shrieks, but he stepped inside with her. It was the same scenario as at the preschool. Little Davy Garret sat in Kate's lap, telling her the details of a skeleton in a long coat and old hat in between gulping and tears, finally listening to the sound of her magical voice. Kate replaced the boy's memory of the terrifying nightmare with several funny Christmas stories. She rocked him while she talked, using her talent, her gift, to bring him peace, to soothe him, and make him feel that his world was right again.

After Kate spent twenty minutes sitting on the floor with the boy, Matt reached down and took the child from her arms and set him aside to play happily with his toys. "Danny can take over, Kate. Come eat the soup, then I'll take you home. You're exhausted." He pulled her gently to her feet.

Kate nodded. "I am tired. I wish I knew what was going on, though. I've never seen anything like this. How could all these children have the same dream? At the preschool, at first I thought maybe Haley told her dream to the others, and they all became upset because she was; but the parents said, no, the children had woken up that way. And Davy certainly didn't have contact with any of them. I don't like it at all." She slipped into a booth near the window and peered out. "The fog seems to be rolling in again, Matthew." She couldn't keep the apprehension she felt out of her voice.

"I noticed," he said grimly. The bright, blinking Christmas lights and cheerful music couldn't quite dispel the tension in the air. "Tell me more about the diaries."

Kate sipped at the hot tea Trudy brought her and stared out the window, avoiding his gaze. "Each generation in our family records our activities in journals, or diaries as we sometimes call them. They're considered the history of the Drake family. The earlier journals were recorded using a language or code of symbols like the ones we saw in the mill. I could read part of what was written on the seal. Someone in my family sealed that malevolent force in there. If it was that dangerous that they decided to seal it without laying it to rest, it was because they couldn't give it peace. And that's very frightening."

"And Elle's the only one who can read the language?"

"Sarah knows a little, just as I do. The others have some working knowledge as well, but there's a lot of history to go through when you don't have a good understanding of the language. We need Elle, but I'm certain Sarah and the others will keep trying to find the proper entry and hopefully decipher it."

The wind whirled through the room as the door to the restaurant was thrust open and Jonas strode in, coming directly to them, his face etched with deep lines. Without asking, he slid into the booth beside Kate. "It's Jackson, Kate. I've never seen him like this. I need you to come and talk to him."

A chill went down Matt's spine. "What's wrong with him?"

At Matt's tone, Kate looked up quickly and caught an expression passing between the two men. "What is it? Why are you both so worried?"

There was a small, uncomfortable silence. "You know how you said Hannah was a private person and wouldn't want people to find out what happened the other night? Jackson is the same way," Matt said.

Jonas sat up straight. "What doesn't Hannah want talked about?"

"We're talking about Jackson," Kate reminded him.

"What's wrong with him, and why are you both so worried?"

The two men exchanged another long look. Jonas sighed and shrugged in resignation. "I need your help or I wouldn't be telling you this, Kate. I expect you to keep it confidential."

She nodded because he had actually waited for her answer.

"Jackson is—was—is a specialist for the Rangers."

There was another silence. Kate watched their eyes. They looked grave, more than a little worried. When neither was more forthcoming she took a guess. "He's trained in things I don't want to know about, and you don't want to talk about. Right now he's in a bad way and both of you are concerned for his mental well-being. And what do you mean by is—was—is?"

"That about sums it up, Kate. Let's go," Jonas said.

"Once a Ranger always a Ranger," Matt added. "And she needs to eat her soup. Give her a few minutes."

"Do you have any idea what's going on, Kate?" Jonas asked. "Your sisters are all upset, and whatever happened last night to you and Matt sounds bizarre. You were so drained, even I could feel it."

She shook her head. "My sisters are still looking in the old family diaries for an explanation, but I don't have any answers, Jonas. I wish I did."

chapter 6

The time, it was right, for a present or two,
And the fog on the sand holds a secret, a clue.

JACKSON DEVEAU PACED BACK AND FORTH IN complete silence. That was the first thing Kate noticed, how very silent he was. His clothes didn't rustle, and the soles of his shoes didn't make any noise. His eyes were as cold as ice, as bleak and as dead as she had ever seen in a human being. She sat down in the one good armchair and tried to repress a shiver. If the man had any gentleness in him, she couldn't detect it.

"I told you I didn't need a damned psychiatrist, Jonas," Jackson snapped, without looking at her. "Get her out of here. You think I want anyone to see me like this?" Sweat beaded on his forehead, dampened his dark, unruly hair.

"I'm not a psychiatrist, Mr. Deveau," Kate said. "I'm simply a friend of both Jonas and Matthew. I have a gift, and they thought it might help you in some way. Neither meant to upset you."

"Stop growling like a Neanderthal, Jackson, and let

her talk," Matthew said. "You'd think you didn't have a civilized bone in your body."

"How strange that you would choose that particular description when my sisters said the same thing about you, Matthew," Kate replied. "Did you have a particularly disturbing dream, Mr. Deveau?"

Jackson whirled around and stalked toward her from across the room, his body moving like a large predatory cat's. "What'd they tell you about me? That I'm crazy? That I have nightmares and can't sleep? What the hell do you want me to say?"

Kate noted both Jonas and Matt were close to her, ready to defend her if necessary. In spite of the shiver of fear, she calmly looked up at the deputy. "They didn't say anything. They've told me next to nothing about you. Most of the children in town seem to have had a collective nightmare. So far, none of the adults have admitted to it, but everywhere we've been today, there's unexpected tension. I thought maybe you would be able to tell me about it. I'm getting garbled accounts from the children, and so far no adult has been courageous enough to admit they had the dream too."

Jackson raked both hands through his dark hair, the muscles rippling under his thin, tight tee shirt. He looked from Jonas to Matthew as if expecting a trap. "Kids have been having nightmares?"

Kate nodded. "Last night, after the fog rolled in, something bizarre happened. This morning, children from all over town were distressed and in tears, some traumatized by a dream they all seem to have shared."

"About what?" For the first time since she'd entered the room, Jackson sat down, his hands still gripping his head as if he had a violent headache.

"They described a skeleton man in a long coat and old hat."

Jackson hesitated, clearly reluctant to discuss his problem with her. He looked from Jonas to Matt and finally capitulated. "The coat and hat were old-fashioned, a heavy wool, maybe. There was no real face, just white-gray bones. There was a woman and a baby and a shepherd, or at least someone with a shepherd's staff." He scrubbed his hand over his face. "I go after real people, real threats, but this thing, this was from a place I can't get to, and I sense that everyone is in danger." He looked at Kate. "More than the actual dream, it was the feeling the dream left me with that's disturbing. The danger was real. I know it sounds crazy, but dammit, it was real!"

Matt stiffened. Jackson Deveau had never feared very much, certainly not his own mortality, yet he was deeply shaken by the nightmare.

"Then you felt it too. That the threat is real," Kate said, leaning toward Jackson.

Jackson drew back. Matt had forgotten to tell Kate the deputy didn't like physical contact. "I know it is." He looked at Jonas and Matt. "You two probably think I've finally gone around the bend, but I swear, whatever that thing was in my dream, he's looking for a way to walk among us."

"He uses the fog," Kate explained. He was no child to be soothed with Christmas stories and loving smiles. He was a grown man, a warrior, and what he needed was the naked truth. It was the only thing he would accept. He needed facts to assure him he was not losing his mind. "Whatever he or it is, he's growing stronger. I think the earthquake cracked a seal locking him deep in the earth, and he managed to escape. Matthew and I found a broken lid in the basement of the old mill. Something came out of a crack in the form of a noxious vapor. I've smelled the same odor in the fog." She met Jackson's gaze steadily. "If you're losing your mind, so am I. So is Matthew. And so are all the children of Sea Haven."

Matthew heard it then, that magical note that brought absolute peace to a troubled mind. He had become attuned to it, aware of the surge of energy in the room, going from Kate to the person she was speaking with. He was also aware of her absorbing the negative energy, taking it in and holding it away from its victim.

"That's a relief. I thought this time I was really losing my mind. I have nightmares, and I can deal with them, but this was something out of a horror film." Jackson shook his head. "I'm not going into an institution."

"You're the only one who ever thinks that way," Jonas said quietly. "So do your sisters have any ideas,

Kate? This is more your field than ours." He nodded toward the other two Rangers. "We can be your soldiers, but you're going to have to give us a direction."

Kate leaned back in the chair, fatigue in every line of her body. "We're working on it. Abbey and Sarah and Damon were going through the diaries this morning. We'll find the reference and at least have a starting point."

"I notice you didn't mention Hannah," Jonas observed. There was a challenge in his voice. "Is she ill? Is that what's wrong with her?" When Kate didn't answer, Jonas swore. "Dammit, Kate, if she's ill, you owe it to me to tell me. Something's wrong with her."

"Something's always been wrong with her, Jonas, you just never noticed before." Kate folded her arms. "I'm not going to be bullied into telling you something that is Hannah's private business. Ask her."

Jonas swore again and stormed out. Kate rolled her eyes. "His temper hasn't improved much with age."

"Come on, Kate, I'm taking you to dinner at my house. I'm a great cook." Matt reached down and drew her up from the chair. "I think it's the only sanctuary left to us."

"I should go home and help the others."

Jackson stood up too. "You made me feel better. How did you do it?"

Kate smiled at him and offered her hand. "It was a pleasure finally to meet you, Mr. Deveau. Jonas and Matthew speak so highly of you."

He hesitated but took her hand. "Please call me Jackson."

Kate felt the jolt of his heavy burden go up her arm. It was difficult to maintain her smile when she felt the brooding darkness in the man. She wasn't Libby. She couldn't heal the sick, and in any case, she didn't sense that Jackson Deveau was physically ill so much as spiritually so. "I wish you peace, Jackson," she murmured softly, and allowed Matthew to draw her from the house out into the cool air.

"He didn't have a Christmas tree up, or any decorations at all," she said sadly. "If anyone needs Christmas, it's that man."

"He'll work it out, Kate," Matthew assured her. "He has his demons, but the bottom line is, honor and integrity rule his life. He would never do any of the things he's afraid he will, and, just like Jonas, he would protect this town and the people in it with his last breath."

"I'm glad you brought him to Sea Haven. You were right about this place. There's just something about the way the people are here—they're welcoming to outsiders." The interior of his car was warm after the chilling wind blowing in off the ocean.

"Did your sisters really call me a Neanderthal?"

She burst out laughing. "Well, yes, but in a good way. I think they could easily picture you beating your chest and tossing your woman over your shoulder to carry her off to somewhere private."

He nodded. "I can understand that. I do have those urges. Often." He looked at her, his hand still around the key. "I really want to take you back to my house, Kate." He waited a heartbeat before starting the engine.

"Are your brothers going to be there? Because, honestly, I think I'm too tired to have them all laughing at me today. I'd probably burst into tears."

He pressed a hand to his heart. "Don't even say that. I think I'd rather take a bullet than see you cry. And my brothers don't laugh at you." He glanced at her to see if she was serious.

"They *always* laugh at me," she said. "I'm always doing these idiotic things whenever I'm around you. Like the other day when you had that accident and you tried to get out of the truck and I was standing too close." She looked down at her hands. "Danny just about fell out of the truck laughing."

"At *me,* Katie, never at you. My entire family knows how I feel about you, and they think it's a riot that I can make such a complete fool of myself every time you're near."

Kate sat very still, her gaze fixed on his face. "How do you feel about me?"

"I've made that pretty damn clear, Kate."

"Have you? I know you're attracted to me physically."

He gave a small snort of derision. "Is that what you call it? I haven't had a good night's sleep since I looked at you when you were fifteen years old. I hate admitting that. I shouldn't have been looking at you, but I did, and I just knew. I've had more dreams about you, more fantasies, than any man should admit to having." He pulled the car into the driveway of his yard and turned off the engine before facing her. "Hell, Kate, if you didn't know, you're the only person in this town who didn't. Jonas asked me last night if I was stalking you."

"He wouldn't do that. You're his friend. He must have been kidding."

"With his hand on his gun. Afraid not, and here you are, at my house, all alone with me. Are you coming in?"

"Am I supposed to be afraid now?"

"I thought my fantasies might scare you off."

"Did you?" Kate slid out of the car. The wind whipped her hair around and tugged at her clothes. "Actually I'm intrigued."

His entire body reacted to her sultry tone. Maybe she didn't mean it the way it sounded, but he was going to take her words as an invitation to love her every way a man could love a woman.

Kate smiled to herself as she went up the stairs to his home. It was situated on the bluff above the ocean, his deck wrapping around the house providing a view from every direction. The house itself was obviously built for a man of Matt's size. The ceilings were vaulted, there were few walls, so the space seemed enormous, one room running directly into the next.

His furniture suited the house, casual, yet overstuffed to go with the dimensions of the house.

"It's so beautiful, Matthew. I love all the bay windows and the alcoves and the way everything is so spacious. Did you design it?"

He felt a little glow of pleasure. "Yes, I wanted a home I was comfortable living in day in and day out. I need space. Even the doorways are wider and taller than normal, so I don't always feel as if I might have to duck."

"I love the open beams and the rock fireplace. This is what I had in mind for my house, or at least something very similar. I love the beams and the natural-looking fireplace in the mill." She turned to smile at him. "We do have very similar taste."

His heart did a curious somersault in his chest. He gripped the edge of the door. "I think so. It should be easy to come up with a design you'll really fall in love with." He said the words deliberately.

Kate stilled and turned her head to look at him. The movement was graceful and elegant. So Kate. He ached, just looking at her. Color swept her face. She glanced from him to the tall Christmas tree in his front room. It was a silver tip, beautiful and decorated with lights and a few ornaments. "Did you put up your tree?"

"I brought in the tree and hung the lights. Mom insisted I get ornaments. She said I was supposed to have a theme, but I just picked up ones I liked."

Kate wandered around the tree. One of the ornaments was a wooden house carved by a local artist. She was surprised and pleased to see it was her cliff house. She didn't comment on the ornament, but she hoped it meant he'd been thinking of her when he'd bought the miniature replica of her home.

"This is my favorite room. I spend a lot of time in here. My office is straight ahead, and I have a large library. I call it a library; Danny and Jonas call it my den." He grinned at her. "They talked me into a pool table."

She laughed. "Of course they did. I'll bet they had to twist your arm."

Matt hastily gathered up a few shirts he'd tossed aside earlier in the week. There was an old pizza box on the coffee table along with an empty doughnut box overturned beside a half-full coffee cup.

Kate grinned at him. "I see you're into health food."

"I actually like to cook. I used to cook all the time for the men in my unit." He opened a door, tossed his shirts inside without looking where they landed, and hastily closed the door to gather up the dirty boxes and coffee cup. "I haven't been home much. Dad's running a big job, and all of us have been working to bring it in on time."

"Matthew." Kate put her hand lightly on his arm. "Are you nervous?"

He stood there looking down at her upturned face. Her enormous soft eyes. Her tempting mouth. Could she be any more beautiful? "Hell, yes, I'm nervous. I don't even know what a woman like you would be doing in the same house with a man like me."

"A woman like me?" She looked genuinely puzzled.

Matt groaned. "Come on, Kate. Are you telling me you haven't known I've been wild about you for years? I can't even have a good time with another woman. I've tried dating numerous women. We have one date, and I know it isn't going to work."

"You're wild about me?" she echoed.

He tossed the boxes on the couch and pulled her into his arms. Hard. Possessive. Commanding Ranger style. "I can't even think straight around you."

There was no way to think when his mouth took hers, hot and hungry and devouring her. Her body melted into his, her arms sliding around his neck, her fingers brushing the nape of his neck intimately, creeping into his hair while she met his ravenous hunger with her own.

He couldn't kiss her and not touch her soft, tempting skin. Without conscious thought, he slid his hand beneath her blouse to move up the soft expanse of skin. Just that slight contact brought him such deep pleasure it bordered on pain. He trembled, his hand actually shaking as he brushed the pads of his fingers over her rib cage, and up to cup the soft weight of her breast in his palm. His body went into overdrive, his heart slamming in his chest and his jeans growing uncomfortably tight.

"Aren't you going to stop me, Kate? One of us

should know what we're doing." He wanted to be fair with her. She was exhausted and obviously not thinking straight, arching into his hand, pushing closer, rubbing her body against his. Soft little moans came from her throat, driving him right over the edge. He found himself kissing her again and again, long hot kisses that pushed their temperatures even higher.

Her lips smiled under the assault of his. "I know exactly what I'm doing, Matthew, you're the one who's unclear." Her hands dropped to the buttons of her blouse.

There was a strange roaring in his ears. He had waited years for this moment. Kate Drake in his home. In his arms. Kate's body open to his exploration. It would take a lifetime to satisfy him. More than that. Much more. Her blouse fell open, exposing the creamy swell of her breasts. White lace cupped her skin lovingly.

Matt stared down at her body, mesmerized by the sight of his large hand holding her, his thumb brushing her nipple through the white lace. For one moment, it occurred to him he was making the entire thing up. Kate Drake. His Christmas present. He bent his head to her breast, his mouth closing around soft flesh and lace. His tongue teased and danced over her nipple while his arms enfolded her closer.

The pounding on the front door was abrupt, loud, and unexpected. Kate cried out, and he felt her heart beneath her skin jump with fear.

Matt lifted his head, his gray eyes appearing silver as they smoldered with a mixture of anger and desire. "Don't worry, Katie." He pulled the edges of her blouse together. Why couldn't the world leave them alone for one damned hour? Was that too much to ask?

Kate buttoned her blouse and tried to finger comb her hair. He caught her wrist and brought her hand to his mouth. "You look beautiful. Whoever it is can just go away."

She waited in the middle of his living room while he yanked the door open. The sheriff stood there, his fist poised for another assault. "Jonas, I'm beginning to think our friendship is going to suffer," Matt greeted with a scowl.

Jonas pushed right past him. "Come on out here and take a look at this." His voice was grim. He stalked through the house to the ocean side, pushing open the double doors leading to the deck overlooking the sea. "What the hell is going on, Kate?"

The fog whirled around the house as if alive. Dark and gray and gloomy, the mist was thick, almost oily. It crept up the walls and swirled around the chimney. Jonas glared at the fog. "No one can drive anywhere. Car accidents are happening all over town. Your sister Elle called. She's in the islands and yet she had *the exact same dream as Jackson and the children.* How could she have the same dream? She said to tell you the symbols meant something. When I asked her what they meant she said you would know."

Both men looked at Kate. She hesitated, trying to remember, but there was nothing that seemed to be of great significance. "There were symbols on the seal, but the only thing of importance I could read was that a locking spell had been placed on the lid to hold something in the ground. I'll call Elle and ask her to give me details. Is she on her way home? She was going to try to make it back for Christmas."

"She said she'd be catching a late flight." Jonas stared at the thick gray blanket of mist, frowning as he did so. "The worst of the fog seems to be centered here. It's much heavier around your house, Matt. People are going to start dying if we don't figure out what's going on. We've been lucky, most people pulled their cars over to wait it out and the accidents that have occurred have been minor. But it would be very easy to drive off the cliff in this dense fog. We've asked the radio stations to alert everyone to the driving hazards."

"I'm guessing you called the weather station and the meteorologists there told you this fog is unnatural," Matt said with a small sigh. The supernatural wasn't his realm of expertise, but he had the feeling he was going to have to learn more about it very fast. A part of him had hoped it would all go away. Instead, the fog was wrapped tightly around his house. He glanced at Kate. She stood very still, her hand to her throat, staring out into the dark gray mist. There was fear on her face.

Anger began to smolder in the pit of his belly, not

hot and fiery, but ice-cold and clear, dangerous and deadly, an emotion he recognized from his combat days. Matthew took Kate by the shoulders and pulled her back, away from the deck and into the safety of the house. "Did Sarah say whether or not they found anything in the diaries, Jonas? They were all looking, hoping to find an explanation."

Jonas shook his head. "Sarah said she doesn't have a clue as to what's going on, but she thought with all the sisters concentrating, they might be able to drive this fog back to sea to give us more time to figure it out."

Matt's hands tightened on Kate's shoulders. "I don't want you to do it again, Katie. I think you're making it angry, and it's striking back at you. Why else would it have followed us to my house and stayed here?" He couldn't articulate the emotions the fog gave off, but there was something dark and ugly about it that reeked of pitiless hostility. He didn't want Kate anywhere near it.

"We can't take chances, Matthew," Kate said, her voice trembling. She pressed her lips together. Instinctively she moved back toward Matt as if for protection. "Jonas said there have already been traffic accidents."

Matt could feel her reluctance. Whatever was in the fog had grown in strength and intensity. The previous night it had been an eerie annoyance; now it seemed darker . . . more aggressive and dangerous.

"The fog swept through town, Kate, right after the

two of you left Jackson's house," Jonas explained. "People came out of their houses to stand there and watch it. The sheriff's office logged well over a hundred calls. When it receded, it left behind a mess. All over town gifts left outside, everything from bicycles and ATVs to garden furniture, were smashed and covered with sea trash—sand, kelp, driftwood, smashed seashells, you name it. Even crabs crawling around." Jonas pushed back his hat and rested his gaze on Kate's face. "The worst damage was done to the town square. The three wise men statues were all but destroyed, and the gifts they carried were ground into the lawn. The statues had kelp wrapped around their necks and wrists and ankles. It was bizarre and ugly and it scared everyone enough that the folks on the committee are concerned about the safety of the men playing the parts of the wise men in the pageant. Do you think it was a warning?"

Kate rubbed at her throbbing temples. She was already so tired. She felt drained and just wanted to lie down for a few hours. "I honestly don't know, Jonas, but the entity is accelerating its destructive behavior."

"Dammit, Kate, what the hell could be alive in the fog?" Matt burst out, wanting to throttle the thing. "I don't want you anywhere near this stuff. Why do you have to be the one to face it?"

"My voice. The others can channel through me. And Hannah can call up the wind to drive it back to sea."

He wasn't touching that. It sounded like witches and spells and things he saw in movies, not in real life.

Matt began a slow massage at the nape of Kate's neck to help ease the tension out of her. "Katie, why would this thing smash gifts? If it's capable of destroying things and moving objects as it did with the wreaths on the doors, why such a silly, almost petty display? Why do the gifts bother it? What would be the significance?"

Jonas followed them back to the sliding glass door. "That's a good question. Is that all it can do? When the calls started coming in I thought it was kids and childish pranks. Smashing gifts and outdoor ornaments and leaving behind dead fish are relatively harmless acts of vandalism a kid might do. Well, at least I thought a kid might be the culprit until I saw the three kings smashed to pieces. Jackson came out to the square to take a look at the damage, and he said the scene was reminiscent of his nightmare."

Kate shook her head. "I think it's growing stronger, testing its abilities. It doesn't feel childish to me. It used wreaths, a symbol often associated with Christmas, and now gifts. Elle said the symbols matter. Gifts obviously are another symbol of Christmas." She sighed and rubbed at her temples. "Obviously this thing does not like Christmas at all. Any guesses as to why?"

"I have no idea," Matt said. He used his body to gently shepherd her farther back into the room, wanting to close the doors against the fog.

She turned in his arms and pressed her body close to his for strength and comfort. "My sisters are waiting. Even Libby. It isn't easy to sustain a channeling for any great length of time."

Matt tightened his arms around her, holding her captive, holding her safe. He buried his face against her neck. "I hate this, Kate. You have no idea how much. I want to pack you up and take you far away from this place. I know you're in danger."

"If I don't do this, Matthew, one of my sisters will try, and they don't have my voice." She hugged him hard and slowly pulled away from him.

Matt allowed her to slip from his arms, taut with fear for her when she stepped onto the deck. He stepped beside her. Close. Protective. Daring the thing to come through him to get to her. Jonas took up a position on her other side. Kate closed her eyes and raised her face to the sky.

A breeze from the sea fluttered against her face. She felt the cooling touch. She felt the joining of her sisters. All seven, together yet apart. Strength flowed into her, through her. She lifted her arms and knew Hannah stood on the battlement of their ancestral home and simultaneously did the same.

Matt heard the moaning of the wind. Out on the ocean, the caps on the waves reached high and foamed white. The fog became frenzied, whirling and spinning madly, winding around Kate so that for a moment it obscured Matt's vision of her. He reached out blindly, instinctively, and yanked her into the protection of his body. “This is bullshit, Kate.” He pressed her face against his chest and wrapped his arms around her head to keep the fog from getting at her.

Kate didn’t struggle. She didn’t act in any way as if she noticed. Her voice was soft, barely above a whisper, yet the wind carried it into the bank of mist, and it vibrated through the vapor, taking on a life of its own. Kate remained against him, her eyes closed but her chanting continuing, a gift of harmony and peace, of contentment and solidarity. She called on the elements of the earth. Matt heard that clearly.

Voices rose on the wind. Seawater leaped in response to the chant, waves rising high, bursting through the fogbank and breaking it into tendrils out over the ocean. The wind howled, gathering strength, rushing at them, bringing the taste of salt and droplets of water to brush over their faces. Thunder crashed, shaking the deck. Still the voices continued, and the tempest built.

“Hannah.” Jonas said her name softly, slightly awed by the raw power forged and controlled between the sisters.

Kate took a deep breath and let go. Let go of her sisters and her body and the physical world she lived in to enter the shadow world. Far off, she heard the echo of Hannah’s frightened cry. The world wasn’t silent as one would expect. She never got used to that. There were noises, moans and cries, not quite human, unidentifiable. Static, the sound of a radio not tuned properly. And the terrible howl of the wind endlessly blowing. It was cold and bleak and barren. A world of darkness and despair. She looked around carefully, trying to find the one she was seeking.

She wasn't alone. She could feel others watching her. Some were merely curious, others hostile. None were friendly. She was a living being, and they were long gone. Something slithered close to her feet. She felt the touch of something slimy against her arm. Kate took another breath and called out softly. At once she saw it. A terrifying sight. Tall, bare white bones, the skull ghastly with a gaping mouth and empty sockets for eyes. It wasn't fully formed. A great hole was in the chest cavity. The ribs were missing. It came striding toward her, and she noticed that the skeleton wore old-fashioned boots stuck at the end of the sticklike bones of its legs. She might have laughed had it not been so frightening. The bones rattled as it rushed toward her, deadly purpose in every bone.

"Kate!" Abigail's cry echoed Hannah's and Sarah's.

Kate held up her hand to ward the thing off as it reached her.

Matt felt Kate's energy crackling in the air around them, a fierce force never wavering, yet her slender body shook with the effort, or maybe with fear, crumbling beneath the strain. Without warning he felt every hair on his body stand up. Kate went sickly pale. Afraid for her, he swept her up into his arms and held her tight against his chest, the only thing he could do to shelter her from the onslaught of the wind and the menace of the fog.

Kate wrenched herself from the shadow world, opened her eyes, expecting to see Matt. Empty sockets stared back at her. The skull's mouth gaped wide, the jaw loose, bony fingers wrapping around her throat. She screamed and pulled away, trying to run when there was nowhere to go. The pressure on her throat increased. She choked.

The wind rose to a howl. Feminine voices became commanding. The bony fingers slid from Kate's throat. She fell to the ground and stared in horror as the voices of the Drake women forced the skeleton away from her one dragging step at a time. Those pitiless empty eye sockets stared at her with malice. Kate tried to scoot crablike in the opposite direction, feeling sick as the entity clacked white bones together in a dark, ugly promise of retaliation.

The wind blew sand into the air, obscuring Kate's vision. She squeezed her eyes closed tightly against the new assault. At once she felt Matt's body pressed close to hers. Afraid to look, she lifted her lashes, hands out in front of her for protection. Matt's reassuring face was there, the planes and angles familiar to her. She buried her face against his throat, felt the warmth of his body leeching some of the icy cold from hers.

The fog crept back toward the ocean slowly, almost grudgingly, retreating from around the house and deck to the beach, with obvious reluctance. With Kate safely in his arms, Matt stared in horror at the wet sand. Distinct footprints were left behind, as if someone had backed toward the ocean with short, dragging steps, a man's boots with run-down heels. A cold chill swept down his spine. His gaze went from the prints in the sand to Jonas. "What the hell are we dealing with here?"

chapter 7

As lovers meet beneath mistletoe bright,
Terror ignites down below them this night.

MATT STARED DOWN AT KATE'S FACE. SHE LAY in his bed, sound asleep, the signs of exhaustion present even as she slept. She looked more fragile than ever, as if fighting back the entity in the fog had taken most of her spirit and drained all of her strength. The curtains over his sliding glass door were pulled back to allow him a clear view of the ocean. He had always enjoyed the sight and sound of the waves pounding, but now he searched the horizon for signs of the fog. Kate was worn out. He worried that if the entity returned, she wouldn't have the strength to fight it, even though she'd slept for hours. The day had disappeared, and night had fallen.

He rubbed his hands over his face to wipe away his own exhaustion. He hadn't slept the night before, standing watch at Kate's bedside, and he was feeling the effects. He had stripped her of her clothes and wrapped her in one of his shirts. It was far too big for her and covered every curve. He'd tucked her in his bed and all the while she lay passively, making little effort to do anything but close her eyes. He had the feeling she'd faced something far worse than the fog, but she hadn't been ready to talk about it with him. Recognizing the signs of exhaustion, he hadn't pushed her.

Matt removed his shirt and shoes and socks and stretched out beside her. He had built his home in the hopes of finding a wife when he returned from serving his country, but no matter how many women he had dated, there had been only one woman for him. Kate had been in his dreams from the moment he'd first laid eyes on her. He would never forget that moment, driving his father's truck, his rowdy brothers cranking up the music and laughing happily. He had glanced casually to his right not realizing that his life was about to change forever. Kate was standing in the creek bed with her six sisters, her head thrown back, laughing, her eyes dancing, totally oblivious to his gaze. A jolt of electricity had sizzled through his entire body. In that one moment, Kate Drake had managed to burn her brand into his very bones, and no other woman would do for him.

"Matthew?" Her voice was drowsy. Sexy. It poured into his body with the force of a bolt of lightning, heating his blood and bringing every nerve ending alive.

"I'm here, Katie," he answered, wrapping his body around hers as he slipped his arm around her waist.

"Didn't Sea Haven always seem like home to you?

When you were far away, in another country, in danger, didn't you dream of this place?"

"I dreamed of you. You were home to me, Kate." There in the darkness with the ocean pounding outside his bedroom he could admit the truth to her. "You got me through the gunfire, and the ugliness, and it was the thought of you that brought me back to Sea Haven. My family always kept track of you for me."

Kate turned her face into his shoulder, snuggling closer to him. "I heard you were doing things that seemed so scary to me. I have such an imagination, and I would wake up in the middle of night picturing you rising up out of the desert sand in your camouflage fatigues with your rifle and enemies all around you. Sometimes the dreams were so vivid I'd actually get sick. I've never told that to anyone, not even my sisters. They saw the differences in us and knew we weren't right for each other."

"Kate." He said her name tenderly. With an aching need in it. "How can you say that? Or even think it? I was made for you. To be with you. I feel it so strongly, the rightness of it. You feel it too. I know you do." He held her possessively, his arms locking her to him. Matt buried his face in the soft warmth of her neck. "Katie, you can't hand a man his dream, then take it away. Especially not a man like me. I stood back and gave you all the room in the world when you were too young for me. Later, when you were grown, you were busy and happy with your life, traveling around the world doing what you do. I never once made a move on you. I knew you needed your freedom to pursue your writing. But now you're home, telling me you're ready to settle down, and I can't just step back and pretend we don't feel anything for one another. Every time you looked at me, you had to know we belonged. You should never have kissed me if you weren't willing to give a relationship between us a try."

Kate closed her eyes, feeling tears welling up. His lips moved over her neck, drifted lower to nudge the collar of the shirt aside. Her pulse pounded frantically. Her heart went into overdrive. "I'm not brave the way you are, Matthew," she admitted in a small voice. "I can't be like you. I'm not at all a person of action. In a few months when you realize that, you'll be so disappointed in me, and you'll have too much honor to tell me."

Matt lifted his head and looked down at her. Tears shimmered in her eyes, and his heart nearly stopped beating in his chest. "What the hell are you talking about, Kate?" He bent his head to kiss the tears away. He tasted grief. Fear. An aching longing. "Dammit." He muttered the words in sheer frustration, then kissed her hard, his mouth claiming hers. A ravenous hunger burst through him, over him. There was a strange roaring in his head. His chest was tight, his heart pounding with the force of thunder. He had faced enemy fire without flinching, but he couldn't bear the idea of Kate walking away from him.

He poured everything he felt into his kiss. Everything he was. His hands framed her face, held her to him while he ravaged her mouth. Heat spread like a wildfire, through him, through her, catching them both on fire until he thought he might ignite. She melted into him, her arms sliding around him, nearly as possessive as he was. He lifted his head to look at her, memorizing every beloved line and angle of her face. He was gentle, his fingertips stroking caresses and tracing her cheekbones, the shape of her eyes, the curve of her eyebrows. The pad of his thumb slid back and forth over the softness of her lips. He loved her mouth, loved everything about her. "Kate." He kissed her gently. Once. Twice. "How could you think I don't know you? We've lived in the same town practically all our lives. I've watched you. I've listened to you. Do you know how many times I've dreamed of you?"

"Dreams aren't the same as reality, Matt," Kate said sadly.

Her gaze moved over his face, examining every inch of his features. Matt waited, holding his breath. He was rough and she was elegant. He was a man who protected the ones he loved. And he loved Kate Drake.

"Matthew . . ." There was that catch in her voice again. Need. Caution.

Matt couldn't imagine why Kate would fear a relationship with him, a life with him, but the thought that she might pull away had him bending his head. His teeth tugged at her delicate ear. His tongue made a foray along the small shape. She shivered in reaction. He grew harder. Thicker. His body was heavy and painful, straining against the confines of his jeans. "Katie, unzip my jeans." He breathed the words into her ear, his lips drifting lower to find her neck. Her soft, sensitive neck.

Kate closed her eyes as his teeth nipped her chin, her throat, as his lips found her collarbone, his chin nudging aside the shirt collar again. She ached with wanting him, her body hot and sensitive. Her breasts felt swollen, begging for his attention. What was so wrong with reaching for something, just this one time? He was everything she'd ever wanted, yet was always out of her reach. Matthew Granite was a fighter, larger-than-life. He'd done things she would never comprehend, never experience. He felt like a hero from one of her novels, not quite real and too good to be true. She knew she'd thought of him when she'd written each and every one of her books. She'd used him as her role model because, to her, he was everything a man should be. Why would he ever choose to be with a woman who looked at life, wrote about life, but refused to participate in it?

Kate was certain she was going to leap from the bed and run, but her body had a mind of its own. She was already working on the button at the waistband of his jeans, finding the zipper and dragging it down. The air left his lungs in a rush when her hand shaped the thick, heavy bulge, caressed and stroked with loving fingers.

"You're wearing too many clothes, Matthew," she pointed out, determined to have her time with him, even if it couldn't be forever.

"So are you." His hands dropped to the buttons of her shirt, sliding them open so that the edges gaped apart. He raised his upper body in order to stare down at her, to drink in the sight of Kate Drake in his bed. She shrugged out of the shirt and allowed it fall to the floor before lying back. His mouth went dry.

Outside, the continual booming of the sea seemed to match the pounding of his heart. In the soft light, her skin was flawless, inviting. Her breasts were full and round, her nipples taut inviting peaks. Kate's long hair spilled around the pillows, just as he'd always fantasized. For a moment he was caught and held by the sight of her, unable to believe she was real. "There was more than one night out in the desert when I was lying half-buried in the sand, surrounded by the enemy. It was important to get in and out without being seen. The enemy showed up and set up camp virtually on top of us. It was the fantasy of you lying just like this in my bed, waiting for me at home, that got me through it."

"Then I'm very glad, Matthew." She tugged on the loop at the waistband of his jeans. "Get rid of those things."

He didn't wait for a second invitation. "I've always loved you, Kate. Always." She would never know how often he thought of her, in the hot arid desert and the freezing nights, in the painful sandstorms. Lying in a field with the enemy not ten feet from him. He had been all over the world, performing high-risk covert missions in places no American leader would ever admit to sending troops, and Kate had gone with him every single time.

He stroked his hand down her leg, more to ensure she was real than for any other reason. He felt her shiver in response. Her lips parted slightly. Her sea-green eyes watched his every move. Matt knelt on the bed, tugging on her ankles, a silent command to open her legs. She complied, parting her thighs wide enough to allow him to slide between her legs.

Matt was a big man. At once Kate felt vulnerable, the cool night air teasing the tiny curls at the junction of her legs. His hands, sliding up her thighs, were gentle, removing her anxiety as fast as it rose. She loved the way he looked at her, almost worshiping her skin, her body, his hot gaze exploring in the same thorough way as his hands. A wave of heat rushed through her, of anticipation. Matt took his time caressing every curve along her slender leg, even the back of her knee as if memorizing the texture of every inch of her was terribly important.

His touch sent darts of fire racing over her skin, penetrating every nerve ending until she could hardly lie still beneath his touch. Her breath was coming in a gasp, and heat coiled deep inside her, a terrible pressure beginning to build.

Matt couldn't contain himself another moment. She lay there like a beautiful offering. He bent over her, kissed her enticing navel, his tongue swirling in the small, sexy dip, his hands continuing their foray lower. He felt her reaction, a warm, moist welcoming against his palm as he pushed against her. He kissed his way up her smooth body to the underside of her breast. Kate gasped and arched her body, her hips moving restlessly. She flushed, her luminous skin taking on a faint peach-colored glow.

He groaned. His body reacted with another swelling surge. Fire raced through his veins. His tongue flicked her nipple, once, twice, and his mouth settled over her breast. Kate cried out, her hands grasping handfuls of his hair, tugging him closer to her. She was magic. He could think of no other word to describe her. His body pressed into the softness of hers, while he lavished attention on her breasts. He'd dreamed of her skin, of the feel and shape of her every curve, and his imagination hadn't come close to the real thing. He cupped her other breast, teasing her nipple, feeling the response in Kate. She was very sensitive to his touch, to his mouth, to every caressing stroke. And she showed him she loved his touch.

Her soft moans heightened Matt's pleasure. He hungered for the sounds and responses Kate showed him. He needed them. She was generous in her reception, her hands moving over him, her body restless with the same hunger. He flicked her nipple one more time with his tongue and took possession of her lips, swallowing her moan, robbing her of breath.

Matt kissed her mouth over and over because no amount of kissing Kate would ever be enough. He trailed kisses down her throat, in the valley between her breasts. Her fingers dug into his hips, urging a union, but he took his time. He rained kisses across her stomach, pausing to dip again into her fascinating belly button.

"Matthew, really, I don't think I'm going to live through this." Her breath came in a series of ragged gasps.

"I waited a long time, Kate. I'm not rushing things." He ducked his head, his tongue sliding wickedly over her wet, hot sheath. She nearly jumped out of her skin. He grinned at her. "I may only have this one chance to prove my worth to you. I'm not about to blow my chances by charging the battlefield." He bent his head and blew softly against her sensitive body. He caught her hips more firmly, dragged her closer to him, and bent his head to taste her.

Kate screamed and nearly rose off the bed. He held her hips firmly, locking her to him while he feasted. She was hotter than he had ever imagined, a well of passion, and he had just begun to tap into it. He felt the first strong ripple of her muscles rushing to overtake her, and his body swelled even larger in response.

"I think you're ready for me, Kate." He didn't bother to hide the satisfaction in his voice. It was still a miracle to him that she chose to be with him. He pushed her thighs a little wider to accommodate his hips, pressing against her so that the sensitive tip of his penis slipped into her hot, welcoming body. The breath slammed out of his lungs. He pushed deeper so that she swallowed the tip, her tight muscles gripping with soft relentless pressure that sent violent waves of pleasure shooting through his body.

Kate gasped and clutched at the bedsheets. Matt froze, understanding dawning. He bit back a string of swear words, took a deep breath, and let it out. "Relax, honey, just relax. I swear, we fit together perfectly."

She smiled at him. "I'm not afraid, you idiot, I've never felt this before, and it's amazing. I want more, Matthew, all of you. Stop being so careful." If he didn't quit moving so slowly, she was going to spontaneously combust. She wanted to push her body over his. It was difficult to hold back when every instinct demanded she lift her body to receive his.

"Dammit, Kate, you're not experienced." He was sweating now. It was impossible to hold back. She was squirming, her hips pushing hard into his, and he was inching his way deeper into the hot core of her. Pleasure was building at such a ferocious rate he was losing all control just when he needed it the most. She was so damned tight, squeezing and gripping him, the friction like a hot velvet fist pumping him dry. Matt thrust deeper because he had no other choice. It was that or risk death. He was certain of it. She took him in, gasping with pleasure, when he'd been so worried.

Matt let go of his fears and took the ride, thrusting deep, tilting her body until she could take all of him. He moved the way he wanted, the way he needed, hard and fast and deep, joining them together in a rush of heat. The ocean pounded the shore just outside the glass door. Matt was unaware of it, unaware of anything but Kate and her body and the way she gave herself so completely to him. She came over and over, crying out, clutching his arms, lifting up to meet him as eagerly as he surged into her. The explosion started somewhere near his toes and blew through his entire body. His voice was hoarse, a roar of joy, as he emptied himself into her.

He sank on top of her, completely spent, completely sated, his lungs burning for air and his heart pounding out of his chest. And it was a perfect moment in time. Her body was soft and welcoming beneath his. He turned his head to capture her breast in his mouth, to lie there in contentment, to have her with him. He had been in hell many times in his life. But he had never been in paradise until now. His arms tightened around her possessively. "Dammit, Katie, don't ask me to give you up." He said the words around her tantalizing breast.

Kate combed her fingers through his hair, lying back with her eyes closed, savoring every aftershock while his mouth pulled strongly at her breast, and his tongue did delicious things to cause fiery sparks zinging in her deepest core. "Silly man," she murmured, clearly amused by his reaction. "I'm right here. Did you think I was going to grab my clothes and go slinking off?" The smile faded from her mind. There was a small part of her that wanted to do just that, run while she still had the chance. Self-preservation was strong in her. Everything about Matthew appealed to her. His lovemaking dazzled her, but she wasn't so far gone that she couldn't look ahead to the future and realize they couldn't spend every moment in bed.

Matt shifted position enough to take most of his weight off of her smaller body, but his arms held her in place and he turned her so he could keep access to the temptation of her breasts. His tongue flicked her nipple. "I want you forever, Kate. I want to grow old and have you here in my arms. I want children. I've wanted you for so long. I don't think that's about to change." He noticed that when he drew her breast into his mouth her hips moved restlessly. It was a wonderful find and one he intended to spend time exploring. He stroked her stomach and moved his hand between her thighs to cup her heat. She jumped but pushed against his hand. His thumb caressed her, his finger pushed deep to find the one spot that could give her another release.

Kate was Kate. She didn't try to pull away or pretend she wasn't ready for another orgasm, she rode his hand, gasping with pleasure, her fingers digging into his shoulder with one hand and the other curled in his hair directing his mouth. He wanted this every damn day of his life. Not just a Christmas present. He wanted to go to sleep with her breast in his mouth. He wanted to wake up with his body buried deep in hers. He wanted to be the man to bring her pleasure in every way possible.

"Marry me, Kate. Stay with me."

She heard him through a haze of piercing fulfillment, so sated with contentment, with the throbbing fire spreading through her like a storm, she could only lay there dazed by the gift he was holding out to her. The temptation.

Matt lifted his head to look at her, his fingers still buried deep inside of her. "Kate. I'm serious. Marry me. I'll make you happy."

"I am happy, Matthew," she said. "I lead a relatively quiet life. I work hard, meet my deadlines, and I'm looking forward to renovating the old mill."

Sensing her withdrawal, he turned to lie over the top of her, his head resting on her stomach. He pressed a series of kisses along her sensitive skin and flicked her enticing navel with his tongue. "We can renovate the old mill together, Katie."

"You're moving a little too fast for me, Matthew."

His Kate was becoming cautious again. He should have known she would. He nibbled his way down her body to her thigh. "We don't have to move fast. We don't have to go for the wedding and children and the entire package if that's too much for you right now."

His teeth nipped as his fingers moved deep inside of her. He wasn't above a little persuasion. "We can keep it to great sex. Incredible sex."

She heard the note of pain in his voice, and it upset her. "Matthew, I'm not normal. I'll never be normal. You think you know me, but you don't. You can't. My sisters and I inherited a legacy that we have no choice but to use. It comes with a price. Sarah has phenomenal athletic abilities, and she can sense things before they happen. Abigail can demand the truth. I can bring peace to people in need. Libby heals people. Joley has incredible powers, and so does Hannah. Both command the wind and the sea. And our Elle." Kate shook her head. "Elle's legacy is tremendous and important and very frightening. She has it all, along with the responsibility to bring the next generation into the world. We each have gifts, but when we're together, we are very powerful. We try to lead our own lives, but we keep the cliff house so we always can be together."

He lifted his head, his silver eyes darkening to smoldering charcoal. "You think I can't understand honor and commitment? You live by a code the same as I do. I understand codes. You have a way of life that's important to you. Why would you think it would be any less important to me? I don't mind sharing you with your sisters, Kate."

She sighed. "I'm sorry. I didn't mean to upset you, Matthew. I just want you to know what we do isn't going to go away, even if we wanted it to. And it isn't only sharing me with my sisters, but with a lot of other people as well." But it was more than that. She wasn't like her sisters, embracing life in the way they did. In the way he did.

"I know a lot of ways to be happy with you," he promised, dipping his head to her breasts, not wanting her to see his face. "We'll take it slow if that's what you need, Katie. Just don't shut me out because you're afraid."

She tried not to react to his words. Of course she was afraid. She was afraid of everything, and that was *exactly* why she couldn't agree to marry him.

He kissed her ribs, her belly button. The phone rang, startling them both. He ignored it, dropping kisses over her stomach. The shrill ringing of the telephone persisted. Matthew sighed heavily and reached lazily across her small body, deliberately brushing across her bare breasts. "Hello." It was the middle of the night. He didn't have to be polite. He didn't want to waste a single moment of his time with Kate, especially when she needed persuasion to stay with him.

"This is Elle Drake. I need to speak with Kate." It was Kate's youngest sister, reputed to be traveling home for Christmas. There was anxiety in her voice. Without a word, Matt passed the phone to Kate.

She sat up, dragging the sheet over her breasts. "Elle? What's wrong, hon?"

"Something's there, Kate. Something's where you are. Below you. It's dangerous, and it's below you."

"Are you certain?" Kate leaned over the bed to examine the floor. Matt could clearly hear the terrified voice on the other end of the phone. "Calm down, Elle, I'm fine. We're both fine."

"Kate, I'm really afraid for you. What's going on? I saw you clearly. You were kissing Matthew Granite. There was mistletoe very close to you, but not directly over your head. And then something bright burst out from under you, a flash and flames and it was truly frightening. What is it?"

"I don't know, but we'll find out."

Matt was already out of the bed, pulling on his jeans, his eyes searching every inch of the floor. Moonlight pouring through the sliding glass door provided enough light for him to search every corner of the room. With his training ingrained in him, Matt chose not to turn on the light and give their position away to the enemy. He might have dismissed the phone call as hysteria or a nightmare, but he had been around the Drake sisters long enough now to see the strange things Jonas sometimes spoke of and to know to take them seriously.

"I'll call you later, Elle," Kate said, her eyes mirroring her fright. "Thank you for the warning." She placed the receiver in its cradle and looked up at Matt. "She's never wrong, Matthew. Do you have a basement? Maybe whatever it is has found a way to get in through the basement."

He shook his head. "There is no actual basement. I did take the space beneath the deck and create storage rooms and a lab to develop photographs." Their eyes met in sudden silence.

Kate slid out of bed and caught up his shirt, the nearest article of clothing she could wrap herself in. "Do you have mistletoe in the house, Matthew?"

"No, but it grows in several of the trees outside near the deck. I've stood on my deck to knock it out of the branches a few times."

Quickly buttoning the shirt, she followed him on bare feet. He didn't like her exposed to danger, but at least he could keep an eye on her if she were with him. He reached back to take her hand. She looked small and vulnerable in his too-large shirt with her hair tousled from their lovemaking. He bent his head and kissed her, a brief hard kiss of reassurance. Kate's public image was always neat and elegant. He liked that Kate very much. He loved the one with him now. His sexy, passionate, private Kate, with her hair mussed and her delicate skin red from his five o'clock shadow. Nothing was going to harm her. *Nothing.*

Kate felt her heart beating wildly in her chest. She tightened her fingers around Matt's hand. Matt slid open the glass door leading outside. The wind rushed in, bringing a cold chill and the scent of the salty air. The roar of the ocean was loud, whereas before the walls of the house had muffled it. She glanced nervously out toward the open sea, afraid of seeing the gray fog, but the ocean's surface was clear.

"Kate." Matt said her name as a warning.

Kate froze and dropped her gaze to the sand below them. It was wet from the continual pounding of the waves, rolling up onto the beach and receding according to the tide. There was a clear trail of boot prints, coming out of the ocean, and marks alongside them that indicated something heavy had been dragged. Kelp lay in tangles along the path toward the stairs leading up to Matthew's home. There was a heavy dark stain, much like oil in several spots in the sand. Kate wanted a closer look and stepped out onto the deck.

Matt pulled her back and thrust her behind him. "It doesn't feel right to me." He had long ago learned to rely on his survival instincts when something wasn't right. "Stay in the house, Kate."

"The fog isn't out there anymore," she pointed out, but she stayed behind him, holding tight to his hand. "Should we call Jonas?"

Matt sighed. "I imagine Elle called him. Don't all your sisters call him when something supernatural happens? I don't think the poor man's had a night's sleep since Sarah came home."

"Supernatural? I never thought of it like that. We've always had certain gifts. We were born with them, and using them seems as natural as breathing. Some people call us witches, and others just think we're able to use magic, but it's different. More. And less. I wish I could explain it." Kate frowned up at him. "It's natural to us."

Matt pushed her hair from her face, his fingers lingering in the silky strands. He tucked her hair behind her ear, the gesture tender. "You don't have to explain it. I'm a believer, Kate." He paused and drew in a deep breath. "Something's wrong. We're not going out on the deck. Come through the house with me." Matt silently slid the glass door closed, lifting his gaze to the night sky, where patches of dark, ominous clouds floated lazily.

Deliberately he didn't turn on any lights as he led her through the house. He paused long enough to slip a leather sheath around his calf. Kate's eyes widened as he shoved a long knife down into it. "Do you think that's necessary?"

"I believe in being safe. You're with me, Kate. Nothing's going to take you away from me. I don't care if it's a monster in the fog or something crawling out of the ocean." He pushed open the door to his house and stepped outside. His eyes searched the terrain restlessly, never stopping. "Do you smell something burning?"

The breeze shifted again, but Kate caught the peculiar pungent odor. "Oily rags?"

Matt hurried over the stepping-stones leading around to the back of the house. He had a good ocean view on three sides, but the bedroom was to the back. The dark stains led from the beach to the stairs and straight to the small photography laboratory he had built. The door was closed and appeared locked, but there were oily smudges all over the door, the same oily smudges they'd seen on the beach.

Kate's heart began to pound. She felt the danger swamping her. Glancing up, she could see the branches of the tree spread over the top of the deck, reaching over the bedroom where she and Matt had been kissing. In the branches were nests of mistletoe and the base of the tree was covered in the oily substance. "Matthew, let's wait for Jonas."

"I have photo-developing chemicals in there, Kate. I'm not losing my house to this thing." He set her away from him. "You stay back. I mean it, Kate. If I have to run, I'll need the way clear. Drag the hose over here for me, but don't get too close."

Matt felt the door. It wasn't hot to the touch. He opened it cautiously. The stench was overpowering, smelling of the sea, dead fish, and heavy oil. Black smoke seeped from a pile of photo paper and rags piled with smashed glass and a mixture of what he knew was lethal chemicals. He dragged some of the papers from the pile, trying to stop the inevitable. Tiny flames licked up the sides of the pile. There was a flash of white and a popping sound.

Kate thrust the hose into his hands. The water was running full out. He turned it on the greedy flames. "Get out of here, Kate," he ordered.

Kate stifled a scream when Jonas emerged out of nowhere and pulled her back, away from the deck. "Call the fire department," he snapped. "Use my car radio and stay out of the house." He pointed to the driveway, where he'd pulled in and left the door on the driver's side open. "I have a jacket it in the car, put it on, you aren't wearing very much."

Kate heard the wail of a siren and saw the deputy's car tear up the driveway. She ran to Jackson as he stepped out of his car. "Jonas says to call the fire department."

He made the call from his radio, pointing silently to the car, as if that was enough to make her stay, then he quickly joined Jonas and Matt. Kate dragged on Jonas's jacket, nearly sagging with relief. There was something utterly reassuring about the three men being together. They exuded complete confidence and worked as a team, almost as if each knew what the others were thinking. They had the fire out before the fire trucks even arrived. It took longer to go through the mess in the photo lab, searching for evidence. She was grateful to be able to return to the house where it was warm. Kate curled up in a chair and waited for Matt to return to her.

chapter 8

And the blood runs red on the pristine white snow . . .
While around all the houses the Christmas lights glow.

MATT STARED OUT THE LARGE BAY WINDOW OF his kitchen at the pounding sea. He frowned at the foaming waves, peering toward the darkness far out in the distance, almost at the horizon where a mass seemed to be congealing. Dark clouds had spread across the entire sky by the time the three men had sifted through the mess in his photography lab. Matt had taken calls from his parents and his brothers making certain he was alive and well and the house was still standing. Kate had received calls from her sisters.

Kate, fresh from her shower and wrapped in his robe, sat in the chair nearest him. "It's out there, isn't it?" she asked quietly. "I'm sorry about all your equipment."

He spun around to look at her. "Do you think I blame you for this?"

She hesitated. "I don't think he would have come here if I hadn't been here. I don't know why I draw him," she said, shaking her head. "Maybe he got my scent in the old mill, or maybe he perceives me as a threat."

"So it's definitely a he. I think it's taking shape, gaining a form," Matt said.

"I need to go home and help find the appropriate entry in the diaries. There are quite a few written in the symbols, and my sisters will need help. I don't think we have a lot of time to figure this out, Matthew. It's only a few days until Christmas, and I think this thing means to stop the town from having a Christmas." It sounded melodramatic even to her own ears. How could she expect to have any kind of a relationship with Matthew Granite and still be who and what she was?

"Time enough, Kate. We'll go right after we take care of things here. I promise."

She lifted an eyebrow. "What things? I thought you and Jonas and Jackson took care of everything."

Matt padded over to her on his bare feet and simply lifted her in his arms. "It takes some getting used to."

Kate clasped her fingers at the nape of his neck. "I'll admit I've never faced anything like this before." She wanted him. Suited or not, for just this space of time, Matthew belonged to her.

"I wasn't referring to our foggy fiend. I was referring to you. Having you in my house. Having you right here where I can look at you or touch you." He set her on the tiled counter and slid his hand inside the warmth of the robe.

He loved her instant response, the way she pushed into his hand. Welcoming him. "Remind me to thank your sister for the warning." Matt leaned forward to take her offering into the warmth of his mouth.

"I think you're a breast man," she teased.

"Mmmm, maybe," he agreed, his hands sliding down her waist and over her hips inside the robe. "But you also have a beautiful butt, Kate. I absolutely love the way you walk. I used to get behind you just to breathe a little life into my fantasies."

He was wedging himself between her legs, and Kate opened her thighs wider to accommodate him. "You've had fantasies about my rear end?"

"More than you'll ever know." He leaned in to capture her mouth. To spread heat and fire. Her fingers tangled in his hair. His fingers tangled in hers. Their mouths welded together so that they breathed for one another. He pulled her bottom closer to the edge of the counter and yanked her robe all the way open. "I've had fantasies about every separate part of you." Very gently he slid her legs apart.

"Matthew." There was a gasp in her voice. Kate stared at the long bank of windows, her hands still in his hair. "What are you doing?"

"Having you for breakfast. I've always wanted you for breakfast."

If Kate had thought to protest, it was far too late. He

was already devouring her, and she was too far gone to care where they were. It was a deliciously decadent moment, and she reveled in it as wave after wave of pleasure crashed over her and rushed through her. The room spun dizzily, and colors mixed together, while his tongue and his fingers worked magic on her body. Her hands grabbed the edge of the smooth-tiled counter to keep herself anchored when she was flying so high, but then he was lifting her and laying her on the table, his body buried deep inside of hers, and there was no room for thought. No room for anything but feeling. The sound of his body joining with hers, their pounding hearts and heavy breathing, was a kind of music accompanying the strong orgasms as they broke over her and through her. His heat was so deep inside of her, she felt as though she were melting from the inside out.

She stared up into his face, the hard angles and planes, the rough shadow on his jaw. His eyes held secrets, things he had seen that should never have been witnessed. She realized how alone he seemed, even in the midst of his family. Like Jonas. Or Jackson. A man apart, not by choice, but by experiences. Kate framed his face with her palms, her thumb sliding in a caress over his faint whiskers. "You're a very wonderful man, Matthew Granite. I hope you know how special you are."

He gathered her to him as if she were the most precious being on the face of the earth, carrying her tenderly to the bathroom so they could shower. He said little, but he watched her all the time, would reach out and touch her body, her face, his fingers lingering against her skin, almost as if he couldn't believe she was real.

"My clothes are dirty," she said, pulling them on. At least she managed to tame her hair, braiding the long length and swirling the braid around the back of her head in an intricate knot.

He smiled at her. "Your clothes are never dirty, you just think they are." He dragged out a fresh pair of jeans from his drawer. "How can we find out what this thing is, Katie? I need to know what we're facing."

"My sisters are poring over the diaries, and I think Damon is helping them. I can try as well, and Elle's on her way home. We should be able to find some clue."

"What's your gut telling you?"

She pressed her lips together to keep from smiling. There was something raw about the way Matt talked, something that always intrigued her. "I think it has to do with the history of our town, possibly an event that happened around Christmas, maybe the pageant itself. I think whatever is in the fog is gaining strength and becoming more destructive, but I'm not entirely certain why. The tree beside the deck with the mistletoe in it is a fir tree, and you had lights strung in it. You didn't have them on, but the dark stain, which seemed to be oil of some kind, was all around the bottom of the tree and going partially up the trunk."

"I noticed that," he agreed. "But there was nothing to ignite it."

"If Elle hadn't called and warned us, we never would have gone outside, Matthew. We would have been above the room when the fire took off, and it might have exploded. I think the fire would have raced to the tree, and he was hoping it would go up in flames as well."

"Strange way to kill us."

"Maybe not just us. Maybe it was the fir tree." She sat on the edge of the bed to watch him dress. He moved with such power, so fluidly, with a masculine grace he didn't seem aware of having. "Each symbol attacked so far has been attached to the Christian belief. There were ancient beliefs far before Christianity ever celebrated Christmas. It's widely believed the birth of Christ was in April, not December."

He paused in the act of buttoning his shirt. "I didn't know that."

She nodded. "I'm not Elle, or the others who sometimes are able to see things clearly, but I *feel* it's connected in some way."

"I get feelings when there's danger near." He suddenly grinned, transforming his face from man to boy. "Unless I'm otherwise occupied."

Kate couldn't help smiling back. In spite of everything, he looked more relaxed than she'd ever seen him. She always thought of him as a great tiger prowling through town. "We can forgive you that." She stood up. "The fir tree's needles rise toward the sky, and the fir tree stays green all year round."

"And that means something?"

"Everlasting hope, and, of course, the raised needles are reputed to represent man's thoughts turning toward heaven. If I were right, why would he want to destroy those symbols? He's not attacking Santa Claus. He isn't someone thinking Christmas is too commercial, he's actually destroying the symbols themselves." She looked up at him, rubbed her temple, and smiled a bit tiredly. "Or not. I could be way off base."

"I doubt it, Katie. I think your guess is as close as we can get right now." Matt looked across the room at her, still astonished that she was in his bedroom. "Let's go shopping for groceries. We can take them to your house and spend the day going over those diaries until we find something."

"Sounds good. I want to get home and put some decent clothes on."

She wandered out of the room while he pulled on his socks and boots. The house was so open, it beckoned her to walk the length of it. Entering the kitchen, she found herself smiling. In her wildest dreams she had never considered making love on a tabletop. A character in one of her novels might do such a thing, but not Kate Drake, with her every hair in place and her need for order. She'd never be able to look at a kitchen counter or table in quite the same way again.

Matt listened to Kate moving around his home. He

liked the scent of her, the soft footfalls, the way her breath would catch when she looked at something she liked.

"Matthew?" Kate called out to him. "You have a very interesting kitchen. I wanted to put the cups in the dishwasher, and it seems to be a bread bin."

There was a small silence. Matt cleared his throat. "I've never actually used the dishwasher, Kate. I just do dishes by hand."

"I see. I guess that makes sense. But why would you put all the fruit in the microwave?"

He hurried into the kitchen. "It's convenient. What are you looking for?"

She grinned at him. "You don't really cook much, do you?"

He rubbed the bridge of his nose. "I do a mean barbecue."

"I'll just bet you do. Are you ready?"

Matt took her hand and drew her close to him as they went out into the morning air. She fit with him, belonged with him. She didn't believe it. He could see the reservations in her eyes, but he was determined to change her mind.

All the regulars considered the grocery store the center of town. Inez Nelson had a way with people. She didn't know the meaning of the word *stranger* and nearly everyone shopped at the local market, more to catch up on all the news and see Inez than for any other reason. She had known every one of the Drake sisters since their births and considered them akin to family.

Matt parked his car in front of the town square just to the left of Inez's store. "The Christmas pageant is growing, so many people want to participate that I think we're going to have to get a larger town square. The actors can barely get through the crowd as they walk up the street to the manger."

"I love the fact that everyone participates. It's so fun for the children afterward, when Santa shows up with his reindeer and gives out candy canes." Kate took the hand Matt held out to her. They stood together looking at the nativity scene in the town square, astonished that the statues, minus the wise men, had already been cleaned and the scene put back together. It would be reenacted with humans Christmas Eve, but a local sculptor had created the beautiful statues and several artists had done woodwork for the manger and life-size stable, and others had painted the entire backdrop. This year, Inez had managed to find a powdery substance that looked exactly like snow and had sprinkled it on the roof of the stable and on the surrounding ground, to the townspeople's delight and amusement. Snow was rarely seen in their coastal town.

"How many kids do you think have snuck into the square for a snowball fight?" Matt lowered his voice and looked around, half-expecting Inez to hear him even though she was a safe distance away inside the store.

Kate turned her laughing gaze on him. "You would have, wouldn't you?"

Fast-moving shadows slid across the ground, blocking out the sun's rays. "Damn right. Jonas and I would have made a snow fort and pelted everyone within throwing distance." His smile faded even as he finished his sentence. His hand gripped her arm to draw her attention. He nodded toward the sky. Seagulls filled the air overhead, winging their way fast inland. The birds were eerily silent, their great wings flapping as they hurried away from the ocean.

Kate shook her head and looked out toward the sea. The gray fog was rolling in fast. It roiled and churned, a turbulent mass, displaying raw energy. Lightning arced, chains of red-orange flashing within the center of the gray mist.

Matt swore and tugged her toward the store. "Let's get inside."

"It's growing stronger," Kate said.

Matt could feel her trembling against him. He pulled her closer to him. "We knew he would get stronger, Kate. You'd think the damned thing would take a vacation and give us a break. We'll figure this out."

"I know." She walked with him to the store. The entity was growing stronger and she felt stretched and tired and breakable. She couldn't very well tell Matt. He was already worried about her. She could read it in his eyes. How had she never managed to see the stark loneliness in him before? The aching desire? It was deep and intense and swamped her sometimes when he looked at her. Yet still, as he walked beside her, a tall, formidable man with wide shoulders and a thick chest and eyes that were never still, she could barely take in that he loved her.

Matt slid his arm around Kate's shoulders as they entered the building. As always, the small store had more than its share of customers. Inez greeted them loudly, gazing at them speculatively with bright eyes and a cheerful smile. "Kate, how lovely to see you, dear. And with Matt. I swear you grow taller every day, Matt."

Her comments effectively turned him into a boy again. Only Inez could manage to do that. "I feel a little taller today, Inez." He winked at Kate.

"Are you two coming to the pageant practice?" Inez asked. "I organized another one after the big fiasco the other night. No one blames Abbey, Kate. It certainly wasn't her fault that rat Bruce Harper is having an affair with little miss hot pants Sylvia Fredrickson."

"Abbey felt terrible, Inez," Kate said. "I'm sure it must have caused problems."

"Well, Bruce's wife left him. You know she's due to give birth any day now. They all dropped out of the production, and I had to find replacements." Inez glared at Matt. "Danny was in a fine snit saying he wasn't certain he could work with *amateur* actors. I told him he was an amateur actor."

"Inez," Kate protested. "You probably broke his heart."

For a moment Inez pursed her lips, looking repentant. "Well, he deserves it. I've got enough trouble without that boy complaining about his part. The three wise men are nervous, and I'm afraid they're fixing to drop out. I don't want to cancel the pageant. It's been put on every year since this town was founded."

"Danny won't drop out. He likes to herd those sheep around," Matt said.

Inez scowled. "He likes to chase them toward the kids and get a huge reaction."

"That is the truth." Matt grinned at her, but his eyes were on the wisps of gray-white fog slipping into town. He moved away from the women toward the plate-glass window, where he studied the fog. The enemy. It was strange to think of the fog, a nearly everyday occurrence on the coast, as the enemy.

The dark tendrils stretched toward houses, reached with long, spiny arms and bony fingers. The image was so strong Matt took a step closer to the window, narrowing his eyes to peer into the fog. "Katie, come here for a minute," he said softly, and held out his hand without taking his eyes from the fog. Something was moving inside of it.

Kate immediately put her hand into his and stepped up beside him. "What is it?"

"Look into the fog and tell me what you see."

Kate studied the rapidly moving vapor. It was darkening and spinning, almost boiling with turbulence. She shivered as long streaks stretched across the highway and began to surround the residences. It made her think of a predator hunting something, sniffing for the right scent. She thought something moved in the middle of the thick fogbank, something shaped vaguely like a tall man in a long, flowing coat and an old hat. She glimpsed a form, then it disappeared in the seething mass, only to reappear moments later, fading into the edges of the whirling mists. It was tall with bare white bones, pitiless eyes, and a wide, gaping mouth. She stepped back, gasping. The skeleton had more than taken shape. This time the entire chest was intact, and small pieces of flesh hung on the body, making it more grotesque than ever.

Kate put a hand protectively to her throat to stifle the scream welling up as she backed completely away from the window. She realized the store was eerily silent. Inez and the patrons stared out the window fearfully.

"It's taking shape, isn't it?" Matt asked.

Jonas and Jackson stalked into the store, Jonas's expression grim. "Kate, get out there and get rid of this before we start having fatalities," Jonas snapped without preamble, ignoring everyone else. "No one can see to drive the highway. I issued a warning on the radio, but we're going to have people not only driving over cliffs but also walking over them. Unfortunately, not everyone listens to the radio."

"Go to hell, Jonas." Matt was furious. *Furious.* At the thing in the fog. At Jonas, and at his own inability to stop the entity. "You're not sending Kate out there to battle that damned thing alone again. She's scared and tired, and I'll be damned if you bully her into thinking she's responsible for taking this thing on by herself. You want someone to fight it, be my guest."

"Dammit, Matt, don't start with me. You know I would if I had a chance in hell, but I don't. This is the Drakes' territory, not mine," Jonas bristled.

Kate put a restraining hand on both men's arms. "The last thing we need is to fight among ourselves. Jonas, I can't manage it alone. I really can't. I need Hannah." She leaned her head against Matt's chest. "I don't bring the wind, Hannah does. She's exhausted with fighting this thing. My sisters have been working with me the entire time. Without Hannah, we can't do anything."

Matt glanced down at her face, saw the lines of weariness there, the look of far too much energy expended, and for the first time, uncertainty. He wrapped his arms more tightly around her, and addressed Jonas. "How bad is it out there? Can they pass on this one and get some rest?"

"I'm getting damned sick of this secrecy where Hannah's concerned," Jonas said, obviously trying to get his temper under control. He felt every bit as impotent against the entity as Matt did, and it was clearly wearing on him. "We may have a running battle going; but if she's ill, it matters to me, Kate. You've been my family for as long as I can remember."

Kate felt Matt stirring, a fine tremor of anger rippling through his body at the tone Jonas used with her. She rubbed her head against his chest. "I know that, Jonas. Hannah is aware you're angry too. You know we all have a difficult time after we use our gifts. Hannah has to expend a tremendous amount of energy controlling something as capricious as the wind. Using our gifts is very draining. And whatever is in the fog has been growing in strength and resisting us, so we're having to expend more effort to contain it."

"Can you get rid of it, Kate?" Inez asked.

Everyone in the store seemed to hold their breath, waiting for her answer. Kate could feel the hope. The fear. All eyes were on her. "I honestly don't know." But she had to try. She could already hear the feminine voices whispering in the soft breeze heading inland from the sea. She felt her sisters calling to her to join with them. Hannah was already on the battlement, drooping with weariness, but facing the fog, waiting for Kate. Sarah and Abbey stood with her, and Joley had arrived. She'd been traveling for two days, yet she stood shoulder to shoulder with her sisters, waiting for Kate.

Kate closed her eyes and drew in a deep breath in

an effort to summon her strength. Her courage. A paralyzing fear was beginning to grip her, one she recognized and was familiar with. Like Hannah, she suffered from severe panic attacks. Unlike Hannah, she was not a public figure. As a writer, her name might be known, but not her face. She could blend into the background easily, yet now everyone was watching. Waiting. Expecting Kate to work some kind of magic when she didn't even know what she was dealing with.

Matt felt the fine tremors that ran through Kate's body and turned her away from everyone in the store, his larger body shielding her. "You don't have to do this, Katie." He whispered the words, his forehead pressed against hers.

"Yes, I do," she whispered back.

Jonas instinctively stepped in front of her to protect her from prying eyes. Jackson spoke. His voice was utterly low, so soft one felt they had to strain to hear his words, yet his voice carried complete authority. "Inez, move everyone to the center of the store away from the windows, and let's give Kate some room to work. We have no idea what's going to happen, and we don't want to take chances with injuries."

Kate was grateful to the three men. She took another breath and pulled away from Matt, deliberately yanking open the door and slipping outside before her courage failed her. At once she felt the malevolence, a bitter, twisted emotion beating at her.

The dark fog wrapped around her body, and twice she actually felt the brush of something alive sliding over her skin. She pressed her teeth together to keep them from chattering. Strength was already flowing into her—her sisters, reaching out from a distance, calling to her with encouraging words.

Matt joined her outside, slipping behind her, circling her waist with his arms, drawing her back against his hard, comforting body so that she had an anchor. Jonas took up a position on her right side, and Jackson was at her left. Three big men, all seasoned warriors, all ready to defend her with their lives. It was impossible not to find the courage and the strength she needed when it was pouring into her from every direction.

Kate faced the dark, boiling fog, lifting her arms to signal to Hannah, to signal to bring in the wind. She began to speak softly, calmly, using the gift of her soothing voice in an attempt to bring peace to the swelling malevolence in the fog. She spoke of peace, of love, of redemption and forgiveness. Gathering every vestige of courage she possessed, Kate made no attempt to drive it away. Rather she summoned it to her, trying to find a way to pierce the veil between reality and the shadow world where she could see into the soul of what was left behind and, hopefully, find a way to heal the broken spirit.

The fog spun and roiled in a terrible frenzy, a reaction to the sound of her voice. Her sisters protested for a moment, frightened by what she was trying, but joining with her when they recognized her determination. Jonas made a small sound of dissent and moved closer to her, ready to jerk her back into reality.

Moans assaulted her ears. The shadow world was vague and gray, a bleak hazy place where nothing was what it seemed. She chanted softly, her voice spreading through the world with little effort, stilling the moans and alerting whatever lived there to her presence. Kate felt the impact when the entity realized she'd once again joined him in his world. She could feel his blazing rage, the fierce anger, and the intensity of his guilt and sorrow. The thing turned toward her, a tall skeleton of a man, blurred so that he was nearly indistinct in the gray vapors surrounding him. He wore a long coat and shapeless hat, and he shook his head and pressed his bony hands over his ears to stop the enchantment of her voice. Flesh sagged from the bones, a loose fit in some places, stretched tight in others.

Kate whispered softly to him, calling, beckoning, trying to coax him to reveal the pain he suffered, the torment of his existence. She used her voice shamelessly, cajoling him to find peace. The shadowy figure took a few steps toward her. Kate held out her hand to him, a gesture of camaraderie. *There is peace. Let yourself feel it surround you.*

The being took another cautious step toward her. Her heart pounded. Her mouth was dry, but she kept whispering. Speaking to him. Promising him rest. He was only a few feet from her, his arm stretching out toward her hand. The bony fingers were close. Inches away from her flesh. She remembered the feel of the finger bones closing around her throat, but she stood her ground and kept enticing him.

Something slithered around his boots. Snakelike vines wrapped around bony ankles. Out of the barren rocks bounded a huge creature with matted fur and yellow eyes. In the cold of the shadow world, she could see the creature's vaporous breath mingling with the fog. The eyes fixed on her, an intruder in their world.

The tips of her fingers touched the bony ends of the skeleton as it reached toward her. The creature howled, sending a shiver of fear down Kate's spine. Her sisters held their collective breath. Jonas stiffened, communicating his apprehension to Matt and Jackson.

Kate continued to whisper of peace, of aid, of a place to rest. The being took more shape, the pitiless eyes swimming with tears, extending its hand as far as the snakelike vines allowed. Abruptly the skeleton threw back its head and roared, rejecting her. Rejecting the idea of redemption and forgiveness. She glimpsed a raging hatred of self, of everything symbolizing Christmas, of peace itself. *There can be no peace.* She caught that as the being began to whirl around, furious, using the vortex of its wild spinning to hurl objects at her. The moans rose to shrieks. The huge creature bounded toward Kate, breathing as loudly as any bull. Kate made one last grab for the hand of the skeleton, but it had turned on her completely, rushing at her along with the beast.

"Get her out of there!" Jonas shouted, catching the collective fear that ran through the Drake family. He gripped Kate's arm hard, shaking her. "Matt, pull her back to us!"

"Kate," her sisters cried out, "leave him, leave him there."

"Hannah!" Jonas cried the name desperately. "The wind, Hannah, bring in the wind."

Kate stared at the terrible figure coming straight at her, fury in its every line. The eyes glowed red through the dark fog; the face was made of bones, not flesh. The mouth gaped open in a silent scream. She was trapped there in the world of shadows, real, yet not, unable to find her way back. The worst of it was, she caught sight of a second insubstantial figure coming at her from the left.

"Kate." Matt whispered her name, lifted her into his arms. Her body was an empty shell, her mind caught somewhere else.

"Kate, darling, go with the other one, he'll lead you out." Elle's soft voice pushed everything else away.

The dark demon was almost upon her. Kate felt a hand on her arm. She looked down and saw Jackson's fingers circling her wrist like a vise. She didn't have time to go voluntarily; he yanked her out of the shadows, back into the light. She heard a roar of rage, shuddered when she felt bones brush against her skin. Matt was real and solid, and she gripped him hard, needing to feel grounded. She felt physically ill, her stomach a churning knot. She closed eyes, sliding into a dead faint.

The wind swept in from the sea, a strong tempest of retaliation. Hannah's fear added to the strength of the storm. Rain burst down on them. The dark fog swirled and fought, not wanting to give ground. For a brief moment there was a confrontation between the entity and the Drake sisters, sticks and debris flying in the wind. The three men could hear the desperate cries of seagulls. And then it was over, the fog retreating to the sea, leaving behind silence and the rushing wind and rain. Matt stood there on the sidewalk, Kate, safe in his arms, staring in shock at the mess left behind.

Clouds overhead obscured the sun, the day overcast and gloomy. Christmas lights twinkled on and off where they hung over the buildings in rows of vivid colors, a terrible contrast to the scene left behind in the town square. Feathers were everywhere and in the pristine white snow by the manger there was a bright red pool of blood.

chapter 9

A star burns hot in the dead of the night,
As the bell tolls it's now midnight

"NEVER AGAIN. NEVER AGAIN." MATT SHOVED both hands through his hair and glared at the Drake sisters. "I swear, Kate, you are never doing that again." He paced restlessly back and forth across the living room floor.

Sarah, Kate's older sister, rested her head against her fiancé's knee, and watched Matt in silence. Abbey sat on the couch, Joley's head resting in her lap. Joley lay stretched out, her eyes closed, appearing to be asleep in spite of his tirade. Hannah lay on the couch closest to the window, lines of exhaustion visible on her young face.

"It doesn't do any good to get upset," Jonas said. "They do whatever they want to do without a thought for the consequences."

Sarah sighed loudly. "Don't start, Jonas. That's not true, and you know it. If you were the one trying to get rid of this thing, you wouldn't worry about your own safety, and you know it. You'd just do whatever had to be done."

"That's different, Sarah," Jonas snarled back. "Dammit anyway. Look at Hannah. She can't even move. I think she needs a doctor. Where the hell is Libby when we need her?"

"Are you ever going to stop swearing at us?" Sarah asked. She rubbed her face against Damon's knee. "Hannah needs rest and maybe some tea."

"I'll make tea," Damon offered. "I think all of you could use it."

"Damon, you are a darling," Sarah said. "The kettle's boiling."

Matt glanced into the kitchen, and, sure enough, the kettle was steaming. He knew very well it hadn't even been turned on minutes earlier.

Damon leaned down to brush a kiss across Sarah's temple before making his way into the kitchen. "This feels like old times," he called out, reaching for the tea kept for just such occasions.

"We could use a little more festive atmosphere," Abigail decided. She stared at the row of candles on the mantel until they spluttered to life, flames leaping and flickering for a moment, then taking hold. At once the aroma of cinnamon and spice scented the air.

"Good idea," Sarah agreed and focused on the CD player. Instantly Joley's voice filled the room with a popular Christmas carol.

"Not that one," Joley protested. "Something else."

"Are you all insane?" Jonas demanded. "Kate could

have been killed. Are we going to pretend it didn't happen and have a little Christmas get-together?"

"Jonas, it does no good yelling at them. What do you want them to do?" Damon returned, carrying a tray with several cups of tea on it. He distributed them among the Drake sisters.

"And you were the one asking me, no, telling me to get out there and stop the fog," Kate pointed out.

Jonas muttered something ugly under his breath and reached down for Hannah's limp wrist to take her pulse. As he did a breeze swirled around the room, and his hat sailed from the chair where he'd placed it and landed in the middle of the room. Jonas straightened and glared down at Hannah, who didn't stir.

"Jonas, we didn't know the entity was going to try to hurt Kate," Abbey pointed out. "We have to know what his motivation is."

Sarah shoved a heavy book across the floor. "Trying to read this thing without Elle is impossible. She's the only one that can read the language our ancestors used. The writing is in that strange hieroglyphic language we were all supposed to study back when we were teens. Mom told us to learn it, but we kept putting it off, wondering why we needed to delve that far back into the past. With the little bit we know, it's impossible to find a single entry in all of this."

Matt stopped pacing, coming to a halt beside Kate, his hand resting on the nape of her neck. "Elle's on the way home, isn't she? It shouldn't be long. How come she learned the language when the rest of you only know a little?"

Abbey blew on her tea. "She learned it in order to teach the next generation, just as our mother did."

"Speaking of Elle, how did she connect with you, Jackson? How did she know you were able to go into the shadows and bring Kate out?" Sarah asked.

There was a sudden silence, and all eyes turned to regard the man sitting in absolute stillness just to the side of the window. His cool dark eyes moved over their faces, a brooding perusal. "I don't know what you're talking about. I don't even know Elle."

Abbey sat up straighter. "That's not the truth, Jackson."

Jonas sucked in his breath sharply. "Don't, Abbey!" His warning came a heartbeat too late. She'd already said it, her voice pitched perfectly to turn people inside out, to reach into their darkest depths and pull the truth from them.

Jackson stood up slowly, his eyes hard steel. He walked across the floor without a single sound. Joley sat up and blinked at him. Matt moved in on one side of Abbey, Jonas on the other. Ignoring the two men, Jackson bent down until he was eye level with Abbey. "You don't ever want to ask me for the truth, Abbey. Not about me and not about Elle." He hadn't raised his voice, but Abbey shivered. Joley put her arm around her sister.

"I'll be outside," Jackson said.

"He's never met Elle," Sarah said, after the door closed behind the deputy. "Jonas, he hasn't, has he?"

Jonas shook his head. "Not to my knowledge. And he's never mentioned her. They both had the same nightmare, but so did half the kids in Sea Haven."

"He scares me," Abbey said. "I don't want Elle near him. She's so tiny and fragile and so sweet. And he's . . ."

"My friend," Jonas said. "He saved my life twice, Abbey."

"And mine too," Matt added. "You shouldn't have done that."

Abbey looked down. "I know. I don't know why I did. It's just that he's so frightening, and the thought that Elle was out there in the shadow world too . . ."

"But she wasn't," Kate interrupted. "She wasn't there. I heard her voice, but she wasn't in the world, she was in my head." Her voice trailed off in sudden speculation. The sisters exchanged a long look. "Jonas, is Jackson telepathic?"

"How the hell would I know?" Jonas asked.

"Well, because you are. Sort of." The sisters looked at one another again and burst out laughing. Their bright laughter dispelled the air of gloom in the room.

Jonas made a face at Matt. "See what I have to put up with?" He stomped across the room to reach down and retrieve his hat. Before his fingers could close around the rim, the flames on the candles flared from a sudden gust of wind, and the hat leaped away from him to land dangerously close to the fireplace. Jonas straightened slowly, his hands on his hips, glancing suspiciously around the room at the Drake sisters. They all wore innocent expressions. "You are not going to get me to believe that the wind is in the house without a little help."

Unexpectedly the logs in the fireplace burst into flame. Jonas took a step toward his hat. It went up on the rim and rolled a few inches toward the burning logs. "My hat had better not go into that fire," Jonas warned.

"Really, Jonas." Joley didn't open her eyes. "You're becoming paranoid. Hannah's already asleep."

He continued to study their faces and finally crossed to the couch where Hannah lay asleep, looking almost a child. "I'm taking the baby doll to bed. It's the only safe thing to do." He simply lifted her in one quick movement and, before anyone could protest, started out of the room.

"The tower," Sarah called after him.

"What a surprise there. I can see Hannah as the princess in her tower," Jonas called back.

The sisters looked at one another and burst out laughing. Matt shook his head. "You all are downright scary."

Joley leaned her head back and grinned at him. "I'd like to know what's going on with my sister and you all alone up in that house of yours. I was going to help Hannah whip up a little love potion and stick it in your drink the next time I saw you, but they tell me you've been playing fast and loose with her already."

Kate turned a particularly fetching shade of crimson. "Joley Drake, that will certainly be the last we hear on that subject."

Joley didn't look impressed with the stern tone. "In case anyone is interested, I took a good look at Kate's neck, and she has a particularly impressive love bite."

Kate clapped her hand over her neck and shook her head. "I most certainly do not. Drink your tea."

"What's even more impressive," Joley continued, "is that Matt seems to be sporting one of his own."

A collective gasp went up. "We want to see, Matt," Abigail pleaded.

"Only if I get to make a wish on the snowglobe," he bargained.

There was instant silence. Sarah sat up straighter. "Matt," she paused and glanced at Kate. "Wishing on our snowglobe is not like making a silly, frivolous wish. It's very serious business. You have to know what you want and really mean it. You have to have weighed your decision very carefully."

"I can assure you I have. If you want to see the love bite, you can produce the snowglobe." Matt folded his arms across his chest.

"Matt," Kate cautioned, "if you're thinking about wishing for anything we already discussed—don't. It wouldn't work."

Joley lifted her head off the back of the couch and

eyed them both. "This sounds very interesting. Does anyone else want Christmas snacks to go with the tea, because I really could go for those little decorated sugar cookies." She waggled her fingers in the direction of the kitchen. "Tell us more, Matt. The snowglobe is right over there by the fireplace. Please do step on Jonas's hat. It always livens things up when he does his sheriff he-man routine." She turned her head to glance at the stairs. "He's been up there a long time. You don't suppose he's taking advantage while Hannah is asleep, do you?"

Sarah nudged Joley with her foot. "You're terrible, Joley."

Matt skirted around Jonas's hat and reached for the snowglobe. It felt solid in his hands. He glanced at Kate. She shook her head, looking fearful. The globe warmed in his hands. He stared at the scene, the snowflakes whirling around the house until they all blended together to become fog. The lights on the tree sprang to life.

"You activated it," Sarah said. "That's nearly impossible."

"Not unless he's . . ."

"Joley!" Kate interrupted her sister sharply. "Matt, really, it isn't something to play with."

"I've never been more serious. Tell me what to do." He looked at Sarah.

She glanced at Kate, then shrugged. "It's relatively easy, Matt, but be sure. You look into the fog and picture what you want most in the world and wish for it. If you meet the criteria, the globe will grant your wish."

"And it works?"

"According to tradition. Family is allowed one wish a year, no more. And you can't wish for harm to anyone."

"That's why we don't allow Jonas access to it," Joley said.

Matt inhaled the fragrance of the candles and fresh-baked cookies wafting from the kitchen. He didn't question who made the cookies. He wasn't even surprised by the fact that there were cookies. He stared into the fog inside the snowglobe and conjured up the exact image of Kate. With everything in him, body, soul, heart, and mind, he made his wish. The fog was still for a moment, then swirled faster, dissipating until the globe was once more clear and the lights on the tree dimmed. He placed the globe back on the shelf carefully and grinned at Kate.

"Let's hope you know what you're doing," Joley said.

Suddenly in a much better mood, Matt flashed her a smile. "At the risk of sounding like an adoring fan, I love your collection of blues. You have the perfect voice for blues." He grinned at her. "Or Christmas music."

Joley winced. "I just sent that to my family for fun."

"It's beautiful," Abbey said. "Are you having fun on your tour?"

Joley frowned. "Yes, it's tiring, and there are always the freaks out there, but there's nothing quite like the energy of forty thousand people at a concert."

"What freaks?" Jonas demanded, walking back into the room. "Hannah didn't even wake up, not even when I called her Barbie doll. Are you certain she's okay, Sarah?"

Sarah paused for a moment, seeking inside herself, reaching out to her sister. "She's exhausted, Jonas, and needs sleep. We'll have to find a way to get some food into her soon."

Jonas rolled his eyes. "We can't have Miss Anorexic gaining an ounce. She's probably worried the camera won't love her, and she won't be able to parade around half-naked on the cover of a magazine for the entire world to see."

Kate tossed her napkin at Jonas. "Go away, you're annoying me. We have to have clear heads to decide how to handle this, and you just stir everyone up."

Jonas shrugged, in no way perturbed. "I have to go back to work anyway. But I want to hear about these freaks of yours, Joley. You haven't been getting any nut-cases stalking you, have you?"

Joley took a sip of tea and looked up at Jonas. "I don't know. I hired a couple of bodyguards, bouncers really, just to protect the stage. Each concert hall has a security force, of course, but I thought if these two traveled with us, we'd have a little extra protection. Stalkers come with the territory, you know that. The more famous you get, the more crazies you attract."

Matt sat down beside Kate. "Do writers have that kind of problem?"

Before Kate had a chance to deny it, Jonas answered. "Of course they do. Anyone in the public eye does, Matt. Writers, musicians, politicians, and—" he glanced toward the stairs—"supermodels."

Joley laughed. "You worry so much, Jonas, you ought to go into law enforcement. It's right up your alley."

"Ha-ha, very funny. I'll call you later to see if anything new has happened." Jonas glanced out the window. "I never thought I'd dread nightfall."

Matthew looked out the window to the pounding sea. "Is Elle expected tonight?"

"She said around midnight. She's flying into San Francisco and renting a car to drive here. I offered to pick her up," Abbey said, "but she didn't want any of us on the road with the fog. She promised she'd check the weather station before she came into Sea Haven."

Jonas scooped up his hat. "I'll keep an eye out for her. You all rest and stay out of trouble." He left, banging the door behind him.

At Sarah's urging, Damon nodded toward the kitchen and Matt obliged.

Abbey waited until the men were out of the room. "I didn't mean to challenge Jackson like that." She pressed her hand to her mouth, her eyes enormous. "That's twice now. And the house should have protected me. How could that happen in our home?"

"You were relaxed," Sarah said. "You let your guard down."

Abbey shook her head. "I haven't let my guard down since I caused such a problem during the committee meeting. Poor Inez called me this afternoon and told me no one realized it was me, but Sylvia knew."

"She went to school with us," Joley pointed out.

Hannah walked back into the room. Tall and blond and beautiful, she looked so fragile she could have been made of porcelain. "Don't worry about Sylvia. I'm certain she's very sorry she hit Abbey."

Joley held out her arms. "Come here, baby, sit by me. You look done in. You were very bad teasing poor Jonas that way and making him think you were sleeping." Joley kissed Hannah. "You really should be in bed."

"I couldn't sleep," Hannah admitted. "I needed to be with all of you."

Joley stroked back her hair. "You didn't do anything awful to Sylvia, did you?"

Hannah's eyes widened in a semblance of innocence. "You all think I'm so bent on revenge all the time."

Sarah paused in the doorway to the kitchen. "That's not an answer, you bloodthirsty little witch. Exactly what did you do to Sylvia?"

Hannah leaned against Joley. "I'm glad you're home.

You don't give me that stern face like Sarah does."

"Hannah Drake, what did you do to Sylvia?"

Hannah shrugged. "I *heard* from a reliable source . . ."

"Inez at the grocery store," Abbey supplied.

"Well, she's reliable," Hannah pointed out. "I heard Sylvia developed a bright red rash on the left side of her face. It appears to be in the shape of a hand. I couldn't help but think it was fitting."

Sarah rubbed her hand over her face, trying to stare down her younger sister without smiling. "You know very well you can't use our gifts for anything other than good, Hannah. You're risking reprisal."

Hannah stretched her legs out in front of her and gave Sarah a sweet smile. "You never know what a humbling experience can do for someone's character."

"I'm getting your tea for you, but I hope this is a big joke, and I won't hear about it later at the store." Sarah turned away quickly to keep Hannah from seeing her laughter.

Abbey squeezed Hannah's hand. "You didn't really do anything to Sylvia, did you?" There was a hopeful note in her voice she couldn't quite hide.

"Drink your tea," Sarah said. "And eat some cookies. You're too pale. Matt and Damon are making us dinner tonight."

"Did I miss anything important while I was making Jonas carry my deadweight up those long and winding stairs?"

"Only Matt wishing on the snowglobe," Joley said. "And we're all fairly certain what he wished for."

"You're so brave, Kate," Hannah said. "I could never be with a man so absolutely frightening. They have those cold eyes and those scary voices, and I just want to curl up and fade away." For a moment tears shimmered in her eyes. She looked over the rim of her teacup at Kate. "You thought I was so brave to go out into the world and be seen, while you chose to stay out of sight and share your wonderful stories with the world, but you're willing to try with a man to have a real life with him."

"I haven't made up my mind yet," Kate admitted. "I'm afraid he'll wake up one day and realize what a coward I am. You'll find someone though, Hannah."

Hannah shook her head. "No, I won't. I don't want some man snarling at me because I forgot to put the dishes in the dishwasher, or angry because I had to fly to Egypt to do a photo shoot. And I could never live with a man who always seemed on the edge of violence, or even capable of violence. I'd be so afraid I'd be paralyzed."

Kate laid her hand on Hannah's knee. "Matt isn't capable of violence against a woman. He's protective, there's a difference."

"That's how everyone describes Jonas, as protective, but he's really a bully. He'll order his wife around day and night."

"If Jonas ever falls in love with a woman, I think he

would move heaven and earth to make her happy," Kate said. "He looks after all of us, and we're sometimes very aggravating. He has a job to do, and he works hard at it. We often make his job much more difficult. And it must be very disconcerting to be so connected emotionally to us. He senses when we're in trouble or hurt, and unfortunately we're in trouble quite often."

Hannah sighed. "I know. He's just so annoying all the time. I closed the window in the entryway; too much fog was drifting in, and it scared me." She forced an uneasy laugh. "I never thought I'd be afraid of the fog."

Kate stood up and looked around the house. "What do you mean too much fog was drifting in?" She stared out the window toward the sea. "You *saw* it? You weren't dreaming? What did it look like?"

Sarah stood up too and began to move uneasily about the room, checking the windows.

"It looked like fog," Hannah said. "I came down the stairs and, to be honest, was a little unsteady, so I sat on the floor in the entryway for a couple of minutes. I could see fog drifting in through the open window. It appeared to be normal fog, a long wisp of it, but the fact that I could see it in the house upset me. So I closed the window."

"Nothing can get into the house, Sarah," Abbey said. "It's protected. You know that the house has always protected us."

Sarah shook her head. "Mom told us we needed to know the ancient language of the Drake sisters, and we all shrugged it off with the exception of Elle. She also told us we needed to renew our safeguards every single time we came home, but did we do that? No, of course not—we've become complacent. Mom has precog, we all know it. It was a foreshadowing, but we didn't take her instructions seriously."

Abbey put a hand to her throat. "Do you think the entity was influencing me to use my voice on Jackson as well as at the committee meeting?"

Sarah nodded. "There's a good chance of it. We have to be very careful. None of us are handling this very well. We've never faced such a thing before."

"And I never want to again," Kate said fervently.

"Dinner," Matt called from the kitchen. "Come eat. And bring Hannah with you. Jonas said she had to eat something."

Hannah rolled her eyes. "There's my point exactly, Kate. Men always try bossing women around. It's their nature, they can't help themselves. We know the thing in the fog is a male, and I'll bet he's seriously upset with a woman."

They all started into the kitchen. Sarah and Kate helped steady Hannah. "Actually, I felt guilt and sorrow and rage coming from him," Kate said. "I could feel the connection, but he tossed it away because he feels he doesn't deserve forgiveness. Something terrible happened, and he believes he's to blame for it."

"Why is he causing terrible things to happen now?" Hannah asked.

"I don't know," Kate admitted. "But it has something to do with Christmas. Sarah's right. We have to really pay attention to every detail now. He can't get any stronger, or we won't be able to stop him."

Matt spent the rest of the day poring over the entries in the diaries and listening to the easy teasing back and forth between the sisters. The women slept on and off throughout the day. Damon and Sarah spent a lot of time kissing every chance they could steal away, and he was a bit jealous that he didn't have the right to be as openly demonstrative with Kate. As the hours slipped by, all he could think about was Kate and being alone with her.

He slipped his arm around her shoulders. "It's late, let's go back to my house."

"Elle's driving in tonight. I'd like to wait for her. She's supposed to be here any minute, and we slept most of the day after that horrible encounter this morning," Kate replied.

"The fog is coming in," Matt announced. He opened the door and wandered out to the wide, wraparound veranda to stare out over the ocean.

"Elle should be here any minute; she told us midnight," Kate said, studying the wisps of fog as they drifted toward land. "She'll make it before the fog hits the highway."

"Who decorated your Christmas tree?" Matt indicated the huge tree covered in lights and adorned with a variety of ornaments.

Kate went down the porch stairs to stand in front of the tree. She touched a small wooden elf. "Isn't it beautiful? Frank, one of the local artists, did this carving. Many of these ornaments have been handed down from generation to generation."

"Don't you worry about them out in the weather?" The tree was inside the yard, and two large dogs protected the area. Sarah's dogs. No one would sneak in and steal the ornaments, even the more precious ones, but the sea air and the continual rain could ruin the decorations.

"We never worry about weather," Kate said simply. "The Drakes have always decorated a tree outside and, hopefully, we always will."

The fog burst over them in a rolling swirl, wrapped around the tree, and filled the yard, streaming in from the ocean as if pushed by an unseen hand.

"I think our old nemesis is attacking another Christmas symbol," Matt said, pointing to the top of the huge Christmas tree in the front yard. "What does the star stand for? There has to be a meaning."

The fog tangled around the branches, amplifying the glow of the lights through the vapor. Kate looked up at the star as it shorted out, sparks raining down through the fog. It brightened momentarily, then faded completely. She was looking up and saw through the wisps of clouds a hot, bright star streaking across the sky, plunging toward Earth. She went still, the color draining from her face. "Elle." She whispered her sister's name. "He's coming for Elle. That's what he was doing in the house. He's after Elle." The fog was choking the road, making it impossible to see.

"What the hell do you mean, it was in the house?" Matt raced back inside the house just as her sisters hurried outside to join Kate. He caught up the phone and called Jonas. He had no idea what Jonas could do. No one could see in the fog. They didn't know exactly where Elle was, only that she was close. She had said she'd arrive sometime around midnight. It was close to that now. She might be on the worst section of narrow, twisting highway leading to Sea Haven.

Kate whirled around, facing toward the town as a bell began to ring loudly. The sound reverberated through the night. "The bell is the symbol for guidance, for return. She's here now. She's coming up the highway now, returning to us. Returning to the fold. Sarah—" she caught her sister by the hand—"she's nearing the cliffs right now. Even if Hannah had the strength to bring in the wind, it's too late. He's warning us, telling us what he's going to do. Why would he do that?"

Kate reached for her youngest sister, mind to mind. She wasn't the most telepathic of her siblings, but Elle was a strong telepathic. Kate heard music, Joley's voice filling the car with her rich, warm tones. Elle's voice joining in. Elle drove slowly, crawling through the thick fog, knowing she was only a mile from her home. It was impossible to see in front of the car; she had no choice but to pull off the road and park until the fog lifted.

Elle peered at the side of the road, trying to see where the shoulder was wide enough to get her car off the highway in case another vehicle came along. She steered slowly over, aware the cliff was high above the pounding sea. Joley's voice was comforting, a sultry heat that kept the chilling cold from entering the car. Elle turned off the engine and pushed open the door, needing to get her bearings. If she could see the lights from any direction, she would know where she was. She knew she had to be close to her home. The fog surrounded her, a thick, congealed mass that was utterly cold.

Kate drew in her breath, tried to touch Elle, tried to warn her of the impending danger. Elle kept her hand on the car. *What is it, Kate?*

Kate cursed the fact that she couldn't form an answer and send it to her sister. She could only send the impression of danger very close. They all knew when their siblings were in danger, or tired or upset. But Kate didn't have the ability to actually tell Elle something was in the fog, something that was taking enough of a form that it could cause bodily harm. She didn't even know whether to tell her to stay in the car or to get away from it. She could only hope that Elle was sufficiently tapped in to all of her sisters and would know what was transpiring. Elle turned in the direction of their home and began to walk along the narrow path.

Matt rushed past Kate, heading toward the highway. The fog swallowed him immediately. "Try to clear it out, Kate," he called back. His voice sounded muffled in the thick mist, even to his own ears. He knew the trail; he'd walked it enough times over the years and was certain Elle would do the same.

Jonas and Jackson were converging from their locations as well, all of them running to Elle's aid from three different directions, but Matt had no idea if any of them would be in time. He only knew that his heart was in his throat, and he had such an overwhelming sense of imminent danger, he wanted to run flat out instead of carefully jogging his way along the steep, uneven path.

chapter 10

Beneath the star, that shines so bright,
An act unfolds, to my delight.

MATT HEARD VOICES, THE RISE AND FALL OF feminine voices. He knew Kate and her sisters were doing their best to fight against the wall of fog crouched so malevolently on the highway. He picked his way as fast and as carefully as he could. The ocean pounded and roared beneath him, waves slapping against the cliff and leaping high so that every now and then, as he jogged, he could feel the spray on his face. Rocks and the uneven ground impeded his progress. The wind picked up, blowing fiercely against the fog, taking chunks out over the roiling sea.

"Matt!" Jackson's disembodied voice called to him from deep inside the fog, somewhere ahead of him. "She's gone over the cliff. She's not in the water, but she's not going to be able to last much longer. Search along the edges." The voice was muffled and distorted by the fog.

"Watch yourself, Jackson, the cliff is crumbling in places," Matt cautioned. He didn't ask how Jackson knew Elle had gone over. Hell, he was beginning to believe he was the only person in the world without some kind of psychic talent. "Dammit, dammit, dammit." He couldn't return to Kate and tell her Elle was dead, that they'd been too late. He'd never be able to face her sorrow.

Matt inched toward the cliff, testing the ground every step of the way, making certain it would hold his weight. "Elle!" He shouted her name, heard Jackson, then Jonas echo his call. The ocean answered with another greedy roar, lifting higher, seeking prey. "Dammit, Elle, answer me." He felt desperation. Rage. Fear for Elle was beginning to swirl in the pit of his stomach. He detested inaction. He was a man who took charge, got the job done. He could have endless patience when needed, but he had to know what he was doing.

It seemed a hundred years until Jackson called out. "Found! I'll keep calling out so you both can get a direction. She's not going to be able to hang on, so I'm going down after her. I've tied off a safety rope."

Even with the fog distorting the voice, Matt got a sense of Jackson's direction and moved toward him. Jackson's voice was far more distant the second time he called out, and Matt knew he'd gone over the side of the cliff to try to get to Elle before she plunged into the sea. He'd been in combat with Jackson, had served on many covert missions with him. He wasn't a man to rush headlong into anything. If he was already going over the cliff to get to Elle, she needed the help. He was counting on Jonas and Matt to rescue them both. He knew they'd come for him.

Matt felt the crushed grass with his hand and flattened his body, belly down, reaching along the crumbling edge of the cliff until he found the rope. Jackson had tied off the end, using an old fence post. Matt sucked in his breath. The fence post was rotted and already coming out of the ground. "I'm tying off again, Jackson, give me a minute," Matt called down to him. He peered over the cliff.

Jackson was climbing down almost blind, feeling with his hands and toes for a grip. Elle lay sprawled out on a small ledge, clinging to a flimsy tree. He caught only glimpses of her as the fog was pushed out toward the sea. The heavy mist crawled down below the cliff line, hovering stubbornly in the more protected pocket to obscure the vision of the rescuers.

"Pass the rope back to me," Jonas said, coming up behind Matt.

Matt did so immediately, not taking his eyes from the scene unfolding below him. The fog was thick and churning, but the wind kept attacking it, driving it out in feathery clumps. It was the only thing that provided him with glimpses of the action. Jackson made his way, with painstaking care, down the sheer side of the cliff. Jonas tied off the rope to a much more secure anchor behind them, where Matt couldn't see.

"We're ready up here, Jackson, say the word," Matt

called when Jonas signaled him the rope was safe to use. "Elle, I'm not hearing anything from you." He hadn't. Not a moan, not a call for help. It was alarming. He thought he could see her actively holding on to the small tree growing out of the side of the cliff, but the more he tried to pierce the veil of the fog, the more he was certain Elle wasn't moving.

As Jackson reached her, Matt held his breath, waiting. Afraid to hear, afraid not to hear. His heart beat loudly over the sound of the sea.

"She's alive," Jackson called up. "She has a nasty bump on the head, and she's bruised from head to toe, but she's alive."

Matt leaned farther over the cliff to hear the conversation below him. Jackson's voice drifted up to him. "Lie still, let me examine you for broken bones. I'm Jackson Deveau, the deputy sheriff."

"This ledge is crumbling." Elle's voice trembled. "Someone pushed me. I didn't hear them, but they pushed me."

"It's all right. Don't move. You're safe now." Jackson's voice was soothing. "Do you remember me? We met once a long time ago."

Matt recognized instantly the calming quality to Jackson's voice. He was talking to keep her from being agitated. "Jonas, I think Elle's injured. I can tell by the way Jackson's acting." Keeping his voice low, he gave the news to the sheriff, aware that Jonas was anxious to know Elle's condition.

"I heard your voice, in a dream," Elle said. Her words blurred around the edges, sending Matt's heart tripping. "You were in pain. Terrible pain. Someone was torturing you. You were in a small closet of a room. I remember."

Matt went still. Jonas froze behind him, obviously hearing Elle's response.

"Then you know you're safe with me. You helped me when I needed it. I'll get you out of this. That's the way the buddy system works."

It was the most Matt had ever heard Jackson say to anyone. He glanced back to look at Jonas's face. The fog along the highway was clearing. The wind gusted, careening off the cliff face in order to push the heavy mist away from Elle and Jackson. Jackson never talked about being captured. Never talked about the treatment he'd endured. He never spoke of the escape that followed or how difficult it had been as he led a small ragtag group of prisoners back through enemy lines to join their forces.

That a Drake sister might be aware of details Matt and Jonas weren't privy to no longer surprised either of them.

"Can you hold on to me as I climb up?" Jackson asked. "I can send you up by the rope. Matthew Granite and Jonas Harrington are up top waiting for you. You're bound to accumulate a few more bruises being hauled up that way."

"I'd feel safer going up with you, but I seem to keep

fading in and out. Things sort of drift away," Elle answered.

Matt felt the tug of the rope, knew Jackson was tying the safety line around Elle.

"Then we'll go up together," Jackson said. "I'm not going to let anything happen to you."

"I know you won't." Elle circled his neck with her arms and crawled carefully onto his back. Matt felt more tugs with the rope and knew Jackson was tying her body to his.

"Your arm is broken. Can you hold on?"

"I don't exactly like the alternative, and Libby is blocking the pain for me."

Matt shook his head. Libby Drake, the doctor. A woman reputed to have a gift for healing the impossible. "Did you know Libby was anywhere near here?" he asked Jonas.

Jonas shook his head. "I knew she was coming home for Christmas, but not that she was on the way. But that isn't unusual for the Drakes. They're all connected somehow, and they tend to do things together."

Jackson's voice drifted up to them. "Good. I'm going to start climbing, Elle. It's going to hurt."

Elle pressed her face against Jackson's broad back. Matt watched Jackson start up the cliff, testing each finger- and toehold carefully before committing to the climb. Matt and Jonas kept the rope just taut enough to allow him to scale the vertical rock face. When Jackson was halfway to the top, the fog simply gave up, retreating before the onslaught of the wind. Matt leaned down to grasp Elle, as Jackson gained the top of the cliff.

Matt untied the rope and gently laid Elle on the ground. "I'll get to a car and radio for an ambulance," Jonas said.

Elle shook her head. "Libby's on her way. She'll fix me up." She turned her head to look at Jackson. "Thank you for coming for me. I didn't think anyone would find me." She touched the bump on her forehead. "I know the fall knocked me out."

Jackson shrugged and glanced at Matt and Jonas, shook his head, and remained silent. A car pulled up beside them and Libby Drake leaped out, dragging a black leather case with her. "How bad is she hurt, Jonas?"

"I'm fine, Libby," Elle protested.

Libby ignored her, looking to Jonas for the truth as she knelt beside her sister. Jackson answered her. "I think her left arm is broken. She definitely has a concussion, and she's either bruised her ribs or possibly fractured them. She's very tender on the left side. There's one laceration on her left leg that looks as if it could use a few stitches. Other than that, she's a mass of bruises."

"I don't want to go to the hospital, Libby," Elle protested.

"Too bad, baby, I think we're going to go and check you out."

Libby's word was obviously law. Elle protested repeatedly, but no one paid any attention to her. Matthew found himself holding Kate's hand in the waiting room while Libby went through all the required tests with Elle and finally settled her in a hospital bed for the remainder of the night.

Kate leaned into Matt's hard frame, looking up at him. "Thank you. I don't know what we would have done if you, Jonas, and Jackson hadn't found her. She looks all cut up." There was a little catch in her voice.

Matt immediately put his arms around her. "I'm taking you home. To my home, where you can get some rest, Kate. Elle's in good hands, you've kissed her ten times, and Libby's going to stay overnight with her. She can't be safer than that. Jackson brought her car to your house and left it for her, so everything's taken care of. Come home with me, Katie. Let me take care of you."

"You need a shave," she observed, her hungry gaze drinking him in.

They walked together to his car, their steps in perfect harmony. Matt smiled because he loved being with her more than anything else. He rubbed his jaw. "You're right, I do. You're not only going to have whisker burn on your face, but if I'm not more careful, you'll have it other places too."

She blushed beautifully. "I already do."

He opened the door for her, caught her chin before she could slide in. "Seriously?" Just the idea of it made his body hard.

Kate nodded. "It's nice to have a constant reminder." It was more than nice. Just the thought of how the marks had gotten there made her hot with need.

Matt dragged her close to him, his mouth taking command of hers. It seemed far too long since he'd been able to kiss her. To have her all to himself. "I want to get you home where I can put you into my bed. I still have such a hard time believing you're with me."

She laughed. "Imagine how I feel."

Kate leaned her head back against the seat of his car and looked at him, the smile fading from her face. "Matt, you shouldn't have wished on the snowglobe. It isn't an ordinary Christmas globe."

He glanced at her, then back at the road, his expression settling into serious lines. "Nothing about you or your family is ordinary, Katie. I knew what I was doing."

She opened her mouth to speak, shook her head, and stared out the window into the night.

Matt searched for something to say to reassure her. Or maybe it was he that needed the reassurance. Kate was still resistant to the idea of a long-term relationship, and he wasn't certain he could change her mind. He couldn't begin to explain the sense of rightness he felt when he drove up to his house with Kate beside him. He sat in his car, looking up at the house with its bank of windows for the view, and the wide, inviting decks going in every direction. "I built this house for you. I even put in a library and two offices, just in case you wanted your own office. I asked Sarah a few years ago, when I first came back, if you had a preference where you wrote, and she said you preferred a room with a view and soft music. I added a fireplace just in case you needed the ambience."

Kate blinked back tears, leaned over, and kissed him. What could she say? Everyone in town knew Sarah. Sarah was magic. She could scale cliff walls and she knew things before they happened. She could leap out of airplanes and climb tall buildings. Sarah lived her life. She didn't dream the way Kate did or live in her imagination.

Matt took her hand and pulled her out of the car. "I soundproofed your office so the noise wouldn't bother you."

"What noise?" She knew better than to ask, but she couldn't stop herself.

"Our kids. You do want kids, don't you? I'm afraid the Granites tend to throw males. I don't have a single female cousin. You do like boys, don't you?"

Kate looked away from him, out to the booming sea. Sarah would have children. All of her sisters would have them. She'd probably tell them all stories. Maybe she should have been the one to wish on the snowglobe. Maybe she should have wished for the courage to do the right thing.

"Katie, if you don't want children, I'll be happy with it being just the two of us. You know that, don't you?" He unlocked the door to the house and stepped back to let her in. “Children would be wonderful, but not necessary. If we can have them. Sometime in the future, after I’ve spent endless time making love to you all over the house.”

Kate went straight to the Christmas tree. She wanted him. She wanted him for as long as she could have him. She swallowed her tears and lifted her chin, smiling at him. “I like that idea. Making love to you all over the house. Would you turn on the Christmas lights? I love miniature lights like these.”

Matt plugged in the lights for her. His house was dark and quiet and a bit on the cool side. He’d never bothered with heavy curtains in the living room because he had no close neighbors, and the bank of windows faced the sea. Kate dropped her purse on the nearest chair and kicked off her shoes. “It’s nice to come home. Just for tonight, I want to think about Christmas and not some awful thing coming out of the fog to hurt everyone.” She looked up at him, her large eyes sad. “Do you think we’ll manage to get one night together, Matthew?”

“I don’t know, Katie. I hope so. I’m going to check the house and downstairs, and I’ll be right back.” He didn’t think he could sleep, not even holding her in his arms, until he checked the sand outside for any peculiar footprints.

“That’s a good idea. I’ll make us up a bed. You don’t mind if we sleep out here by the tree do you?”

Matt looked around the huge, spacious living

room. The miniature lights winked on and off, colors flickering along the walls and the high ceiling. "I'd like that, Kate."

He circled the house, checked the rooms beneath the deck and the beach for any signs of intrusion. He had the feeling the enemy was as fatigued as they were. He glanced out to sea. "How about giving us a break, buddy," he murmured softly. "Whatever has you all upset, Kate had nothing to do with it."

Above his head the skies opened up and poured down rain. Matt grinned wryly and hurried back to the house. Back to Kate. The gas fireplace was lit, the "logs" burning cheerfully. On the mantel were several lighted candles. The scent of berry permeated the air. In the flickering lights, he saw Kate, lying naked on the sheets, her body beautiful, sprawled lazily on the covers while she watched the lights of the Christmas tree. His breath rushed from his lungs, so that he burned for air, just standing there in the doorway staring in surprise at the most incredible Christmas present he could imagine. That was how he thought of her. His Christmas present. He would love this time of year forever.

"Matthew." She turned over, smiled at him. "Come lie down with me."

He could see the real Kate Drake. On the outside, she seemed flawless, perfect, out of reach, yet she was really vulnerable, and as fragile as she was courageous. Kate needed a shield and he was more than happy to be that shield, for her. He could stand between her and the rest of the world. "Give me a minute, Kate."

Kate turned back to the tree, watching the lights blinking on and off, so many colors flickering across the wall. It was heaven just to lie down and rest. To relax. More than anything she loved to feel Matt's heated gaze on her. He made her feel beautiful and incredibly special. He was a large man, and the feel of his hands on her body, the way his body came alive at the sight of her, was a gift. A treasure.

Kate lay with the sheets cool on her skin and the lights playing over her body. She imagined his hands on her. His eyes on her. Thinking about him made her grow hot with need. A small sound alerted her, and she looked up to see him towering over her. For a moment she couldn't breathe. She drank him in. His strong legs and muscular thighs. His amazing erection. His flat stomach and heavily muscled chest. Finally, his eyes. His eyes had turned smoky, seductive, and now they smoldered with intensity and heat. "You take my breath away." It was a silly thing to say, but it was true. She patted the blanket beside her. She wanted to touch him, to know he was real. To feel him solid and strong beneath her fingertips.

"I'm supposed to say that to you." He stretched out beside her, gathered her into his arms to hold her to him. "I want to lie here with you for a very long time."

She rested her head on his shoulder, fitting her body more closely to his. "I wouldn't mind staying here for the rest of the winter, locked away in our own private world." She stretched languidly, pleased to be able to relax. To have him holding her with such gentleness.

Matt knew she was tired, and it was enough to hold her in his arms, even with his body raging at him and her body so soft and inviting and open to his. His mouth drifted down the side of her neck. She snuggled closer, turning her head toward the Christmas tree, giving him even better access.

"I love the way you smell," he said. Because he couldn't resist, he slid his palm over her skin. He'd never felt anything so soft. He traced her ribs, a gentle exploration, not in the least demanding, simply wanting to touch her. Her soft belly called to him, a mystery for a breast man, but he loved the way she reacted each time he caressed her there.

Kate smiled. "I love the feel of your hands."

"I've always hated my hands. Workingman hands, rough and big and meant for manual labor."

"Meant to bring pleasure to a woman, you mean," she contradicted, and caught his hand to bring it to her lips. She kissed the pads of his fingers, nibbled on the tips, and drew one into her mouth.

He caught his breath, aching with love, burning up with need. "Everything about you is so damned feminine, Kate. Sometimes I'm afraid if I touch you, I'm going to break you." He measured her wrist loosely by circling it with his thumb and index finger.

She laughed and rubbed her body against his affectionately, almost like a contented cat. "I doubt you have to worry about breaking me. This thing with the fog is draining, but I recover quickly." She frowned, even as she ran her fingertips along the hard column of his thigh. "I am a little worried about Hannah though, and now Elle."

He was very much aware of her fingers so close to his throbbing erection. She was tapping out a little rhythm on his upper thigh. His stomach constricted, and his blood thickened. The lights on the Christmas tree blinked on and off in harmony with the drumming of her fingers. Every tap brought a surge of heat through his body. "The doctors said Elle was going to be fine. She'll have a whale of a headache, though, and Jackson was right about her ribs and arm, but she'll heal fast with Libby around."

Matt cupped her breast in his hands, his thumbs teasing her nipples into taut pebbles. He felt her response, the swift intake of breath. The flush that covered her body. "It seems such a miracle to me to be able to touch you like this. I wonder if every other man knows what a miracle a woman's body is."

"And all this time, I thought the miracle was a man's body." Kate ran her fingernails lightly along his belly.

"Maybe the miracle is just that I finally managed to stop you from hiding from me," Matt decided. He bent his head, flickered her nipple with his tongue, made a lazy foray around the areola. She moved slightly, turning to give him better access.

"I've been thinking about the fog. Something isn't quite right."

"Quite right?" He lifted his head to look at her, arching his eyebrow. The Christmas lights were playing red and green and blue over her stomach. A bright red light glowed across the small triangle of curls at the junction of her legs. It was distracting and made it hard to concentrate on conversation. He slipped his hand in the middle of the flashing light, watched his fingers stroke the nest of curls, felt Kate shiver, and pushed his fingers deep into her warm wet sheath. She pushed back against him, a soft moan escaping. He dipped his head to find her breast, suckling strongly. "What are you thinking, Kate?" His tongue swirled over her nipple, and he pushed deeper inside her until her hips began a helpless ride.

"He isn't going after Hannah. Why attack me? Or Elle? Or even Abbey? He should go after Hannah. She summons the wind to drive him out to sea. She stops him." Her words came in little short bursts. She gasped as she pushed against his hand, as her body tightened with alarming pressure, with the pure magic of passion shared with Matthew.

"Take the pins out of your hair," he whispered, his voice raw. "I love your hair down. You look very sexy with your hair down."

"You think I look sexy no matter what," she pointed out.

His teeth teased her nipple, nibbled over her breast. "True, but I love the hair."

"You won't love it when it's falling all over you." But she was lifting her arms, pulling out pins and scattering them in every direction while he shifted her, lowering his body into the cradle of her hips, thrusting deep inside her.

She cried out when he surged forward. Whips of lightning danced through her blood. "Matthew." There was a plea for mercy, and he hadn't even gotten started.

"We have all the time in the world, Katie," he whispered, his lips sliding over her throat, her chin, and up to her mouth. His strong hips paused, waiting. She held her breath. He thrust hard, a long stroke surging deep to bury himself completely within her. A coming home. She was velvet soft and tight and fiery hot. He wanted a long slow night with her. His hands shaped her body, stroking and caressing every inch of her.

"I don't feel like we have all the time in the world." She protested, breathless, arching her hips to meet the impact of his. "I feel like I'm going to go up in flames."

"Then do it," he encouraged. "Come for me a hundred times. Over and over. Scream for me, Kate. I love you so much. I love watching you come for me. And I love your body, every square inch of it. I want to spend the night worshiping you."

Kate wanted the same thing. She did scream, clutching at the bedcovers for an anchor as her body fragmented, and she went spinning off into space. She couldn't tell if the whirling colors were behind her eyes or from the Christmas tree lights. She found it didn't matter when he caught her hips firmly, held her still, and began surging into her once more with his slow, deep strokes.

chapter 11

In the stocking hung with gentle care,
A mystery, I know, is hidden there.

MATT WOKE ALREADY AROUSED. HE WAS thick and aching, so tight he thought he'd burst through his own skin. The blankets had fallen onto the floor as if he had spent a long, restless night. His body was stark naked and mercilessly aroused. He looked down at Kate. She smiled up at him, her sea-green eyes sultry, her hands moving gently over his flat stomach. Her long hair spilled over his hips and thighs, teasing every nerve ending. He knotted a long strand around his fist. "I dreamed of you, Kate."

Her smile was that of a temptress. "I hope it was a good dream." She bent her head to her task, lovingly stroking her tongue over the thick inviting length of him, sliding the velvet knob into the heated tightness of her mouth.

Matt gasped as the pleasure/pain of it rocked him. "How could it not be?" he asked when he got his breath back. Her tongue made a teasing foray along the rigid length and stroked over him before she once again slid her mouth around him.

He closed his eyes, his hips surging forward, wanting more, needing more, as waves of heat spread through his body, as every muscle clenched and tightened. Kate's fist wrapped him up while her mouth performed miracles. "I don't know if I'll survive this, Kate."

Her answer was muffled, her breath warm and enticing, her mouth hot and tight. He was certain he felt her laughter vibrate through his entire body. There was joy in Kate. That was her secret, he decided. Joy in everything she did with him. She didn't pretend not to enjoy his body, she reveled in exploring him, teasing him, driving him to the very edge of his control.

Kate kissed her way up his belly and over his chest. She mounted him, the way an accomplished horseback rider smoothly slides aboard a horse, settling her body over his with exquisite slowness. She put up her hands and he took them so she could use leverage as her body rose and fell, stroking his. Her hair spilled around her, adding to her allure as her full breasts bounced and beckoned with every movement. She threw her head back, arched back, moving differently, tightening muscles until he was certain he would explode.

"Kate." Her name was a husky, almost hoarse sound, escaping from his constricted throat. His lungs burned. A fire spread through his belly, centered in his groin, and gathered into a wild conflagration. He couldn't take his gaze from her. There was a sheen to her skin, a flush over her body. She moved with a woman's sensuous grace and mystery. "The feel of your hair on my legs and belly makes me crazy." It should have tickled his skin, but the silky fall brushed over sensitive nerve endings and added to the heat and fire building in the deep within him. He felt as if every part of his body was being pulled in that direction.

Kate moved with exquisite slowness, undulating her body, sending him right out of his mind. The erotic visual only increased his raging hunger for her. In the soft morning sunlight, her hair flashed red streaks, and her pale skin seemed made of dewy petals. Most of all, the expression on her face, deeply absorbed in the ride of lust and love and passion, shook his entire being. He could read the way her body began to build pressure, her muscles clenching tightly, gripping him strongly. He could see it on her face, the rapture, the passion, the intensity of the orgasm as it overtook her. He watched her ride it out, watched the excitement and pleasure on her face, in her body. Seeing her like that heightened his own pleasure, and he wanted more, wanted her flushed body to feel it again and again and bring his body to his own explosive orgasm.

He caught her hips in his hands, taking control, guiding her ride, thrusting upward hard as she slid down over him, encasing him in a fist of hot velvet. He shuddered with pleasure, feeling the pressure building relentlessly. He could feel her body preparing for a second shock, the muscles tightening around him, adding to the intensity of his explosion. It shook him, a volcano going off, detonating from the inside out, taking everything in its path. He caught her to him, fighting for air, fighting to regain some sense of where he was, of a time and place, not fantasyland, where his every dream came true. It seemed impossible to be lying on his living room floor, his heart raging at him, his body in ecstasy, and the love of his life in his arms. His world had been guns and sand and jungles and an enemy fighting to kill him. Women like Kate were not real and they didn't wind their arms around his neck and rain kisses all over his face and tell him he was too sexy to be alive.

They lay together just holding one another, trying to get their heart rates back to normal and to push air through their lungs. Kate lay stretched out on top of Matt, pressing her soft body tightly against his. Beneath her, he suddenly stiffened.

"What the hell is that?" he growled, hearing a noise outside the house.

Kate gasped and rolled off of him, landing on the pile of blankets. "We have company, Matthew," she whispered, gathering the sheets around her.

He sat up abruptly, his breath hissing through his teeth. He'd asked for a night with Kate, he should have asked for the entire damned week. He was never going to get enough of her, never be sated. "I thought I'd at least get you for a few more hours," he groused as he padded naked across the floor. He suddenly halted halfway to the door and uttered a string of curses. "It's my parents."

Kate's eyes widened. She clutched the sheet to her naked breasts. "What?"

"My parents," he announced. He reached down to help her up. "Why is it that even when you're grown, parents can make you feel like a teenager caught in the act?"

Kate wrapped the sheet around her and hurried toward his bedroom while Matt scooped up the blankets and followed her. "Did you get caught in the act often?"

"Are you laughing at me?" he asked, a dangerous glint in his silver eyes.

"Only because I'm disappearing into the bathroom to leave you to face the music alone. You might get dressed." She grinned mischievously at him as she gathered up her clothes and retreated behind a securely locked door.

Matt caught sight of the wisp of peach-colored lace that lay on the floor and found a wicked smile stealing over his face. He stooped down and picked it up, bunching it into his hand before shoving it into the pocket of his jacket, which was lying on the back of a chair. He dragged on clothes as fast as he could, combing his hair with his fingers just as the polite knock on his door came.

He could hear Kate laughing, and it was contagious.

He couldn't wipe the grin off his face as he opened the front door. Victoria Granite threw her arms around her son and hugged him hard. "You frightened us, Matt! We called and called and you never answered. First there was a fire here and Danny told us about that horrible incident at the store and then a call went out and . . ."

"Victoria, take a breath," Harold Granite advised. He smiled lovingly at his wife, used to her run-on sentences. "We heard the fog came in last night, and Elle Drake went over the cliff. Victoria was worried."

Matt's mother made a face. "Really, Harold, I knew he was perfectly fine; you were the one who spent the entire morning trying to call him and pacing back and forth like a wild tiger. I was fine!"

Matt met his father's gaze over the top of his mother's head. They both stifled a knowing grin. "I'm sorry, Dad. I should have remembered after all these years, how you worry."

Victoria smiled and patted Harold's arm. "There, dear, you see there was nothing at all to worry about. All that pacing." She shook her head, stopping in midsentence as she looked up at the mantel and the candles that had burned down to the holders. "Oh my goodness." She looked around carefully. "Matthew Granite, you had a woman here last night, didn't you?"

"Mom, once I turned thirty, I thought we agreed I didn't have to talk about women with you."

From the bedroom came the sound of a door closing. His parents exchanged a long, satisfied look. Victoria arched her eyebrow at her son. "She's still here?"

"As a matter of fact, yes. And don't start on her, Mom. I don't want her scared off. This is the one."

There was another startled silence. "Kate's here?" Harold asked, clearly astonished. "Kate Drake?"

"Of course it's Kate," Victoria said.

Kate came out of the bedroom with a bright smile and desperation in her eyes. She was wearing one of his shirts over her thin white blouse. Matthew was instantly mortified. He thought he would tease her, and at the same time, he'd have the added pleasure of knowing she was sitting beside him in the warmth of his car without a bra. He'd planned to slip his hand inside the white silk of her blouse and caress her soft creamy skin. The idea alone had made him as hard as a rock. It hadn't occurred to him that her blouse was sheer enough that her darker nipples would show so alluringly.

Kate always presented a near flawless appearance to the world, and he realized immediately when he saw the desperation in her eyes that it was her armor. She wore her clothes and hair and makeup to keep people from seeing the real Kate. The vulnerable Kate. The Kate she shared only with her sisters, and now with him.

"Hello Mrs. Granite, Mr. Granite," she greeted.

Matthew drew the edges of his shirt together

around her, sliding several buttons in place. He bent to kiss her, shielding her from his parents' scrutiny for a brief moment. When he was certain she was sufficiently covered, he circled her waist with his arms and held her in front of him. He could feel her soft unbound breasts pushing against his arms. Instantly his body reacted, thickening, hardening, an ache pounding through his blood. He held her close to him, covering the painful bulge stretching the material of his jeans. Kate was without mercy, slowly and sensuously rubbing her round bottom over the hard ridge. "I would very much like to visit, but Elle's in the hospital, and we have to go by Kate's house before we go to see her." Was that his voice? It sounded thick and husky to his ears. He was even afraid color burned in his face. His palms itched to cup Kate's breasts in his hands. The soft weight on his arms was driving him crazy. His mouth had actually gone dry. And if she didn't stop the way she was rubbing against him, he was going to shock everyone right then and there. "Let's have dinner tonight," he suggested, in desperation making eye contact with his father.

Harold, taking the cue, caught Victoria's elbow firmly.

"Danny will be spending the evening with Trudy Garret and her little boy at the Grange. Santa Claus is stuffing stockings and delivering presents around seven. We were going to watch," Victoria said. "Can we plan for another night?"

"Tomorrow is the pageant rehearsal," Matt said. "You all are in that. Maybe we can grab dinner afterward."

"There's never time." Harold shook his head, but headed across the living room to the front door. "The pageant rehearsal never runs smoothly, and we're always there until midnight."

"Good point," Matt agreed. "Don't worry, Mom, we'll have dinner together soon." He walked them to the door. "Who's playing Santa Claus this year?"

Harold grinned. "No one's supposed to know, Matt." He went out into the light drizzle and paused. "Jeff Burley broke his leg a couple of weeks ago. He's done it every year, and we had a bit of trouble finding a replacement. Everyone's afraid of the fog. Some of the townspeople think it's some kind of alien invasion."

Victoria put up her umbrella and made a little face. "People are so silly sometimes."

"I hope you're not trying to ask me to be Santa Claus this year, I'm more afraid of the kids than I am of aliens." Matt sounded as stern as he dared with his mother.

Kate made a move to retreat back into the house, but Matt held her firmly as if she were his only refuge. The cold air hardened Kate's nipples into tight buds, and she was acutely aware she wore no bra beneath Matt's shirt. The drizzle was penetrating straight through the material and turning the silk blouse beneath it transparent. She crossed her arms over her chest and kept her smile firmly in place.

"There aren't any aliens," Victoria said, exasperated. "And no, you don't have to play Santa. I know better than to ask any of you boys. You'd frighten the children with your nonsense."

"Not Dad!" Matt suddenly sounded authoritative, and Kate looked up. "Dad, the doctor told you not to overdo."

"Playing Santa Claus wouldn't overdo anything." Harold was clearly annoyed. "And no, it isn't me. We had someone come forward, but he wishes to remain anonymous. It would ruin all of his fun if I revealed his identity."

Matt followed his parents to their car, taking Kate with him. "I'm not going to tell anyone."

"The last man you'd ever expect," Victoria said primly.

"The last man I'd ever expect to play Santa would be Old Man Mars." Matt laughed. "Can't you see Danny's face? He'd run from Santa."

Victoria and Harold looked at one another and burst out laughing. Victoria waved gaily at Kate. Matt stared after them. "You don't think they meant that mean old man is going to play Santa."

"I can't imagine it. I think they were teasing you. Do you have the car keys? I'm getting cold, and I have to stop by my house to pick up some clothes before we go to the hospital."

"I've got them. Come on. Let's get you out of the rain." Matt drew her bra from his jacket pocket and held it out to her. "I'm sorry, Katie. I couldn't stop thinking about playing out my little fantasy of being able to touch you when I was taking you home. It was childish of me."

Kate merely looked at the peach-colored bra in his outstretched hand, but made no move to take it. "And you wanted to be able to touch me how?" She walked past him to the car. There was a distinct sway to her beautiful rear, one he couldn't resist. Kate settled into his car, slowly unbuttoned the wet overshirt, and allowed the edges to gape open to reveal the transparent silk blouse underneath. She leaned back against the seat.

Matt drove slowly along the coastal highway, fighting for air when there was none in the car. The shape of her breasts was not only outlined beneath the see-through material, but highlighted. "Kate, you're an incredible woman."

"I'm a lucky woman. I rather like your fantasies. By all means, tell me whenever you get one."

He couldn't resist. Matt slipped his hand inside her blouse, cupped the soft, creamy flesh in his palm. His knuckle rubbed gently over her breast, the pads of his fingers possessive as he caressed her body. Right at that moment he could think of a hundred fantasies. He turned the car onto the drive leading to the bluff overlooking the sea. The moment he parked, he caught the back of her head and held her still while he devoured her mouth.

They spent an hour in the car, laughing like children, necking like teenagers, wildly happy as they held hands, touched and kissed and whispered of dreams and hopes and erotic fantasies.

When they arrived at the Drake house, no one was home; the sisters were all at the hospital. There was a note for Kate telling her Elle was doing much better and instructing her to join them when she could. Kate took the time to shower. Matt joined her and spent a long while leisurely lathering soap over her and rinsing her off. He made love to her under the spray of water, then dried her off with large towels. He couldn't take his eyes off of her while she dressed. "I've never been happier, Kate," he admitted, as she pinned the thick length of hair on top of her head into her "perfect Kate" style.

"Me either," she answered, and leaned over to kiss him.

Matt caught her hand and dragged her through the house into the living room. "Kate, do you love me? You know I love you. I tell you. I show you. I want to spend my life with you, and I've made no secret about that. Do you love me?"

Kate nearly stopped breathing. She touched his face. "How could you not know, Matthew? I love you so much I ache with it sometimes."

"Then why won't you agree to marry me? I don't

think your family objects to me, and obviously my family would welcome it."

She let her breath out slowly. "I have some things to work out, Matt. I want to marry you. I do. But I have to be certain it's right for you. That I'm right for you."

"Katie. Honey. I know you're right for me." He looked around the room. "Where's that damned snowglobe anyway?" He retrieved it from the shelf.

Kate took it out of his hands. "You only get one wish, Matt, and you've had yours." She went to place the globe back on the shelf, but it came alive in her hands, the fog swirling. Waiting. Kate closed her eyes and made her wish. She couldn't stop herself. She wanted Matthew Granite more than she'd ever wanted anything in her life.

Matt said nothing, asking her no questions. He simply took her hand in a gesture of solidarity.

Kate and Matt spent most of the afternoon in the hospital with Kate's sisters in Elle's room. Matt and Damon played a game of chess while the seven sisters caught up on news. Joley helped Damon, and when Matt expressed disapproval, Abbey immediately took Matt's side. They did their best to entertain Elle, who looked bruised and very young. Her bright red hair tumbled around her white face and heightened her pale skin and deepened the purple in the bruises. She was in good spirits but weak and still had a headache.

Matt and Kate left the hospital in the evening to

meet the Granites at the Grange, where most of the townspeople were bringing their children for photos with Santa and a small party.

The Grange hall was packed with parents and children. "Jingle Bells" blared through the building, mistletoe was hung in every conceivable place, and holly decorated the tables laden with cookies and punch. A fake mantel went along the entire length of one wall with holly, candles, and tiny sleighs filled with candy canes adorning the top. Rows of stockings hung on gleaming hooks. The silver-tipped fir tree nearly reached the ceiling and was covered in lights, ornaments, and a multitude of white angels with silver wings.

"The ladies at the arts and crafts shop have been busy," Matt whispered.

Kate shushed him, but her eyes were laughing. Several elves hurried past them, bells tinkling from their hats and ankles. Kate and Matt followed the elves through the crowd to the back of the building, where Santa Claus sat in a high-backed chair surrounded by more elves and a reindeer that looked suspiciously like a dog with plastic antlers attached to his head. The line to visit Santa was long, small children clutching parents' hands and staring with large round eyes at the jolly old man. The Santa suit fit perfectly, and the white beard and mustache seemed natural, both bushy enough to hide the face successfully. Matt tried to get close enough to get a good look at the Santa. Several preteenagers rushed past him laughing loudly, tossing popcorn at each other.

"Do you think it's Old Man Mars?" Matt whispered.

"How could it be?" Kate asked. "He hates Christmas."

"Right height. I could tell if he were talking loud or maybe even by the way he walks." Matt weaved his way through the small children.

"Hey!" A young boy with red hair protested. "No cutting in."

"I just wanted to ask Santa if he'd give me Kate for Christmas," Matt explained.

Unimpressed, the boy wrinkled his nose, and all of his friends made faces. "Well, you got to stand in line like everyone else."

Kate laughed and dragged Matt away from Santa Claus. He spotted Inez and pulled Kate toward her. "If anyone knows who Santa Claus is, it'll be Inez. She knows everything."

"Doesn't that come under the heading of gossip?"

"News, Katie. How can you even use the word *gossip?*" Matt stopped moving abruptly and brought her up short, staring out the window. He bit out a string of curses. "The damned fog is rolling in, Kate. It's coming right this way."

Kate looked at him, then looked around at the children. "I don't want people to panic and run for their cars to get away from here. No one would be able to drive in the fog. I'll find a way to distract the kids." She hurried toward Santa Claus, whispering softly to the children so that the throng parted like the Red Sea to give her access to the jolly old man sitting with a child on his lap. She leaned in and spoke to him.

From a distance, Matt watched Santa stiffen, listen some more, and nod. Kate straightened up and directed the children into a large circle. Santa gave out candy canes, patting heads and laughing as he did so. Several mothers began distributing cookies and punch while Kate started an enthralling Christmas story. Matt had never seen anyone hold an entire room in her hand, but there was no sound other than the faint background of Christmas music and Kate's spellbinding voice. He found himself caught up in the sheer beauty of the magical tone, even when the fog began to seep through the cracks of the doors and windows.

There was no way to keep the fog out. It was only the magic of Kate's voice, the anonymous Santa Claus's cheerful punctuation of ho, ho, ho woven cleverly into the storyline, and the Granite reputation in the community that kept panic from spreading as the gray-white vapor filled the room, bringing with it the scent and feel of the sea. Kate smoothly incorporated the fog into the storyline, having the children hold hands and interact with Santa's ho, ho, ho. The children did so with enthusiasm, laughing wildly at the antics of Kate's characters in the fog. Matt realized she was creating the illusion that the fog was deliberate, a part of the story she was telling, used for effect. He could see parents relaxing, thinking Kate had found a way to keep the children from fearing the incoming fog, a part of life for anyone who lived on the coast.

It seemed hours to Matt, watching the fog churning, swirling in deeper shades of gray, spinning when there was no breeze to create the effect, yet it was only a few minutes before the fog began a hasty retreat . . . almost as if it couldn't take the sound of Kate's voice. It was a silly notion. Fog had no ears to listen, but it also shouldn't have been able to leave footprints in sand or do damage to property. He made his way closer to Kate, knowing she would pay a steep price using her energy to keep such a large crowd under the spell of her voice. As he moved toward her, he felt something in the fog, something tangible brush against his arm.

Matt whirled toward it, hands going up in a fighter's defensive position, but there were only coils of vapor surrounding him. He heard a sound, a growling voice muttering a warning. A chill went down his spine. He felt the touch of death on him, bony fingers reaching for him, or someone who belonged to him. The hair on his body stood up in reaction to the half moan, half growl that could have been wind, but there was no wind to generate the sound. Matt knew it was a warning, but the words made no sense.

Anger was impotent against fog. He couldn't fight it, couldn't wrestle it; he couldn't even shoot it. How could he protect Kate when he couldn't see or get his hands on the culprit? He stood very still as the vapor simply rolled from the building, leaving behind the soft Christmas music and the laughter of the children. He looked around the room, at the sunny faces, at the tree and decorations. Why had the fog come, only to recede without incident?

He made his way to Kate's side, slipping his arm around her waist to lend her strength. She sent the children to the tables of food, a smile on her face, shadows in her eyes. Laughter picked up as if the fog had never been; but Matt continued to survey the room, inch by inch, concerned there had to more, something they were all missing.

Kate leaned into him as they looked out the window. "It's heading out to sea on its own. Why would it do that? Why would it come here and leave?"

Matt watched the children eating. Santa Claus was eating. "Could it have poisoned the food some way?" he asked, his heart in his throat at the thought. His parents were seated at a table with Danny, Trudy Garrett, and her young son.

"I doubt it, Matthew, how could it?"

"How could he do any of the things he's been doing?" His hands tightened on her shoulders. "Santa Claus is a symbol of Christmas, right? What does he represent?"

"You don't think he came to attack the man playing the part of Santa, then decided against it, do you?" Her anxious gaze followed the burly man in the red-and-white suit.

Matt shook his head. "I feel danger, Katie. When I feel it this strong, it's here, close by. Tell me what Santa represents."

She rubbed her throbbing temples. "Goodwill, I suppose. He represents goodwill and generosity. He gives presents, stuffs stockings, eats the children's milk and cookies."

"He spreads goodwill among the people and is generous, teaching by example to be generous." Matt tugged on her hand, moved toward the tree where Santa's pack lay. He peered inside. There were a few netted candy cane stockings holding small toys, candy, and various small personal items the town always generously donated for the event. Santa had slipped most of the candy cane net stockings into the children's stockings hanging from the fake mantel earlier when he'd first arrived, so that each child would have something to take home after the party.

Matt went to the brightly colored stockings, each with a child's name stitched in bold letters across the top. Kate's fingers tightened around his. She already knew, just as he did. They peered inside. She drew back, stifling a cry, looking at him with fear. Inside each stocking, the fog had added to Santa's generous gift. A mass of sand and sea bugs writhed in hideous black balls in the toes of the stockings. All were damp with seawater and smelled faintly of the noxious odor the fog seemed to leave behind. Crushed shells and spiny sea anemone, kelp and small crabs were mixed with the wiggling insects.

Santa Claus joined them, staring at the mess while all around them children ate and laughed and played. "We have to get rid of these. Some of these creatures are venomous."

Matt glanced quickly at the man, recognizing the voice. Old Man Mars was indeed playing Santa. "You're right. I'll get a couple of the men, and we'll get the stockings out of here before the children start trying to collect them. Kate." He pulled out a chair for her. "Sit down before you fall down. I'll take you home when we're through here."

"To my house," she said in a weary voice. "I need to go to my house."

He nodded, his gut knotting tightly.

chapter 12

A candle burns with an eerie glow,
As it melts, the wax does flow

"THE THING IN THE FOG SPOKE TO ME." MATT made the announcement after the Drake sisters had settled Elle firmly in the living room. It was late afternoon before the doctors let her go home, and her family had been so anxious, Matt had steered clear of the subject of the danger in the fog. He and Kate had gone to the mill earlier in the morning to reexamine the seal and see if she could find anything new about the spirit. He hadn't wanted to bring up the subject at the very source of the trouble.

There was a sudden silence. He had their attention immediately. Kate set down her teacup. "You didn't say anything to me about it."

"You were exhausted and worried about Elle last night, Katie, and again this morning. I didn't want to bring it up. Now that she's home and safe, I thought it was a good time to discuss it." En masse, the Drake sisters were difficult to contend with. He could feel every eye on him. There was power in the room, intangible, feminine, but a steady flow of it. An energy he couldn't begin to explain, but he knew it moved from sister to sister.

"What did it say?" Sarah asked. Her voice was gentle, nonjudgmental. Practical, magical Sarah. She was the oldest and the most influential.

"It made no sense. It was a moan and a growl mixed together. The syntax was old-fashioned, but from what I got, it was a warning to keep my loved ones away from one with the staff."

"The staff? He used the word *staff?*" Kate asked.

Matt nodded. "I've thought a lot about it, and maybe it all ties up with Christianity and the staff of life or something. Anything to do with the Christian beliefs of Christmas is under attack?" He made it a question.

Elle lifted the old journal Sarah handed to her. "I'll do my best to try to find a reference to a staff in here," she said. "I don't think I thanked you for coming to my rescue the other night, Matt. One minute I was making my way home, and the next I felt something shove me over the side of cliff. I broke every fingernail on the way down, grabbing at dirt and rocks. I have no idea how Jackson climbed down to get me. I couldn't even call out with a strong enough voice for help, and I was afraid to move. The ledge was literally crumbling under me."

"I know it was frightening, Elle, but we have you, you're safe now," Joley soothed.

"Kate said something the other evening about how the entity didn't go after Hannah. It's strange because Hannah's the one providing the wind to drive him out to sea and away from the town," Matt said. "Do any of you have any idea why he's chosen not to try to harm her?"

Sarah frowned. "It really only went after Elle."

Kate shook her head. "It definitely tried for me, Sarah. And I think it tried to use Sylvia and her amorous ways to get to Abbey, then made a second attempt here in the house, pitting her against Jackson. Jackson's a mercurial man, and Sylvia's unpredictable. I think it wanted Abbey out of the way too. Of all of us, wouldn't Hannah be its main obstacle?"

"What do you all have in common?" Matt asked. He watched as Sarah moved through the living room lighting tall, thick candles at each entranceway. The candles each had three wicks and sat in wrought-iron holders. She murmured something he couldn't hear as she lit each candle. He realized the windows had arrangements of colorful flowers and herbs tied in bundles on either side of the sills and above the window frames. The bundles of dried arrangements hadn't been there before. The fragrance was a blend of outdoors and strong scents of rosemary, jasmine, and something else he couldn't quite identify. The lights of the candles flickered on the walls, dancing and leaping with every movement of the sisters, as if tuned to them.

"Abbey, Kate, and Joley all have special gifts involving their voices," Sarah answered, bending over a tall cranberry candle near the bay window. She glanced over at her youngest sister before lighting the round candle. "Elle has many talents, but she doesn't share their voice. She is, however, a strong telepath, and she can share the shadow world with Kate. Neither Joley nor Abbey have has that ability."

"But nothing happened to Joley," Matt said. He sighed. "So much for my great detective work."

Joley made a small dissenting sound. "That's not exactly true." Immediately, she had the attention of all of her sisters.

"Something happened that you didn't tell us," Kate asked.

"I didn't want to worry anyone," Joley admitted. "I get all kinds of silly threats on the road, and in light of the threat to Kate, I didn't want to worry anyone."

Joley stretched, a sensuous flow of feminine muscle. Everything Joley did, every way she moved or even spoke was sultry. It was as natural to her as breathing. Matt found he could appreciate her looks and voice, yet not react in the least. It was a further revelation to him just how deeply in love he was with Kate. He sank onto the floor in front of Kate and leaned against her knees. At once her fingers tunneled into his thick hair, a connection between them.

"What happened, Joley?" Sarah prompted.

"I went up to my room after we all talked the other day. Hannah said she closed the window because the fog was slipping into the house, and it made her uncomfortable. I was so tired I just crashed on the bed, and I didn't think to pay attention to the feel of the room. I woke up choking, strangling really. At first I thought I'd wrapped a scarf around my neck in my sleep and somehow pulled it tight. But the fog was everywhere, layers of it. I could barely see. I pulled the scarf away from my throat and turned on the fan. My throat hurt and . . ." She hesitated, sighed softly, and dragged the turtleneck sweater away from her throat. Distinct round bruises marred her skin.

"And you didn't think it was important to tell us?" Sarah turned on her younger sister. "That we shouldn't know this thing has advanced to such a sophisticated level of violence? Joley! You weren't thinking."

"I know." Joley rubbed her palm over her thigh. "At first I was terrified, and I went through the house and began to gather the herbs and flowers for the windows, but the entire time I wondered why it just didn't kill me. If it could partially strangle me, why didn't it just do it all the way?"

"Maybe he isn't strong enough," Abbey ventured.

Sarah glanced toward the sea. "He's strong enough. He managed to take shape and, from what Matt says, even find a voice."

"Are you saying he didn't try to kill Joley? He certainly tried to kill Elle," Abbey argued. "Maybe he wasn't prepared for how hard she fought."

"*I'm* saying it didn't try to kill me," Joley said.

"Then what was it doing?" Sarah asked.

"I think it was trying to silence my voice."

Kate put a protective hand to her throat. "In the shadow world, he went for my throat as well."

Something deep inside of Matt went very still. Kate had an incredible voice. "If he wants to still the voices capable of enthrallment, Joley, Abbey, and Kate are definitely on the hit list." He looked at Elle. "But why you?"

She smiled, her green eyes bright. "Maybe he doesn't like redheads."

"I think he doesn't want to be saved," Kate announced. "When I touched him, I felt rage, yes, but it wasn't his primary emotion." She leaned towards Elle. "Didn't you feel sorrow and guilt? You were there, you had to have felt it."

Elle looked down at the journal, her expression sorrowful. "I felt it," she said in a small voice.

Matt raised his head sharply. "Elle shares emotions, doesn't she? You connected with Jackson when he was taken prisoner."

Elle refused to meet his eyes. "Yes."

"But he was halfway around the world," Matt protested.

Libby put her hand out to her youngest sister, and Elle took it immediately. "It's very difficult sometimes,

Matthew," Libby explained. "We're different. We look the same and try to act the same, but we're not normal and sometimes the overload is . . ." She searched for the right word, looking helplessly at her sisters.

"Dangerous," Sarah supplied. "Using our talents is very draining. Each of us has to overcome by-products of her gift."

"I've seen it in Kate," Matt agreed. "Is there any way to minimize it?"

The seven women looked at one another. As usual, it was Sarah who answered. "We all handle it in different ways. Most of us find our own space and live there, as shielded as we can manage to be." She smiled at Matt. "I know it will help Kate to have you. Damon helps me."

"So far I haven't managed to keep her from wearing herself out. Every time I think we're going to get a little respite, the fog comes in again," Matt pointed out. He was extraordinarily happy that Sarah had accepted his relationship with Kate.

"You've helped enormously," Kate acknowledged.

Elle leafed through the journal. "You said there were symbols on the seal, Kate? Could you read it at all?"

"The first Drake settlers must have been the ones to seal the restless spirit, Elle. It was definitely formed around the time the town was settled. From what I could read, it was something about rage and sealing until one is born who could do something. I went back to take another look, but most of the seal was crushed and the actual writing lost," Kate admitted.

"Until one is born who can do something," Sarah repeated aloud. "Something to do with a voice."

"Here it is," Elle said triumphantly. "'He who will not receive forgiveness shall remain sealed until one is born who can give him peace.'"

There was a long silence. Matt stared at the cranberry candle as the three flames leaped and burned. Hot wax poured over the side like a lava flow, forming a thick pool around the holder. It was a fascinating sight, deep purple wax flowing almost like dark blood. "Why would he need peace?"

Elle pushed a pair of glasses on her nose and studied the faded writing. "One of the sisters who helped to seal the spirit must have had precognition the way Mom does. If that's the case, it means we should be able to find a way to allow him to rest."

"Unless the earthquake opened the crack in the ground and allowed him to escape before his time," Matt said.

"I doubt it," Sarah said seriously. "Things usually happen the way they're supposed to happen, Matthew. It's obviously our time. We have no choice but to figure this out. It's our destiny."

Matt wiped his hand over his mouth. He wasn't certain he believed in destiny. He felt Kate's hand in his hair and changed his mind. "Hannah, are you feeling any better?" She didn't look better. Without her, he wasn't positive they could have managed to get Elle back up the cliff in the midst of the thick fog or drive the entity out to sea and away from the townspeople time after time.

"I've been resting. Libby's helped."

Libby Drake. Matt looked at her. She was legendary in the small town. She was the only Drake with midnight black hair and pale, almost translucent skin. She was a natural-born healer, the real thing. He smiled at her. "It's good to see you again, Libby. Maybe you better hide out while you're home. If word gets out you're back, you'll have everyone in town lining up for a cure."

"I do want to visit Irene's son while I'm home. My sisters went to see him and did what they could to make him comfortable, but I promised I'd go see him."

"Libby—" Matt shook his head—"you know he has terminal cancer. Even you can't get rid of that." He waited. When no one said anything he looked at her. "Can you?" The idea was unsettling.

"I won't know until I visit him," Libby admitted.

"What would be the price?" Matt couldn't imagine what it would cost Libby to actually cure someone sent home to die.

Libby smiled at him. "I can see why Kate loves you so much, Matt. You're very discerning. It's a trade-off. I might save one person, but while I'm recovering, I might lose a hundred others."

"That bad?" He reached his hand for Kate. The thought of what the women had to go through on a daily basis moved him. In their own way, they were warriors, and he had a deep respect for them.

"Does anyone want more tea? I'm getting another cup," Hannah volunteered.

"I can get it," Matt offered. He felt a little useless.

Hannah paused just a few feet from the entrance to the kitchen. "I'm already up, but thank you," she said, and took two steps, halting abruptly, staring at the flickering candle in the bay window facing the sea. "Sarah, you need to come look at this."

Matt got to his feet, pulled Kate up beside him. Apprehensively, he glanced out the large window to the sea. He already knew what he would see. Anytime anything strange happened, the fog was back, settling over the town like a smoky monster crouched and waiting.

"What is it, Sarah?" Elle asked from her position on the couch. She had pillows piled around her, a comforter over her, and strict orders to remain where she was.

"The wax is forming something as it runs down the sides," Sarah explained. "It looks like a hook to me."

"Or a candy cane." Matt was morepragmatic.

"It's a staff," Hannah corrected. "A long staff, or maybe a cane. Something used to walk with."

"This is getting more bizarre by the minute," Abbey

said, rubbing her hands up and down her arms. "And while we're on the subject of bizarre, Joley, I'm sorry, but there was no excuse for your not telling the rest of us what happened. You take shielding all of us way too far."

Sarah's smile at Joley was gentle. "She's right, hon. You should have told us what happened. Do you have any other bad news you don't want to worry us with?"

Joley hesitated for a brief moment, then shrugged. "I'm sorry, I should have mentioned the strangling fog. Do you have any idea how ridiculous that sounds?" She burst out laughing.

Kate joined her. "I have to admit, it threw Christmas wreaths at me."

"And no one is going to believe the fog *pushed* me over the cliff," Elle said with a small grin. "This one will go into our journal and nowhere else!"

"I plan on telling our children," Matt announced. "It's a great story for around the campfire, and they aren't going to believe us anyway. They'll think I'm a brilliant storyteller."

"Children?" Joley raised her eyebrow. "I love the idea of Kate having children. Don't the Granites produce boys? Very large hungry boys?" Her sisters erupted into laughter while Kate covered her face and groaned.

"You aren't helping, Joley," Matt said, putting his arms protectively around Kate so she could hide her face against his shoulder. "She hasn't even agreed to marry me yet. Don't be scaring her off with the idea of little boys running around."

Sarah continued to study the wax flow over the sides of the candle. "Do you see anything else that could be helpful in that book, Elle?"

Elle rubbed at the bump on her head and frowned at the thin pages. "There was no single predominant religion in the town at the time people first settled here. A faction celebrated the birthday of a pagan god. This is very interesting." Elle looked up at her sisters. "Many of the settlers here came together to celebrate their differences, unable to live anywhere else. The founding fathers wanted a safe haven by the sea, a place they envisioned would one day have a port for supplies. It actually says a lot about the town's founders and perhaps gives us insight to why the people here are so tolerant of others."

"And it explains why our own people settled here."

Kate nuzzled Matt's throat. "If I remember my grandmother and her history lessons correctly, she said Christmas was slow to catch on in America, that the colonists didn't celebrate it, and in some instances actually banned it."

"That's right." Joley snapped her fingers. "It was considered a pagan ritual in some places. But that was a long while before this town was settled, wasn't it?" She swept Elle's hair away from her face and fashioned it into a ponytail. "Does that have anything to do with all of this?"

"Thanks, Joley," Elle said. She smoothed the worn pages. "The townspeople wanted to celebrate the Christmas season and settled on a pageant. They asked everyone to participate regardless of their beliefs, just for the fun of it. They treated it more as a play, a production that included all town members, meant to be fun rather than religious." She looked up with a small smile. "Libby, our however-many-greats-grandmother has your very interesting handwriting. Aside from the language, I have to decipher the worst handwriting on the face of the earth."

"I do not have the worst handwriting on the face of the earth." Libby tossed a small pillow at her sister, missing by a great distance.

"There's something else in the wax," Sarah said. "All of you, look at this! Tell me what you see."

The sisters crowded around the cranberry candle. Kate tilted her head, studying it from every angle. "Where did you get this candle, Sarah? Is this one Mom made?"

"Yes, but I didn't know it would do this."

"Is a candle a symbol of Christmas?" Matt asked.

"Yes; some people say the light of the candle relieves the unrelenting darkness," Kate answered. "My mother makes incredible candles."

"I can imagine. Do they all do this?" Matt indicated the flowing wax.

"It's a face, I think," Sarah said. "Look, Abbey, don't you think it's a face?"

"That wouldn't surprise me." Matt peered at the thick pool of wax. "The spirit found feet, a coat and hat, and bones, why not get himself a face, even if it's made of wax. Does it have eyes? Maybe he wants to get a good look at us."

"Ugh." Kate made a face. "That's a horrible idca. It could never use one of Mom's candles for that. Mom instills a healing, soothing magic in each of them. We were the ones who forgot to guard our home. She insisted we make certain every time, but we just got complacent. I'm not forgetting this lesson for a very long time."

"Me either," Joley agreed.

"I think I found it now," Elle said in excitement. "Most everyone wanted to participate with the exception of a small group of believers in the gods of the earth. They considered the pageant a Christian holiday celebration and felt it was wrong to participate. One of the most outspoken said the pageant was evil and those participating would be punished. His brother-in-law, Abram Lynchman, went against his advice and allowed his wife and child to take part. Because he stood up to Johann, the rest of the group also decided to join the town in the pageant."

"Is this Johann angry because his flock was out of his control?" Joley asked.

Elle held up her hand for silence. Her hand went to

her throat. Matt noticed that her hand was trembling. "Everyone helped with the production, bringing homemade candles and lanterns. The shepherd herded several sheep with his staff, and the sheep got away and ran through the crowd."

None of the sisters laughed. They were watching Elle's face intently. Matt glanced out the window to see the fog solidly in place. For some reason, his heart began to pound. The strange radar that always told him danger was near was shrieking at him, even there in the warmth and safety of the Drakes' home.

"The people were having fun, laughing as the sheep rushed through the crowd with the shepherd running after them. The sheep panicked and ran straight into the small shelter the town had erected to use as the stable for the play. The shelter crumpled, knocking several candles into the dry straw. Fire spread along the ground and across the wooden planks used to make the shelter. Several participants were trapped under the debris, including Abram's wife and child." Elle had a sob in her voice. She shook her head. "I can't read this. I can't read the words. Anastasia, the one writing the journal, was there, she saw the entire thing, heard the cries, saw them die. Her emotions are trapped in the book. I can't read it, Sarah." She sounded as if she were pleading.

Matt wanted to comfort her. The feeling was so strong he actually stepped toward her before he realized he was feeling the emotions of Elle's sisters. They rushed to her side, Sarah pulling the book from her hands, Kate putting her arms around Elle. The others touched her, helping to absorb the long ago, very strong emotions still clinging to the pages of the journal.

"I'm sorry, honey," Sarah said gently, "I should have thought of that. You've been through so much already. Kate, do you think you can get an idea of what happened next? I wouldn't ask, but it's important." She held the book out to Kate.

Matt wanted to yank the book out of her hands and throw it. "Kate's been through enough with this thing, Sarah. You can't ask her to do anymore." He was furious. Enough was enough. "Elle almost died out there. Without Jackson, she would have. You have no idea what a miracle it was that she didn't end up at the bottom of the ocean."

Kate put a restraining hand on his arm. Sarah simply nodded. "I do realize what I'm asking, Matthew, and I don't blame you for being angry. I don't want Kate to touch the journal, but the truth is, if we don't know why this spirit is doing the things he's doing, someone very well could die. We have to know."

Kate took the book from Sarah's hand. Matt muttered a string of curses and turned away from them, feeling impotent. All of his training, his every survival skill, seemed utterly useless in the unfamiliar situation. Not wanting to look at Kate, not wanting to witness the strain and weariness on her face, he stared hard at the cranberry candle and the eerie flow of wax. He stared and stared, his heart suddenly in his throat. He took a step closer, stared down in a kind of terror. "Katie." He whispered her name because she was his world, his talisman. Because he needed her.

Kate put her arm around him, held him. He couldn't take his eyes from the face in the wax, praying he was wrong. Knowing he was right. She looked down and gasped. "Danny. It's Danny."

chapter 13

My last gift now, is a special one,
A candy cane for a special son,

He watches and tends and knows the land,
But not enough to evade my hand.

MATT TOOK KATE BY THE SHOULDERS AND SET her aside. She made a grab for him, but he was already moving swiftly for the front door.

"Danny's at the pageant rehearsal," Kate reminded him. She ran after him, tossing the journal onto the floor, trying to keep up with him. Hannah grabbed Kate's coat and hurried after both of them.

The fog obstructed Matt's vision, but he could hear the women. "Go back, stay in the house, Kate. It's too dangerous." His voice was grim. Authoritative. It made Kate shiver. He didn't sound at all like her Matthew.

"I'm coming with you. Stay to the left. The path leads down the hill to the highway. If we cross right beside the three redwood trees, like we did the other night, we'll end up quite close to the shortcut to town." Kate followed the sound of his voice. Hannah took her hand and held on tightly.

"Kate, dammit, this one time, listen to me. I have to find Danny, and I don't want to have to worry about what's happening to you."

Kate wished he sounded angry, but Matt's tone was chillingly cold. Ice-cold. She tightened her fingers around Hannah's hand but continued hurrying along the narrow path. "Hannah's with me, Matthew, and you're going to need us." She kept her voice very calm, very even. She ached for him and shared his rising alarm for the safety of his brother. The features in the wax had definitely been Daniel Granite. She had a strong feeling of impending doom.

Hannah pressed closer to her. "It's going to happen tonight, Katie." Her voice shook. "Should we try to clear the fog now?"

Matt loomed up in front of them, startling both of them, catching Kate by the shoulders. "It has never gone after me. Only you. Go with your sisters and work your magic. Clear the fog out of town, and this time get rid of it. I'll do what I can to keep Danny alive. I'm safe, Kate." His gray eyes had turned to steel. "I need to know you're as safe as possible in this mess."

She clung to him for just one moment, then nodded. "We'll be up on the captain's walk, where we can better bring in the wind."

Matt dropped a hard kiss on her upturned mouth, turned, and hurried down the narrow, well-worn trail. His mind was racing, working out the route the actors in the pageant used. Had they noticed the fog rolling in and taken shelter in one of the businesses along the parade route, or had they gone ahead with the rehearsal plans? Matt made it to the highway and stood listening for a moment in silence. He couldn't hear a car, but the fog seemed capable of muffling every sound. Still, he didn't want to wait. He felt a terrible sense of urgency, of his brother in acute danger. He cursed as he ran, nearly blind in the fog. It was only his training that kept him from being completely disoriented. He moved more from instinct than from sight, making his way toward the town square. Most of the committee meetings were held at the chamber of commerce building near the grocery store. The players were supposed to be rehearsing, though, and he doubted whether Inez would let a heavy fog and some entity she couldn't see change her plans.

He heard a shrill scream, the sounds of panic, and his heart stuttered. "Danny!" He called his brother's name, using the sheer volume of his voice to penetrate the cries coming out of the fog. He followed the sound of the voices, not toward the square, but away from it, back toward the park on the edge of town, where the river roared down through a canyon to meet the sea. The wall along the river was only about three feet high, made of stone and mortar. He nearly ran into it in his haste to reach Danny. At the last moment he sensed the obstruction and veered away, running parallel with it toward the cries.

He was getting closer to the sounds of the screams

and calls. He heard Inez trying to calm everyone. He heard someone shout for a rope. The river, rushing over the rocks, added to the chaos in the heavy fog. "Danny!" Matt called again, trying to beat down his fear for his brother. Danny would have heard him, would have answered.

Right in front of him, Donna, the owner of the local gift shop, suddenly appeared. Her face was white and strained. He caught her shoulders. "What happened, Donna? Tell me!"

She grabbed both of his arms to steady herself. "The wall gave way. A group of the men were sitting on it. Your brother, the young Granger boy, Jeff's son, I don't know, more maybe. They just disappeared down the embankment, and all the rocks followed like a miniavalanche. We can't see to help them. There were some groans, and we heard cries for help, but we can't see them at all. We tried to form a human chain, but the bank is too steep. Jackson went over the side by himself. He was crawling. I heard a terrible crack, now he's silent. I was going to try to find a telephone to call for help. The cell phones just won't work here."

"What was Jackson doing here?" He knew the deputy never participated in the town pageant. "Is Jonas here?" As he talked he was moving along the wall, feeling with his hands for breaks, taking Donna with him.

"Jackson happened to be driving by when the fog

thickened. He was worried about us, I think, so he stayed. I haven't seen Jonas."

"Don't wander around in this fog. Hopefully, Kate and her sisters will move it out of here for us." He patted her arm in reassurance and left her, continuing the search for the break in the wall with an outstretched hand. When he found it, he swore softly. He knew the section of wall was over a steep drop and the river below had a fast-moving current running over several submerged boulders. The bank was littered with rocks of every size, with little to hold them in place should something start them rolling.

"Danny! Jackson!" His call was met with eerie silence. He began to crawl down the bank, distributing his weight, on his belly, searching with his hands before sliding forward. It was painstakingly slow. He didn't want to displace any more of the rocks in case his brother or any of the others were still alive and in the path of an avalanche.

Matt's fingertips encountered a leg. He forced himself to remain calm and used his hands to identify the man. Jackson was unconscious, and there was blood seeping from his head. In the near-blind conditions, it was impossible to assess how badly he was injured, but his breathing seemed shallow to Matt.

Something moved an arm's length below Jackson. Matt followed the outstretched arm and found another body. The Granger boy. Matt knew him to be sixteen or seventeen. A good kid. The boy moved again, and Matt cautioned him to stay still, afraid he would disturb the rocks.

"You okay, kid?" he asked.

"My arm's broken, and I feel like I've been run over by a truck, but I'm all right. The deputy told me not to move, and the next thing I knew he was somersaulting and smashed hard into the rock right there. He hasn't moved. Is he dead?"

"No, he's alive. What about the others? What about Danny?" He crawled around Jackson to get to the boy, to take his pulse and run his hands over him to examine him for other injuries.

"Tommy Dockins fell too. Danny tried to push him clear when the slide started. We didn't really have any time. I didn't see either of them, but Tommy's yelled for help a couple of times. I couldn't tell from which direction though."

The kid sounded tinny and distorted in the fog, and his voice shook, but he lay quietly and didn't panic. "Your name's Pete, right? Pete Granger?" Matt asked.

"Yes, sir."

"Well, I'm going to slide on around you and see if I can locate Danny and Tommy. Don't move. The fog will be gone soon, and Jonas is on the way with the rescue squad. If you move, you'll send the rest of those rocks right down on top of the others and me. Got it?"

"Yes, sir."

"I'll be back as quick as I can." Matt glanced in the direction of the cliff house, where the Drake family had lived for over a hundred years. He needed the modern-day women to work their magic, to remove the fog so he had a semblance of a chance to save his brother and Tommy and to get Jackson and Pete to safety.

"Come on, baby," he whispered, hoping the swirling clouds would take his voice to her. "Do this for me. Clear this mess out of here."

As if they could hear his words, the seven Drake sisters moved together out onto the battlement and faced the sea. Libby and Sarah both had their arms wrapped around Elle to aid her as they stood in the midst of the swirling fog.

Sarah looked up at the sky, to the roiling clouds gathered over Sea Haven and back to her sisters. "This troubled spirit is in terrible pain and does not believe there can be forgiveness for his mistake. He cannot forgive himself for what he believes to be bad judgment. I am certain his motive was to save others his sorrow. He believes that by halting the pageant, history will not repeat itself. He has lived this unbelievable nightmare repeatedly and needs to be able to forgive himself and go to his rest." She looked at Kate. "Your gift has always been your voice, Kate. I think the journal is referring to you. One born who can bring peace."

Kate could think only of Matt, somewhere out in the fog. She didn't want to be up on the captain's walk facing another struggle, she wanted to be with him. It was the first time in her life she had ever felt so divided around her sisters. She knew at that moment that she belonged with Matthew Granite. It didn't matter that she was an observer and he was a doer, she loved him, and she belonged with him.

As if reading her mind, Hannah took her hand, squeezed it tightly. "He's counting on you to do this, Kate. He's counting on all of us."

Kate took a steadying breath and nodded. She stepped away from Hannah, knowing Hannah would need room. Facing the small town invaded with the fog, Kate began to chant softly. An inquiry, no more, a soft plea to be heard. Her voice was carried on the smallest of breezes as Hannah faced the sea and lifted her arms, directing the wind as she might an orchestra.

Behind Kate, Joley and Abbey began to sing, a soft melody of love and peace, harmonizing with Kate's incredible voice. so they produced a symphony of hope. Power began to build in the wind itself, in the sky overhead. Lightning forked in the spinning clouds. Kate spoke of forgiveness, of unconditional love. Of a love of family that transcended time. She beckoned and cajoled. She pleaded for a hearing.

"You've touched him," Elle reported. "He's fighting the call. He's determined to keep the accident from happening. There is no past life or future life as he understands it, only watching his wife and child die a horrible death over and over, year after year." She staggered under the burden of the man's guilt, of his loss.

Kate didn't falter. Matt was out there somewhere in the fog, and she felt him reaching for her, counting on her. And she knew he was in danger. She talked of the townspeople coming together with every belief represented. Of the elderly and the young given the same respect. She spoke of a place that was a true haven for tolerance. And she spoke of forgiveness. Of letting go.

Power spread with the building wind. The ocean leaped in response. A pod of whales surfaced, flipping their tails, almost in unison, as if creating a giant fan. Joley's voice, a sultry purity that couldn't be ignored, swelled in volume, taking over the lead, while Abbey's voice joined in perfect harmony.

Hannah's voice called on the elements she knew and loved. Earth. Wind. Fire. Rain. Lightning flashed. The wind blew. Rain poured from the clouds. And still the power continued to build. Her hands moved in a graceful pattern as if conducting a symphony of magic.

Kate lured the spirit to her with promises of peace. Rest. A family waiting with open arms, holding him dear, not placing blame. An accident, not the hand of an ancient god angry that he had allowed his loved ones to participate in something different. Simply an unfortunate accident. Joley sang of Christmas, past, present, and future. Of a town committed to all the members celebrating together in a variety of ways. Of festivals for ancient gods and a gala for those who didn't believe. The two voices blended, one in song, one in storytelling, weaving a seamless creation to draw the lost soul back home.

Abbey lifted her voice finally, a call for those lost to welcome loved ones. As she could draw truth, so did she speak truth. She added her voice to the tapestry, promising peace and rest and final sleep in the arms with those he loved most.

"He's coming. He's beginning to believe, to want to take the chance," Elle said. "He's hesitant, but he's so utterly weary, and the idea of seeing his wife and child and resting in their arms is irresistible."

Libby raised her arms with Hannah, sending the promise of healing, not the body, but mind and soul. She added her power to the force of the wind, added her healing energy to Kate's soothing peace.

The wind increased in strength, blowing with the force of a small gale, tearing through Sea Haven, herding the fog, guiding it toward the sea. Toward the house on the cliff and the seven women who stood on the battlement, hand in hand. The feminine voices carried unbelievable power throughout the air, land, and sea. Rising on the wind. Calling. Promising. Leading.

And the fog answered. The thick gray vapor turned toward the sea, drifting reluctantly at first, tendrils feeling the way, hesitant and fearful. The voices swelled in strength. The wind blew through the fog.

Elle reached for Kate. "Now, Kate. Go to him now."

Kate never stopped talking in her beguiling voice,

but she closed her eyes and deliberately entered the world of shadows. He was there. A tall, gaunt man with sorrow weighing him down. He looked at her and shook his head sadly. She held out her hand to him. Beside her, Elle stiffened as a beastly creature with glowing eyes and fur stared down at Kate with hate. As the snakelike vines slithered and coiled and hissed as if alive, wanting to get to her sister. Elle moved them, holding them back with the sheer force of her power, giving Kate the necessary time to lure the spirit of Abram to her.

Kate told a story of the love of a man for his wife and children. A man who made a courageous decision to go against what others said was right and allowed his family to participate in a production designed to bring people together. She spoke of laughter and fun and his pride in his family as he watched them. And the horror of a terrible accident. The candles and dry straw, the heavy planks coming down on so many. The man watching his loved ones die. The guilt and horror. The need to blame someone . . . to blame himself.

Joley and Abbey sang softly, the voice of a woman and child calling for the one they loved to join them. Kate used the purity of her voice, silver tones to draw him closer. The woman and child waited. Loved. Longed for him. His only job was to go to them, to forgive himself. There was no one to save but himself.

Kate kept her hand extended and pointed behind him. Clouds of dark gray fog drifted aside. He turned to see the shadows there. A woman. A child. Far off in the distance waiting.

There was a sharp cry like that of a seagull. The waves crashed against the cliff, rose high and frothed white. Lightning veined the clouds, forked into the very center of the fog. The flash lit up the shadows, throwing Kate out of that world and back into the reality of her own. She landed heavily on the wet surface of the captain's walk, in the middle of her sisters. Libby held her close.

"You're all right. It's all right now. You did it, Kate. You gave him peace," Sarah said.

"We did it," Kate corrected with a wan smile.

They sat together, too weary to move, the rain lashing down at them. Sarah turned her head to calculate the distance to the door. "Damon will be here with tea, but I don't think he can carry us back inside."

Elle draped herself over Abbey. "Who cares about going inside? I want to just lie here and look up at the sky."

"I want to know Matt's safe and that he was able to get to Danny," Kate said. "When Damon comes up, please have him call Jonas."

Matt scooted carefully down the steep bank, skirting rocks until it became impossible to go farther. He had no choice but to go over them.

"I'm Tommy, not Kate," a voice called weakly from his right side.

Matt didn't realize until that moment that he was

whispering her name over and over like a prayer. He glanced up at the sky, felt the wind in his face, the first few drops of real rain. He felt power and energy crackling in the air around him. "Thank you, Katie, you are unbelievable." He said it fervently, meaning it. Already the fog was beginning to thin so that he could make out the boy lying a few feet from him. "Are you hurt?"

"I don't think so. I don't know what happened though. One minute I was falling off the fence and rolling, and the next Danny shoved me. I woke up a few minutes ago and when I tried to move, I dislodged several rocks. I didn't know where anyone was, so I thought I'd better just wait until help came."

Matt remained lying flat, searching carefully for Danny. The wind drove down through the canyon and shifted abruptly, coming back off the river. He caught sight of his brother a few yards away. Danny was lying facedown on the cliff over the water's edge, partially buried under debris. He wasn't moving. The pulse pounded in Matt's temples. He forced himself to go to the boy and examine him first. "You'll be fine. Just stay down until we can get help to you. I'm checking on Danny."

He took a deep breath and called toward the top. "Donna? Is Jonas here yet?"

"He's on his way along with the rescue squad," She yelled back.

"I'm working my way down to Danny. Everyone else is alive. Jackson looks the worst. Could be a concussion. The entire mountainside is unstable. Tell them to be careful moving around up there until I can get Danny out of the avalanche zone."

Matt patted the teenage boy and proceeded to make painfully slow progress through the rocks. The smallest trickle of pebbles could bring down a tremendous storm of boulders on his brother. He inched his way through the rubble until he reached Danny's side.

Danny was precariously balanced at the edge of the bank. It was actually the rocks that saved his life, holding him pinned in the dirt. Matt was very gentle as he examined his brother. He couldn't find a single broken bone, but there were several lacerations, particularly on Danny's hands. His face was pushed hard into the dirt. He carefully turned Danny's head, scooping dirt from his mouth. Danny coughed, and the rocks slid. Some dislodged and one fell to the river below. "Don't move, Danny, don't even cough if you can help it," Matt instructed.

"Tell us what you need, Matt," Jonas shouted down to him.

"I've got to move Danny. When I do, everything above him is going to slide. You'll have to get Pete out of there and Jackson. When you move them, Jonas, don't disturb the rocks. If I take Danny now, there's a chance we'll lose those two. I'll shield my brother, just work fast."

Matt knew Jonas wouldn't bother to argue with him. There was no way Matt would leave his younger brother hanging out over the edge of the fast-moving river with an avalanche of boulders poised to slide. The Drake sisters had managed a miracle removing the fog, but there was still dangerous work to be done.

"Don't forget about me," Tommy called.

"We'll get you," Jonas promised.

"You're going to be just fine, Danny boy," Matt said, brushing more dirt from the lacerated face.

"Get out of here, Matt," Danny barely mouthed the words. "Breathing moves the rocks. If they're working up above, the boulders will smash us both."

"Have a little faith, bro, that's Jonas up there. Are you hurt?"

"What does it look like?"

Matt heard the ominous rumble above him. "Incoming," Jonas yelled from above them. Matt shifted so his upper body protected Danny's head. He put his arms over his own head and tried to shrink as rocks bounced down, knocking a few more loose. The rocks rained down and splashed into the river below. One glanced off his calf and rolled away, dislodging more rocks before it hit the water.

"Dammit, be careful." Matt could hear Jonas snarling at the rescue team. "If you can't move them without setting off a landslide, get the hell back up here and let someone else do that! You all right down there, Matt?"

"We're fine. Just be careful," he called back.

"You weigh more than the rocks do," Danny complained.

"You deserve it, scaring the hell out of me like this. Anything broken?"

"Naw. I'm a Granite. We're tough."

Matt rubbed his brother's head in a rough, affectionate gesture. He glanced up. "They've got Jackson and the boys out, and they're on the way to us. When we move you, Danny, the entire side of the bank is going to come down. I won't be able to be very gentle, but I'm not going to let anything happen to you."

"Just get me the hell out of here."

It was not an easy task. The rescuers inched their way down and worked out a coordinated plan to move Danny, knowing once they pulled him from under the pile of rocks it would set off an avalanche. Matt stayed beside his brother, joking, keeping Danny's spirits up. The men cleared as many of the rocks from Danny as they could without triggering the landslide. It was only the soft damp dirt that saved Danny from terrible injury or death. His body was pressed deep into the muck. They dug around him with painstaking slowness, careful not to disturb the precarious balance of boulders poised over their heads.

"Ready, Danny boy?" It was Matt who locked arms with his brother.

"More than ready." There was fear in Danny's eyes, but he winked at his older brother and managed a weak smile.

Matt didn't wait. They had cleared as much of the ground as possible out of the way of the landslide path so that Matt had a clear trail on the steep embankment to drag Danny quickly out of harm's way. He exerted his great strength, pulling his brother out from under the rocks, moving as fast as humanly possible. The rocks immediately crashed into the river, starting the avalanche. The boulders above, with nothing to hold them, rolled down, taking most of the embankment with it. Matt covered Danny's body a second time, waiting until the debris had cleared.

Danny tried to stand, but his brother held him down. "You made me come down here and play mudcakes with you, you can just get on the stretcher and let the medics carry your butt to the hospital and check you out."

"I'm fine," Danny protested, as they strapped him into a litter. "I feel like an idiot," he said.

"That's good, Danny. You are an idiot." Matt took up a position at the head of the stretcher to help carry him up the steep bank. They were still cautious, worried about the unstable conditions, but managed to get him to the top without incident.

Danny protested more when they put him in the ambulance, but no one paid him any attention. Matt jumped in beside him, keeping one hand on his brother's shoulder. It wasn't until the doctors pronounced Danny bruised, but fine that Matt left him to go check on Jackson and the teens.

By the time he returned to the cliff house, he was tired and only wanting to hold Kate to him. The Drake sisters were sprawled in every chair of the living room, pale and drawn, all greeting him with their brilliant smiles.

Matt gathered Kate to him, holding her close. All he wanted to do was take her home with him where she belonged. She looked exhausted and in need of a hot meal and two or three days of sleep. Kate clung to him, turning her face up for his kiss, burrowing against him.

"I heard there was an accident on the river wall," she greeted.

"Everyone's fine. Shook up, but fine. Did Jonas stop by?"

She shook her head. "Inez called to make certain we were all right. She knew we must have cleared out the fog and that we would be exhausted. She told us what happened. Jackson's in the hospital, but the two boys were treated and released. She said Jackson's going to be fine." Her smile was slow coming but bright. "I have a feeling he'll make a terrible patient."

"Somehow I think you're right. Danny was treated and released also. He's bruised from head to toe, but he didn't have a single major injury." There was elation in Matt's voice. "He's hoping Inez will upgrade his part next year in the pageant due to his, quote, 'heroism.' It was pretty dicey, Kate. Thanks for all you did."

"We all did it. I could never have managed without

my sisters. I'm so glad your brother is fine. The pageant just wouldn't be the same without him in his annual role as the shepherd. Speaking of the pageant—" She broke off as her sisters burst out laughing.

Matt's head went up suspiciously. He was beginning to know the Drake sisters, and their laughter heralded trouble for him. He was certain of it.

"Inez sent over a costume she made for the third wise man. A king," Kate said brightly. "She asked if you would be willing to fill the role at the last minute and of course, with Inez being so distressed, we said we were certain you'd want to help out."

He stiffened. "I'd rather be boiled in oil."

"Acting runs in your family," she pointed out.

He held up his hand. "You can't look at me with those eyes while you're weak and tired, it's unfair tactics."

"I know, Matthew," she said. "I'm trying not to, but Inez is such a good friend, and I couldn't bear her being so upset. The pageant is important to the town after all the near accidents. We need to get our confidence back."

"And I have to be in the pageant in order for our town to do that?" He raised one eyebrow skeptically.

"All you have to do is walk through the town. No lines, nothing awful. You don't mind, do you?"

"Does wanting to be boiled in oil instead sound like I want to do this?"

She turned her face into his chest. Pressed her lips against his skin.

He growled, deep in his throat. The growl turned into a groan. "I can see what my life's going to be like. I'll do it. This one time. Never again."

"Thank you." She kissed him again. "I just want to go home with you and sleep in your arms," she said, uncaring that her family could hear her. "Let's go home, Matthew."

Matt kissed her gently, her lips, her throat, bringing her hand to his mouth as elation swept through him. She had said, "Let's go home." He lifted her with ease. "I'll take good care of her," he promised her family.

Sarah nodded. "We have every confidence that you will, Matt."

chapter 14

All deeds are now done, forgiveness is mine,
As two people share a love for all time.

"WE'RE GOING TO BE LATE," KATE SAID, EVADing Matt's outstretched hand. "We promised the committee you'd be on time. We didn't make rehearsals, and everyone's worried you're going to mess up their play."

"I wasn't the one who agreed to wear that silly-looking robe Inez made. *You* agreed I'd wear it! Is it my fault they lost a couple of their stars to a scandalous affair?" He stalked her through the house, one slow step at a time.

Kate laughed and dodged around the table, putting a chair between them. "You theater people are always involved in scandals."

He moved the chair out of the way and proceeded to back her into a corner. "I'd be more than willing to cause a scandal. Just let me get my hands on you."

"I don't think so. Inez is probably watching her clock and tapping her foot. I'm not about to get a lecture about the benefits of being on time. Put on your costume!"

"I am in my costume. What king travels by starlight from one country to another and wears a satin bathrobe with cheesy lightning bolts sewn all over it? And I doubt very much if he sat on that camel naked under the robe."

Kate held her stomach, laughing so hard she could barely manage to squeak through a small opening he'd left beside the counter. "Somehow I think Inez might object to the idea that you were running around naked in her kingly robes. I, however, am rather intrigued by the idea." She backed down the hallway, holding her hand palm out. "Seriously, Matthew, she'll reprimand you in front of the entire town if you're late."

She was nearing the entrance to the bedroom. His silver eyes gleamed with anticipation. "If you think that's more humiliating than wearing this damned robe, which, by the way, is two sizes too small, you're sadly mistaken. I think Bruce had the affair with Sylvia just to get out of wearing it."

She pressed her hand to her mouth to keep an undignified giggle from emerging. "I think it looks dashing on you." He was right; the robe looked utterly ridiculous on him. His huge muscles strained the material so that it stretched tight over his wide shoulders and back. Instead of reaching the ground, it was halfway up his calves, and the front gaped open to reveal . . . She laughed. "I think it has interesting possibilities."

He spread his arms wide and rushed her, using an

old football tackle. She screamed and turned to run, but he caught her up and carried her across the floor to the bed, where he unceremoniously dropped her. The kingly robe made its way to the floor. "I'm the king, and I demand my rights."

Kate pushed one hand against his chest to fend him off. "You have no rights. Inez has you under contract, and you're supposed to be *on time.* Do you want the entire town waiting for you?"

"I wouldn't mind in the least." He caught her legs, pinning her to the bed, stopping her from scooting away from him. "I think everyone should wait on me. I have this tremendous need to see your breasts. Why don't you unbutton your blouse for me?"

"It doesn't have buttons, oh mighty King."

"Who the hell cares," he growled. "Get rid of the shirt."

"I think that robe went to your head." Excitement raced through her, curled heat in her deepest core. She drew the blouse obediently over her head so that her full breasts spilled over the fine white cups of her bra. "Is this what you're looking for?" She slid her hand over her skin, drawing his attention to the taut peaks.

Matt reached to draw the zipper of her jeans down. "Exactly like that." There was a husky catch to his voice, the playfulness slipping away as he tugged the material from her body. He left her sexy little thong. "Every time I see that thing, I want to take it off with my teeth," he admitted, and bent to the task.

Kate enjoyed the feel of his hands on her body. Big hands. Capable. Nearly covering her buttocks as he lifted her hips and teased her skin with his teeth. Just that fast she was swamped with heat, her body flushed and alive and in desperate need. The thought of the Christmas pageant went out of her head, and much more erotic thoughts took its place. His mouth was everywhere, his tongue teasing and dancing, his teeth pulling at the only barrier between him and his goal.

She felt the sudden release as the material parted, the cool air mingling with her own heat, then the plunging of his tongue going deep while she nearly came off the bed, air bursting from her lungs in a wild rush. It was only his hands holding her down that kept her open to him while he made certain she not only was prepared for him, but that she hungered for him. Laughing, he slid his body over hers, settling over her soft form, gripping her hips to pull her to meet the hard thrust as he joined them together.

"I think that kingly robe works just fine," Kate managed to say, in between gasps of pleasure.

"Maybe I'll keep it if it gets this kind of results," he teased. He began to move, a slow assault on her senses, driving deep, needing her body, needing to feel the way she welcomed him. The heat and fire. Flames licking over his skin. "I love watching you when we make love," he admitted. She was so completely abandoned in the way she gave herself to him.

Kate loved the way he watched her. There was desire etched into the lines of his face. There was hunger in the depths of his eyes. There was steel in his body and a fine hot heat that made her flame, catch fire, and burn with passion. "I love making love with you," she told him, sliding her arms around his neck to draw his head down to hers.

"That's a good thing, Katie." His teeth nibbled at her chin, her full bottom lip. "Because I think we're going to be spending a lot of time doing just that."

Kate gave herself up to the sheer glory of his body driving so deeply into hers. The pressure built and built, and she dug her fingers into his shoulders, holding on as they soared together in perfect unison.

He lay over her, fighting for his breath, trying to slow his heart rate.

"You're laughing," she observed. "I told you, your entire family laughs at me."

"I can't help it, Kate. And I'm laughing at me. I feel like one of those sappy men who run around with a big grin on his face all the time. I feel like grinning all the time around you, and it's so idiotic."

Kate's answering smile was slow. She rubbed her face against his chest. "I'm just beginning to realize how much I mean to you, Matthew."

He kissed her tenderly, his hands framing her face. "I adore you. Why else would I ever put that horrible robe on in front of the entire town?"

Kate looked smug. "And you know what I'll be

thinking about when you come walking down the street looking sexy and kingly."

"I'll tell you what you'd better be thinking, Katie." He took a deep breath. "You'd better be thinking, 'here comes the man I intend to marry.'" He feathered kisses along the corners of her mouth. "Marry me, Kate. Spend your life with me."

She looked up at his beloved face. Her fingers slid through his hair in a loving caress. "I don't climb mountains or swim seas, Matthew. I sit in the corner and read books. I'm not at all brave. You have to be very sure that it's me you want."

"More than anything in the world, Kate. You. With you I have everything."

"Well, I guess that kingly robe is lucky after all." She kissed his throat, his chin. Found his mouth with hers and poured heat and fire and promises into her kiss.

He responded just the way she knew he would, his arms wrapping her close, his body coming alive, growing hard and thick deep inside her. He made love to her slowly, leisurely, as if they had all the time in the world and the entire town wasn't waiting on them. He made a thorough job of it. Kate felt like the most important person in the world. And the happiest.

They lay on the bed in a tangle of arms and legs, fighting to breathe. She turned her head to look at him. "I'm thinking you should wear that robe more often, Matthew."

He snorted his derision and glanced at his watch. "Kate! We're late."

"I told you we were late."

"Not this late, we're holding up the parade." He hastily leaped off her, looking around for his clothes. Kate laughed at him through the entire drive to the park where the members of the production were assembling. He caught Kate by the hand and ran across the lawn to the pavilion.

"Where have you been?" Inez demanded, gesturing toward the huge crowd assembled along the streets. "We've all been waiting for you."

"*And*," Danny added, "you didn't answer your cell phone." He shook his head, hands on his hips, clucking like an old hen. "You aren't even in that lovely costume Inez made for you. What have you been doing?" He wiggled his eyebrows at Kate.

"Are you feeling all right, Danny," Kate asked.

He tugged her hair affectionately. "I'm fine, but don't tell Trudy, she's babying me. And Mom's worse."

Inez all but stamped her foot. "Why are you late?"

"Kate made me late," Matt told Inez, and the interested group of actors crushed together to see the fireworks when Inez told Matt off. Matt exchanged a long, slow smile with Kate while he listened to Inez politely.

"I believe him," Jonas said. "You know how the Drake sisters are. Barbie doll alone takes three hours to get ready for anything. Put them all together, it could take days."

Kate glared at both former Rangers and took Hannah's hand. "Why aren't you participating this year, Jonas?" she asked sweetly. "Inez, didn't he promise you last year? I could have sworn Sarah told me Jonas really wanted to play a major role."

"He likes to stand out," Hannah added, smiling at Inez. "If you don't offer him a lead, he won't cooperate. You know Jonas. He has to be the star."

Inez turned to the sheriff. "Why didn't you sign up this year?"

"I didn't sign up," Matt pointed out.

"We don't have time for this argument," Jonas said, glaring at Kate. "Traffic is going to be backed up from here to hell and back. Get this show on the road, Inez, or we'll have to shut it down."

Inez began barking orders like a drill sergeant. Hannah nudged Jonas. "Don't look so smug. I'm putting your name in for the role of donkey next year. I'm certain Inez will come up with a suitable costume."

Deliberately the sheriff leaned into her, so close her body was pressed up against his. "That's great, baby doll, as long as you're the one riding me." He breathed the words against her ear, then stalked away from her.

The wind rushed over him and sent his hat sailing toward the river. He glanced back, his grin wide. "You have such a bad temper, Hannah. Merry Christmas."

Matt tried to cling to Kate but was dragged firmly away and forced into his satin costume. He did his best not to notice the other actors hiding their smiles behind their hands as they looked at him, or that Inez and Donna looked horrified. The streets were lined with townspeople, from the oldest to the youngest. Even Sylvia had turned up, with one side of her face covered in a red rash.

The parade began, and Matt was forced to endure trudging through the streets where everyone could see Inez's bizarre creation. The other two wise men went before him. He thought they looked somewhat ridiculous in their robes of velvet, but if he squinted enough, he could use the word *regal.* Cursing the fact that his costume looked more like a woman's bathrobe than a king's robe, Matt thought it took an eternity to get through town, with everyone singing slightly off-key, and to finally catch sight of the town square. Worse, he couldn't prevent the silly grin from breaking out on his face. It just wouldn't go away, and he knew it had to look like he was enjoying parading through town in a woman's bathrobe. He knew Kate and her sisters had grabbed a spot near the makeshift stables to wait for him, and he kept a sharp eye out for them. He let out a sigh of relief when he finally spotted them.

"You look really good in that satin robe, bro," Danny declared, nudging his brother with the hooked end of his staff.

"Shut up, Danny, or I'm going to kick your butt," Matt threatened out of the side of his mouth. He kept his eyes straight ahead, trudging like a man doomed, carrying his gift of frankincense on a white satin pillow out in front of him. He'd argued the wise men hadn't had white satin pillows to use carrying the foul-smelling stuff, but not a single person had listened, and his protests had earned him a black scowl from Inez. He kept his eyes straight ahead, not looking at the waving townspeople as he marched stoically onward to the town square with his silly grin on his face.

Danny whistled at him. "That robe manages to show your butt off nicely, Matt." He tapped the offending part of Matt's anatomy with the staff again. "Sorry, little accident, couldn't help myself."

"I hope you have life insurance," Matt said in his most menacing voice. He made the mistake of looking up to judge the distance to the square. He had to know the exact amount of time he would have to suffer further humiliation. Kate stood there with her sisters. Every last one of them had a huge smile on her face. Matt entertained the idea of throwing the frankincense at their feet and hauling Kate over his shoulder like the Neanderthal they all thought he was. He'd keep the robe, it might come in handy.

Danny poked him with the staff again. "Get along there little dogie," he teased.

Matt's furious gaze settled on Old Man Mars. He stood slightly apart, watching the pageant with a peculiar look on his face, somewhere between mortification and shock. It was obvious he shared Matt's view of the idiotic robes. The old man caught his eye, read the pain on Matt's face, and stepped closer to commiserate. He walked alongside Matt.

"She made you do this, didn't she?" Mars asked.

"Damn right. Otherwise, I wouldn't be caught dead in this getup," Matt replied, hope beginning to stir.

Mars nodded as if he understood Matt's total misery and stepped back away from him with his arms folded. Behind him, Danny began the mantra. "Don't say it. Don't say it. Don't say it." He glanced nervously at the old man as he approached him.

"Merry Christmas." Matt turned back with a cheerful grin. "Merry Christmas, Mr. Mars," he said happily.

A black scowl settled over Old Man Mars's face. His craggy brows drew together in a straight thick line. He made a single sound of disgust and spat on the ground. The old man delivered his yearly kick right to Danny's shin and shuffled off, muttering something about tomatoes. Danny howled and jumped around, holding his injured shin. The staff swung around in a wide circle so that the participants had to break ranks and run for safety. Matt kept walking straight past Inez and the outraged look on her face. Kate met him at the stable, lifting her face for his kiss, while Inez followed Danny, giving him her annual Christmas lecture on behavior.

"All in all, Katie," Matt said, holding her close, "I'd say this was a very satisfactory pageant."

EPILOGUE

"So, did your wish come true?" Sarah asked.

Matt reached out to take the snowglobe from her, turning it over and over in his hands. He looked across the room at Kate. His Kate. The flames leaped and danced in the fireplace. The Drake sisters were decorating a live tree they'd brought in for Christmas Day. The next day they would plant it on their property near the many other trees that marked the passing of the years.

The house smelled of cedar and pine and cinnamon and spice. Berry candles adorned the mantel and the aroma of fresh-baked cookies drifted from the kitchen. Jonas appeared in the doorway of the kitchen. Red and green frosting smeared his face and fingers, and an apron covered his clothes. "No one asked me if my wish came true," he complained.

"You're such a baby, Jonas," Joley informed him with a little sniff. She caught the apron strings and dragged him backward. "You were the one who said there was nothing to baking cookies, and we should try our hand at doing it the old-fashioned way."

Jonas escaped and raced back into the living room.

"*You! You!*" he protested. "*Women* bake cookies. That's what they do. They sit around the house looking pretty and hand their man a plate of cookies and a drink when he comes home."

Jonas grinned at the women tauntingly. Matt groaned and covered his face with his hands, looking between his fingers. He already felt power moving in the air. Curtains swayed. Hair stood up. Crackles of electricity snapped and sizzled. The flames on the candles and in the fireplace leaped and danced. Jonas watched the sisters, clearly expecting reprisal. It came from behind him. The small fish tank lifted into the air and tilted part of the contents over Jonas's head. Water rushed over his head. He stiffened, but he didn't turn around, nor did he attempt to wipe it off.

"I just want to point out that this is Christmas Day," he said. "And you all just came back from church."

Joley sat down at the upright, perfectly tuned piano. "And we're all feeling full of love and goodwill, Jonas. Which is why you aren't swimming in the sea with the sharks right now. Shall I play something cheerful?"

"Oh, please do, Joley," Hannah entreated wickedly. "I'm feeling *very* cheerful."

"You would be," Jonas muttered. He took the towel Libby handed him and wiped off his face and hair.

Hannah blew him a kiss.

"Matt didn't answer my question," Sarah persisted.

"The globe only works for family," Abbey said.

Music swelled in volume, filling every corner of the

house with joy. Matt heard the sound of feminine laughter, felt his heart respond. Kate walked around the tree, an ornament in her hand. She moved with grace and elegance, his perfect Kate. Feeling the weight of his gaze, she looked across the room at him and smiled.

"Yes, that's true, Abbey," Sarah said. "It only works for family. Matt? Did the globe grant your wish?"

He cleared his throat. "Yes." The affirmation came out on a husky note.

Joley's fingers stilled on the piano. She turned to look at him. Libby put her hand out to Hannah. Abbey put her arm around Elle. All of the Drakes looked at Matt. Kate's sisters. The magical witches of Sea Haven. He thought he fit in rather nicely.

"What did you wish for, Matthew?" Sarah asked. She sat down in Damon's lap, wrapping her arms around his neck.

"I wished for Katie, of course," he answered honestly.

Kate walked over to him, leaning down to kiss him. "I wished for you," she whispered aloud.

"So that little jewelry box in your jacket pocket means something?" Elle asked.

"It means Kate said yes," Matt said. He believed his grin was a permanent fixture on his face.

Jonas shook his head, still mopping up the water. "You got her to say yes just by wishing on that snow-globe?"

"That's what it took," Matt said. "But they say it only

works for family. I guess it acknowledged that Katie belonged with me."

"Really? It can reason all that out, can it?" Jonas stared at the snowglobe sitting so innocently on the shelf. "Family huh? Well, I've been family for about as long as I can remember."

A collective gasp went up from the seven Drake sisters as Jonas reached for the snowglobe.

"No! Jonas, don't touch that." Hannah sounded frightened.

"You can't, Jonas," Sarah said.

His hand hovered over it. Matt could swear he heard hearts beating loudly in the sudden silence. Jonas picked up the globe. Almost at once it sprang to life, the tiny lights on the tree glowing, the fog beginning to swirl.

"Jonas, put it down right now and step away from it," Joley warned.

"You can't play with things in this house," Elle added. "They can be dangerous."

"Jonas," Abbey said, "it isn't funny."

Jonas turned toward the women, his hands absently cradling the globe. "Aren't you all supposed to be cooking dinner for us? Jackson's going to be here any minute, expecting the full Christmas fare, and all he's going to get is some cookies I made." As he spoke, he kept his gaze on Hannah. All the while his palm rubbed the globe as if he could conjure up a genie.

"Don't you *dare* wish on that globe, Jonas Harrington," Hannah hissed. She actually backed a step away from him. "I'm sorry about the fish tank. And the silly hat thing as well. Just put the globe down and keep your mind blank. We'll call it even."

"Are you watching this, Matt?" Jonas asked, clearly taunting Hannah. "This is called power."

"Not for long," Kate said. She held out her hand for the globe. "Hand it over and stop tormenting Hannah. We're liable to serve you up dragon's liver for dinner."

"All right," Jonas agreed. He looked into the glass. "It's certainly beautiful." Instead of giving it to her, he stared into it for a long moment. The fog swirled into a frenzy, obliterating the house until only the lights on the tree blazed, then it slowly subsided, leaving the glass clear and the lights fading away. Only then did he hand it over to Kate.

There was a long silence. Jonas grinned at them. "I'm teasing. You all take things so seriously." He nudged Matt. "I'm not a dreamer like my friend here. I wouldn't let a snowglobe decide my fate. Come on, let's get that turkey carved."

Kate accepted Matt's kiss and watched him go into the kitchen with Damon and Jonas. She joined her sisters as she did each year in surrounding the tree, hands connecting them in a continuous circle. The overhead lights went off, leaving them in the shadows with the flickering candles and Christmas lights. She felt the familiar power running up and down her arms. Running through her. Tiny sparks leaped into the air like little fireflies. Electricity crackled around them. She could feel the minuscule threads in the tapestry of power that wove them together. Energy sprang from one to the other.

Matt stood in the doorway with Damon and Jonas and Jackson, who had come in through the kitchen, and watched the seven women as they stood hand in hand circling the Christmas tree. The women looked beautiful and fey, with their heads thrown back and the sparks leaping around them like miniature fireworks.

Jonas nudged him. "Welcome to the world of the Drake sisters, Matt. And Merry Christmas."

Matt couldn't imagine a better one.

Christine Feehan

recently took time from her busy writing schedule to talk to us. Here are the highlights of that conversation.

What inspired you to write a novella about a family of witches during the holiday season?

I loved growing up in my family. I have ten sisters. And yes, they are all biological. We had an amazing childhood. Our friendships with one another were, and remain, very strong. Christmas was my favorite time of the year. My uncle was in a wheelchair, and he lived with us. He made Christmas an exciting and special holiday. We collected ornaments from around the world, and to this day I keep that tradition, as do my children. I think loving my sisters and feeling that when we are together there is a special magic, first brought the idea of writing about a family of very magical sisters into my head. All of us have different talents as well as different trials, and we're strong women . . . but when we're together, we're at our strongest. We see one another through every difficult time and every joyous occasion. And we all love to come together at Christmas!

Kate Drake, the heroine of *The Twilight Before Christmas*, is a bestselling author. Readers can't help but wonder how much you modeled her after yourself. Any similarities?

Maybe a few. Kate does things she doesn't think she can do and she doesn't consider herself courageous. I think I started out the same way, believing I couldn't do things, although martial arts definitely changed that in me. But Kate Drake and I share a love of books. My all-time favorite thing to do is curl up in a chair and read a book by my favorite author, or to read a great new find. I'm a reader, and I read everything. I love the written word, and if I could sit in the old mill coffee shop or down on the beach and read, I'd be very content. Kate is more of a composite of two of my sisters and a wonderful, bestselling author, Jayne Ann Krentz, who I thought of often as I wrote this story. I even pictured her in the role of Kate. I've often curled up with Jayne's book and escaped into another world, and it was easy to imagine her as Kate writing her wonderful books for me to read.

Your martial art expertise is fascinating. Can you tell us how old you were when you started training, why you started training, and the level of your ability today?

I started training when most women didn't do martial arts, so in the early years I trained mostly with men. I had always been interested in karate as an art form, the beautiful and powerful katas and, of course, I wanted the benefits of gaining more confidence in myself. I loved the discipline and philosophy of the various arts and studied many of them. I was lucky enough to train under a wonderful man in the Korean art of Tang Soo Do and I hold a third degree black belt in that art. I also hold rank in several other disciplines as well. I taught self-defense to women and martial arts to both men and women and helped with battered women seminars and various other projects to empower women. Martial arts became a way of life for me, one I believe in and highly recommend. I had to retire due to my health a few years ago, but the training I received has enabled me to write realistic action scenes and to develop real characters in difficult situations. My training allowed me to spend a great deal of time around a certain type of alpha male so I developed an understanding of how they act and react when they are attacked or encounter physical danger. And no, it is not always the way our society would prefer them to do so!

No doubt there's a touch of magic in the Feehan household during the holiday season. Are the Feehan family's celebrations anything at all like the Drake sisters' holiday festivities?

Yes, very much so. Christmas is one of the biggest events of the year for my family. Everyone comes home. It's a time we look forward to throughout the year. Our Christmas celebration is huge. My mother has a very large two-story house (and it is needed!) and we all gather there on Christmas Eve. My brothers and sisters are married and have children of their own. My parents have seventy-two grandchildren. The house has high ceilings, and the top of the tree touches the ceiling. My sisters have a traditional party just before Christmas to decorate, and the ornaments are blown glass from all over the world! You can imagine the number of gifts beneath the tree. There's always music and laughter, and my mom loves candles, so the scent is wonderful! Several sisters love to bake, so we have tons of wonderful desserts. Everyone brings an enormous amount of food. Wineglasses have been handed down from generation to generation and the glasses are brought out and we toast the coming seasons and any new babies in the family! Usually at some point a cat runs up the tree. Dogs mill around. We play Ping-Pong and cards and other games. We tell stories and open gifts. And we often attend midnight mass together.

Do you have a favorite holiday tradition you perform every year?

Yes, we always decorate a live Christmas tree. The children love decorating the tree, as I've collected ornaments over the years. I get teased about my ornaments because the children think I have too many! And my husband says I have too many lights to go with my too many ornaments. We spend hours decorating the tree. There's a lot of laughter, but mostly at my expense! The children spend hours playing "I spy" with the ornaments. When Christmas is over, we plant the tree in the yard. My family thinks I have a tree fetish as well as an ornament fetish. We always watch my husband's favorite Christmas film, *It's a Wonderful Life* together as well. Then the children all tease him instead of me!

What is your favorite holiday tune?

"I'm Dreaming of a White Christmas."

Okay, this is a "revealing" interview, so would you please tell us whether you and your family open presents on Christmas Eve or Christmas Day?

My father is a retired fireman and usually worked Christmas Day, so it became a tradition to always open the gifts Christmas Eve. We've continued that, going to my parents' house and spending Christmas Eve with them, and then opening gifts at the Feehan house very early the morning of Christmas Day. The floor is covered with paper, and there's a lot of laughter and teasing!

And who cooks Christmas dinner?

My husband Richard is a fabulous cook and he always cooks Christmas dinner. Some of the grown children bring side dishes, but for the most part, he plans, shops, and cooks the entire thing!

Getting back to your professional life, what prompted you to become a writer?

I believe I was born a writer. I honestly can't remember a time in my life when I didn't write. I used to make up stories as a child, and my sisters would have to listen. Once I could write my brilliant masterpieces down on paper (and they were truly awful) my sisters would read them all dutifully. Writing is a part of me, just like breathing. I can't imagine not writing. When the day comes that I am no longer published, I will still be writing!

Critics and reviewers hail you as one of the most imaginative authors writing today. Where do you get your ideas? And why do you choose to write stories with Gothic elements and paranormal characters?

I love action and very edge-of-the-seat creepy suspense, both in movies and in books. I wanted to be able to combine that with my love of romance and happy-ever-after endings. I also am very intrigued with the paranormal and with myths and legends that have persisted throughout the history of the world, in every country. What better way than to combine them all and write what I love to read? As for my ideas and where I get them—everywhere! Everything I see, or hear, newspaper articles on some strange happenings. It can be something small like the way a woman turns her head, or more intense, such as a freak fog moving into a town that never has fog! My imagination doesn't need much help to take flight.

What was the biggest challenge in writing *The Twilight Before Christmas?*

In all honesty, it was finding the time. I had the town, the characters, and the legacy of the Drake sisters already firmly in my mind. I did research on symbols and settlers and even the history of Christmas, but I had wanted this story, all the Drake stories, to be incredibly magical. To do that, I had to find the time. I stayed in a wonderful little house on the coast and wandered up and down the coastal highway to really get the right feel before I began writing the actual story.

You strongly evoke the atmosphere of a California coastal town in *Twilight.* Have you ever lived in a town like the fictional Sea Haven?

I grew up in a small town very close to the California coast and have lived much of my life in or near a small coastal town. I love the atmosphere and have so many pleasant memories of my mom and my sisters and me walking along the wooden sidewalks and enjoying the year-round flowers growing wild. Herds of wild elk populate the area, and the beaches are wonderful. Seals are in the water, and you can whale watch during certain times of the year. I love the fishing villages and have favorite restaurants I enjoy.

Will readers see more of the Drake sisters in the future?

I certainly hope so! I love the Drake family. In fact I really enjoy all the characters in Sea Haven. Yes, I have plans to give each sister her own unique story.

Finally, is there one special wish you would like to have come true this Christmas?

It sounds sappy to say Peace on Earth, but it sure would be wonderful.

And this interview wouldn't be complete if I didn't ask: How *do* Carpathians celebrate Christmas?

The Carpathians have their own traditions, but as for Christmas, they only began celebrating that holiday recently. Raven Dubrinsky, lifemate to the Prince, was an American and loved Christmas very much. She invited her family and friends to the Dubrinsky home this year. Antoinetta Justicano agreed to make the trip with Byron to play the piano for everyone so they could all sing time-honored carols. Raven had fun insisting that Mikhail decorate the tree using human methods and he ended up wrapping the Christmas lights around the tree, around himself, and around the furniture. Each Carpathian made an ornament to adorn the first Carpathian Christmas tree and mark the occasion. They came from all over to sing and celebrate and join in the festivities. If they had one wish to make on the Drakes' snowglobe, it would be that their women could bring babies safely into the world to live and thrive!

Merry Christmas from the Feehans, the Drakes, and all the Carpathians!

Christine Feehan